Waking Dream

Rhiannon Lassiter graduated from Oxford University in 1998. The first literary agent to see her work encouraged her to finish HEX, which she wrote when she was seventeen, and it was bought by the first publisher who read it. Her mother is the well-known children's author, Mary Hoffman. Rhiannon lives in Oxford with her two cats Shadow and Ghost.

'A young Rhiannon Lassiter grabbed our attention a few years ago with the gripping SF Hex trilogy. Now she turns to magic, with this gripping and terrifying story of three cousins bound together by something much deeper and darker than blood – their dreams'
The Bookseller

Waking Dream

☾

Rhiannon Lassiter

MACMILLAN CHILDREN'S BOOKS

First published 2002 by Macmillan Children's Books

This edition published 2003 by Macmillan Children's Books
a division of Macmillan Publishers Limited
20 New Wharf Road, London N1 9RR
Basingstoke and Oxford
www.panmacmillan.com

Associated companies throughout the world

ISBN 0 330 39701 X

1 3 5 7 9 8 6 4 2

A CIP catalogue record for this book is available from
the British Library.

Phototypeset by Intype London Ltd
Printed and bound in Great Britain by Mackays of Chatham plc, Kent

Let me be no nearer
In death's dream kingdom
Let me also wear
Such deliberate disguises.
                    —T. S. Eliot

I could come here
And concrete the dark
                    —Anon

This book is dedicated to my grandfather –
John Barber.

And also to the rest of my family
in Sussex, York and Oxford;
past, present and future.

With thanks to Matthew Marcus
who might have been,
and to the anonymous fridge poet who was
the inspiration for this novel.

PROEM

~❦~

There are three books lying on the polished wooden desk. Each of them tells a story. Professor Greenwood, whose desk this is, has reason to believe it is the same story. But the titles of the books would appear to contradict him.

The first book has a blue cover and the pages are slightly rough to the touch; the type of book sold by art shops to amateur sketchers. Oblivious to this fact, the owner has filled the pages with neat regular lines of script in uncompromising blue rollerball. Inside the front cover the same hand has printed in blockish capitals: THE DREAM JOURNAL OF BETHANY GREENWOOD.

The second book is bound in black leather and the pages are smooth and creamy. The writer has appropriately selected a thick-nibbed fountain pen and in black spikes and swirls the words march across the pages. The book's title is stencilled in silver on the cover above a delicate red flower: *A Book of Lies*.

The third book is handmade. Hard tanned leather has been carefully sewn around pages of a thin brownish paper. But although the title has been burned on to the cover the same words are written again inside with a plain black biro in a careless scrawl: *Rivalaun's Secrets*.

CHAPTER ONE

Peace, peace! he is not dead, he doth not sleep —
He hath awakened from the dream of life —
'Tis we, who lost in stormy visions, keep
With phantoms an unprofitable strife.
　　　　　　　—Percy Bysshe Shelley

The Book of Dreams
Bethany's Book

I will begin by describing the painting my father left me in his will. I hadn't expected to inherit anything, although if I had thought about it I'd have realized that there would be money. But my mother refused even to speculate as she hustled me out of the car and up the steps of the solicitor's office. I stumbled on the second step and heard my mother's gust of irritation as she helped haul me up again. Looking glumly down at my green school uniform, worn because my mother refused to allow me to put on black for mourning, I saw a streak of blood sliding gleefully down one pale knobbly leg.

'For crying out loud, Bethany,' my mother snapped in a fierce whisper. 'You could at least try to walk properly.' Then she sailed into the solicitor's office ahead of me and I heard her greeting someone in the bright social voice she reserves for clients and relatives. I trailed after her and stopped inside the doorway when I saw my cousin Poppy waiting for us.

She was standing in the hallway with her parents and even in the numb, dazed state I'd been living in since my father's death I felt the same instinctive gush of loathing I always have in Poppy's presence. Most unfairly, I thought bitterly, she was looking artistically pale in an expensive inky black dress and a black ribbon that tied back her red hair. I regarded that ribbon with disgust. It was a typical Poppy touch, a staged quality that I instinctively distrusted.

I stood in the doorway, wondering if my cousin had equipped herself with a black lace handkerchief as well, while my mother accepted my aunt and uncle's con-dolences with brisk politeness. Ten years after the divorce she could hardly be expected to behave any differently, but I annoyed myself by wishing she had pretended to care a little more. My uncle, on the other hand, was genuinely grieving. While my aunt Emily spoke in hushed tones to my mother and briefly pressed my hand sympathetically, Uncle Sylvester stared straight ahead and spoke in monosyllables until the solicitor arrived and ushered us into a room filled with straight-backed chairs.

The reading of the will didn't last long. My uncle was officially appointed a trustee of my father's estate in a complicated legalese that no one attempted to follow. The lawyer paused in the middle of a convoluted clause to ask if my other uncle was expected and my aunt Emily shook her head.

'Daniel is travelling,' she explained with a touch of embarrassment. 'And we haven't been able to contact him.'

'Then we'll move on to individual legacies,' the

lawyer informed us, and turned to a thicker sheaf of papers on a nearby table.

My mother acquired a drawing my father had made of her on their honeymoon, a smiling girl in an Italian garden, and showed little reaction to the gesture. My cousin Poppy looked sorrowful over a small sketch of the flower she's named for: probably wondering how much it would fetch at Sotheby's.

By then I had realized I was due for some kind of bequest and hoped that it wouldn't be in the same vein as the others. I'm embarrassed by paintings of me, unlike Poppy, who glories in them and has her own portrait displayed prominently in her room at school: a serious eleven-year-old crowned with Titian hair.

It was with dread that I watched the lawyer produce another picture frame when he reached my name. But the painting he gave me was a landscape. I took it automatically, puzzled by the choice. It wasn't one of my father's better efforts. The castle in the foreground looked incomplete and the purple mountains behind too artistic to be real. A river flowed sluggishly across the painting but nowhere did it catch the light because the sky above was an unrelieved slate grey. My mother made a slight sound of disapproval and asked if it would need much insurance. I looked up as the solicitor confessed he doubted it, and caught a look passing between my aunt and uncle that I could only interpret as disapproval – although whether that was of my mother or the painting I couldn't tell. Poppy, on the other hand, seemed fascinated by the gift and craned her head to study it intently.

'It's not like Uncle Felix's other paintings,' she said,

stating the obvious in the little-girl voice she puts on when she has an audience. 'More like he was trying to draw a memory or a dream.'

I jerked my painting away jealously and hugged it to my chest, ignoring Poppy's hurt expression. No one said anything for a moment. Then my aunt Emily, the family peacemaker, stepped into the breach.

'If that's the last, we should be leaving,' she said, rising to her feet. 'Sylvester, are you ready to go?'

My uncle staggered upright. Although he wasn't much older than my father, he walked with a limp and used a silver-knobbed cane to support himself. Poppy went quickly and unnecessarily to help him stand and Aunt Emily turned to my mother.

'I'll telephone you, Cecily,' she said quietly. 'About that other matter . . .' She and my mother both glanced at me at that point and I hugged my painting tighter, deliberately ignoring them. I was used to my mother conspiring with other people about me: the problem child. My mother has spent most of my life trying to tidy me away, and I didn't doubt that another plot, like the one that had deposited me at boarding school when she remarried, was under way to rid me of my awkward and socially inconvenient grief.

Surprisingly, my mother held off for a few weeks, leaving me to sit in the apricot-and-cream bedroom she had decorated for me and stare at my painting. I should have realized what was preoccupying her. My father had finally given up the battle against his cancer a month before the long summer holidays – necessitating my early removal from school. In some ways this was not inconvenient since I only missed the end-of-year exams and I invariably did well at them.

However, what my father had failed to consider when he died was that my mother had a very definite schedule for the summer holidays. She and my stepfather celebrated my release from boarding school by packing me off to my father for a month while they went on their annual cruise around the Adriatic with a combination of friends and clients. It would be out of character for my mother to allow her ex-husband's demise to change plans made months in advance. My stepfather, although unfailingly polite to me, doubtless felt that London in the height of summer was an insupportable option. But, in deference to my continued grief, they waited until the evening of the traditional pre-cruise dinner to inform me that they were going ahead with the holiday as planned and I would be spending the summer holidays in Camomile House.

I received this information with a marked lack of enthusiasm. Camomile House meant my uncle's family and a Cornish summer of wondering when the rain would stop. At my glum expression my mother finally lost her temper.

'Honestly, Bethany, you might show a little more enthusiasm,' she snapped, whisking the debris from a recent bout of comfort eating into my apricot-coloured waste-paper basket. 'These last few weeks have been hard on everyone, not just you, and it wasn't as if you were unaware that Felix was ill. He told me you'd spoken about it together and you understood . . .' She broke off as my eyes filled with tears.

My father and I had spoken about his illness, and his last letters included a series of little line drawings: a small black-clad Bethany weeping at the graveside followed by a succession of little Bethanys resolutely enjoying themselves hang-gliding, mountain climbing and white-water rafting. But these private images didn't fit with the successful social funeral orchestrated by my father's admirers. The photos in the national press showed me in the background dressed, as usual, in my school uniform. Fortunately Poppy, who would otherwise have eclipsed me with staged Ophelia-esque misery, was still at school sitting the exams I'd avoided.

'At the least you could appreciate your aunt's kind-ness in offering to look after you,' my mother pointed out, discounting my uncle Sylvester's influence as everyone invariably did. 'And Poppy will be company for you. You could share her room.' I blanched at the thought, the horrific possibility jolting me.

'Poppy's a poisonous witch!' I informed my mother. 'I'd sooner share a room with a scorpion.'

For a second she fixed me with the frozen look that usually means trouble then, unexpectedly, she laughed.

'I admit she does lay it on a bit thick sometimes,' she agreed and sat down on my desk chair. 'Did you really want to wear black, Beth? I thought Poppy looked like an extra from *Macbeth.*'

'Poppy never looks like an extra,' I said in a snuffly voice, disarmed by her sudden sympathy. 'And I don't want to go and stay with her.'

'And I don't really feel like going away,' my mother said, with an edge in her voice. 'But David would be disappointed if I cancelled now. So we're both going to have to live with it, OK?'

'OK,' I replied, accepting the inevitable, and she smiled approvingly.

'Don't worry about Poppy,' she said reassuringly. 'She's probably as scared of you as you are of her.'

I rolled my eyes.

'Mother, that's wasps,' I pointed out.

CHAPTER TWO

~❦~

My mother said, I never should
Play with the gypsies in the wood
If I did, she would say
Naughty little girl to disobey
Your hair won't curl, your shoes won't shine
Naughty little girl you sha'n't be mine.

—Anon

The Book of Lies
Poppy's Book

When I bought this book in Bond Street I was going
to give it the title *A Book of Spells*. But this was just after
the reading of Uncle Felix's will and I was annoyed
enough with my parents to want to scream. So I call it
The Book of Lies because I am lied to every day and I
still don't know if my family thinks I am too stupid to
realize it.

If it wasn't for the fact that my father is obviously
devastated I wouldn't even be sure that Felix was dead.
I've learned not to count on anything I'm told. But if
even his own brother's death can't persuade him to tell
me the truth I am beginning to doubt that anything
will. I don't even know if I'd believe him. My parents
have lied so often and for so long that recognizing the
truth may be impossible.

When I gave up sciences last year Sylvester, my

father, asked me seriously if I thought that was a wise idea. I told him I'd decided to be a Creationist and that I didn't believe in science. He frowned and said I shouldn't be so narrow-minded. Narrow-minded! Maybe he won't think that after the witchcraft scandal breaks. I'm getting tired of the way both my parents refer to my 'coven' with an amused deprecation as if it were a harmless teenage phase. What does it take to get them to believe that I'M SERIOUS!

I can't remember what it was that first gave me the clue that we're not like other families. Certainly nothing my parents did. They preserve their façade at all times – my father the cloistered academic, my mother a charming hostess and talented musician. It's only because I live with them that I can see how much of that glossy exterior isn't really real and even that's been increasingly difficult to tell since they sent me to boarding school. Perhaps it was my uncle Felix who first gave me the clue. He might preserve the family's image in public but he never pretended to find the uncanny or extraordinary humorous. I didn't realize until the reading of the will how much I was going to miss him. I suppose until then I still half-believed he wasn't really dead.

My parents didn't let me go to the funeral, preserving the pretence that it would be healthier for me to sit my exams like any normal child. But my cousin Bethany went and her mother is even keener on preserving normality than mine is. I saw Beth in the photos, looking lumpish in school uniform. She isn't allowed to wear black for some reason and she looked pretty sick when she saw I was wearing mourning at the will reading. Maybe she wouldn't be so jealous if she had to put up with all the little teasing references to 'Poppy and her gothic friends' or 'Poppy's vampire chic'.

Felix gave me the necklace I wear all the time. A poppy, of course. I have so many now that sometimes it's hard to remember who gave me what. But this wasn't *Papaver rhoeas*, the red poppy everyone thinks I am named for; but *Papaver somniferum*, the white opium poppy. He called it a talisman when he gave it to me, and I knew it was important because my parents looked disapproving, just as they did when the lawyer gave Beth her legacy. I *know* the painting's important as well. It's a clue to the strangeness at the heart of my family. Maybe my parents are waiting to reveal the truth suitably dramatically on my twenty-first birthday or something, but I've got news for them: I won't be waiting for it.

I think I'll leave this book behind when I leave home. Then my parents will know why I left. I'm not going to stick this out much longer – that's for damned certain. I cheated on all my exams this summer. If it counts as cheating to have a perfect photographic memory. Another thing my parents dismiss. 'Oh, Poppy's always had a good memory,' they smarm to my teachers. 'She's such a good student.' I'm not. I'm a terrible student. I didn't even bother writing anything in the last two papers. I just concentrated hard on the words in my memory and was presented with pages of my own black-inked handwriting. It was probably a mistake though because I was so *bored* while everyone else scribbled away for the rest of the afternoon.

I'm bored almost all the time now. Either bored or angry. Sometimes I almost hate my parents. Their refusal to admit what's happening to me makes me feel so trapped. The irony is that everyone else seems to think I'm so lucky. Like Beth. When we were kids we were almost friends but since coming to Ashmount she's determined to think that I'm her enemy. It's my popularity that does it – Beth hates the fact that I rule Ashmount and no one even knows she exists. I can't understand her. My cousin is such a mouse about everything. 'She's intimidated by you,' my mother says oh-so-sensibly, as if Beth doesn't share an eighth of my genetic material. Whatever I've got, she's got too, although I confess I haven't seen much sign of it. She's obviously heard my mother's coven jokes because the couple of times I've tried to talk to her about witch-craft she acts as if I'm deluded.

God, why is everyone so blind? Even the Coven, this clique that's formed itself around me, doesn't really believe in the supernatural. Alys and Siona and the rest of them go along with it the same way they'd jump on any bandwagon to be cool. I'd like to show them some of the stuff I can really do but they'd be scared out of their tiny minds and, to be honest, maybe I would be too. I haven't done all that much really, yet. I keep hoping one of my parents will make this big revelation. A kind of 'Hey, Poppy, well done, you guessed it, you are a witch!' speech and explain what's going on.

In the meantime, I just do simple things. I can open any lock – damn useful when breaking bounds at night. I started with levitating pencils but that's so teen-witchy and at least lock-picking has some practical use. But there's weird stuff mostly – like whatever desk I'm sitting in, if I reach into it there's the book I want. In four years though no one's noticed that although we need about a million textbooks and files for lessons I never carry any more than a tiny little black backpack large enough for some make-up and a pen. They just stagger about with their satchels and hockey sticks and endless pieces of paper and wonder feebly why I look so much more cool. And lessons. I mean since *when* am I supposed to be this intellectual genius? But everything I do gets an A.

But that's nothing compared to some of the nasty stuff. Things like making people like me, or making them believe what I say. I used to do a lot of that – making myself more popular. It's how I've got the lead in every school play ever since the fourth form. It's how come I got the head boy of Wooten College to take me to the May Ball when he'd only met me once. Poppy's fatal charisma. Everyone sees it but they don't really SEE it. Or me.

I'm sick of being treated like a child. I'm sick of being lied to. Are my parents ever going to tell me the truth, or am I supposed to just go to school and university and do my exams honestly like a good little witch? Screw that. I want OUT of Ashmount, with its stupid rules about wearing a hat to chapel and turning your mattress every morning. I want to DO something. Anything! I want to use my magic and understand it, instead of having to hide it and have everyone believe I'm making it up. Hell, it's not even Ashmount, I want out of my whole life.

And now I'm about to be shipped down to the

grim south again. I have a month of Beth's company to look forward to while her mother and stepfather cruise round the Adriatic on their annual salute to yuppiedom. My mother's thrilled by the idea — anything to avoid having to spend the summer in my unrelieved company. She's already phoned the stables to arrange a horse for Beth, blissfully ignorant of the fact that Beth rides like a sack of potatoes. I can't see anything to look forward to about the summer. Beth's been like the walking dead ever since the funeral and even at her best she loathes me.

I swear I'm not taking this much longer. I'm sixteen years old. I'm not going to wait about the rest of my life, waiting for my parents to be honest with me. I'm not going to meekly do A-levels and go to school like a kid when I've got all this . . . all this POWER inside me wanting to be let out.

~❦~

That is no country for old men. The young
In one another's arms, birds in the trees
— Those dying generations — at their song,
The salmon-falls, the mackerel-crowded seas,
Fish, flesh, or fowl, commend all summer long
Whatever is begotten, born, and dies.
Caught in that sensual music all neglect
Monuments of unageing intellect.

—W. B. Yeats

The Book of Secrets
Rivalaun's Book

I think my father's stories hide a secret. But if there's a hidden truth to them, I don't know what it is. I don't know whether it's by his choice we travel the worlds or if we suffer under the weight of some curse, but each new transition that leaves *him* eager for discovery makes *me* increasingly weary of change. We walk the long road, my father and I and, just as its beginning is hidden by a veil of secrets, its ending can only just be glimpsed.

I think that in this, our most recent shift between worlds, I can see for the first time the beginning of the end. But Danaan is unusually reticent. We've hardly spoken since we arrived in this cold, wet world full of machines and unquiet minds. Already the village, our

14

home for the last year, is receding like a memory of long ago. The liquid voices of the People and the river and the quiet babbling in the back of my mind don't belong here. Marten made me this book and, fingering the words branded into the cover, I wonder if they were a joke. The People have a strange sense of humour, and what they made of my father I'm still not certain of. Danaan wins people over easily, catching them in the web of his words, but they distrust him easily too. More than once our departure from a world has been hasty, carrying nothing with us but Danaan's winning words.

Just this morning Marten passed me this book, an imitation of those he had seen in my father's hut, with a diffident smile.

'It's so you can have secrets too,' he said as I tried to thank him. 'Like the Storyteller.'

I wonder how he knew that Danaan doesn't share his secrets with me. But then, standing in the grove of lilac trees, while around us the life of the village flowed on in its uncomplicated placidity, I thanked him and meant it. When, a little later, my father came to tell me we were leaving and we were yanked once more through the barrier between worlds, this book is all I cared to take with me. Possessions have been left behind too often for me to care much about them, but writing in this carefully crafted gift I believe that Marten was right. I should have some secrets of my own.

I'll begin with saying that I'm excited about this change. Despite the city, which is a shock after living in a community of fifty people for more than a year, and the rain, the idea of finding out some of my father's own stories makes me eager to get to wherever we're going. Danaan is grimly uncommunicative. All I know is that my uncle is dead and this must be at least as much of a shock to me as it is to him, since before this new piece of information was presented to me I wasn't even aware that I had an uncle. Now I am burning to know more, but Danaan is grieving and I don't feel able to pester him for answers. The long road has taught me to be patient and answers will come soon enough. We travel now in a long rattling vehicle — a train — a journey I enjoy more the further the village recedes in my mind. Danaan has inevitably acquired a book from somewhere and is reading it with the fixed concentration of the scholar. We share the carriage with a woman and her two children. The woman is reading a book as well, one with a bright pink cover, and the two children are alternately playing with and fighting over a toy that makes little trills of sound when they touch it. I am dying to have a go. It seems to have some kind of story inside it and points are awarded. I am filled with avarice. One of the best things about changing worlds is the games. I learn them quickly and win often. Danaan has occasionally capitalized on this skill of mine and learning the games seems to gain friends faster than almost any other activity.

We are travelling to Camomile House. Where and what that is, I don't know. Those two words were all my father said in response to my question. The death of my uncle has made him taciturn and he is moving much faster than usual. I don't know where he acquired the money to travel on this train since we customarily

16

arrive in a world destitute, but he has hustled and bustled the pair of us onwards so quickly that I still haven't had time to work out the rhythms of this new world. Covertly, I study the clothes of the woman and the two children. The children both wear trousers of a blue material and shirts with words on them. Language at least presents no problem, this is one I can both speak and read. But I am mystified by meaning. One child's shirt is emblazoned with colourful animals and proclaims: 'Catch them all!' The other, even more puzzlingly, exclaims: 'Ay Carumba!' The woman, reassuringly, is wearing a dress with a yellow flower print. Well then, time to explore further . . .

I've now walked up and down this train and it appears that clothes at least are similar to those of the village. Homespun is not common by any means, and men wear their hair shorter here, but no one gives me a second glance as I wander up and down the carriages. I think Danaan will stand out more than I do. There seems to be an unspoken rule here that children and new–adults have more freedom in their dress than older people. The woman in our carriage definitely gave him a second glance before settling herself and the children down. Normally, he would have charmed her immediately but now there is nothing in his manner to show that whatever she is reading cannot exercise one fraction of the fascination of my father's stories. The journey does not fit into the pattern of our travels. Danaan is normally a loquacious companion. He seems to be constantly in motion, talking, gesturing, sharing a pipe or a drink with our companions on the road. It's hard for strangers to tell that he is learning, soaking up their reactions, reading an entire culture into the way they laugh or frown. When strangers first meet him he is alien and exotic, a man from far away; when they bid him farewell they see in him one of their own, a traveller from no further than the next township whose customs are the same as their own. Sometimes I find that irritating, the ease with which he gains people's trust. But now I want him to come out of that musty volume and start talking, to tell me where we are travelling, to charm the woman into putting down her book, to draw the children away from their toy with the spell of his voice.

We are going to see family and I don't even know who they are. They'll be a community, a small-knit group, as close to each other as the villagers. But they'll see us as one of their own. That's new to me. My father and I are strangers wherever we go, and suddenly it seems important that this belonging isn't wasted. If I have a family, I want to know who they are. I prepare to put down this book and the pen I found when we arrived in this carriage and to engage my father in conversation . . .

I don't know what to make of the result.

'Father,' I said quietly, conscious that the woman was listening. 'Danaan.' He looked up, his eyes blank for a moment, and I realized that he might not have been reading his book at all but using it to gain a shield of privacy.

'Hmmm?' he murmured, focusing on me slowly.

'I've forgotten the names of the people we're

meeting,' I told him. The lie was an old one. Not knowing the name of your destination, or the name of the world you live in is unbelievable. But forgetfulness is an acceptable lapse. It's the way we ask questions in public when ignorance would be thought peculiar. However, there was an unspoken criticism in my question; after all Danaan *should* have told me where we were going.

'The people?' Danaan lifted an eyebrow but he accepted the ruse. 'I don't know for certain how many of them will be there.'

He paused for thought and then listed a bunch of names quickly, the rhythm of his voice making a half-poem out of the litany:

'My brother Sylver; his wife Emily; their daughter, your cousin Poppy; Cecily, who was the wife of my other brother; and her daughter Bethany, who is also your cousin.'

I blinked, trying to take it all in. Danaan's recitation made it appear that there were hundreds of people waiting to greet us and it was only after a few minutes' thought that I got the names clear in my head. By then he had returned to his book and I didn't have the desire to disturb him again.

Sylver. Emily. Poppy. Cecily. Bethany.

Sylver. Emily. Poppy. Cecily. Bethany. Danaan. Rivalaun.

The names fit easily into the rattling of the train. I can't imagine how we'll fit into their group. I can't envisage the faces behind the names. I don't know if we'll be strangers to them or if, like my father, they'll have that gift of fascination; of seeming both alien and

19

familiar at once. An uncle, two aunts and two cousins. Two cousins, two aunts and an uncle. My father's secrets. The train carries us to meet them as inexorably as my father's stories journey towards an ending.

CHAPTER FOUR

~❦~

Take up our quarrel with the foe:
To you from failing hands we throw
The torch; be yours to hold it high.
If ye break faith with us who die
We shall not sleep, though poppies grow.
— John McCrae

The Book of Dreams
Bethany's Book

I had convinced myself that I was resigned to my stay at Camomile House. But as my stepfather's BMW pulled smoothly past the gates I felt a deep dread sit itself in the pit of my stomach. Sitting in the back of the car, clutching the painting my father left me, I gazed out of the windows at the banks of flowers on either side of the road. Poppies everywhere.

I had forgotten the unholy way Poppy's parents glory in her. Naturally, they wouldn't think of doing anything so vulgar as gloating. Instead they treat us lesser mortals with a dreadful pitying kindness. At parents' days at school they study the work on display with care, deliberately looking at everything, as if every last piece of juvenilia had an intrinsic merit. Other people laud their children's gifts to the skies; Poppy's parents don't need to. They know and we know that Poppy wins every competition before the rules have even been set.

But I wish they didn't try to be so *nice* about it all the time.

Of course, Poppy's sickening habit of excelling at everything she puts her devious little mind to is what landed me at Ashmount to begin with. My uncle and aunt explained diffidently that Poppy's education required a school with a wide range of extra-curricular activities and a firm disciplinary attitude. My father fell in love with the prospectus and my mother with the idea of me getting an identical education to Poppy the Multi-Talented. *Et voilà*. I'm packing my bags for boarding school. I still owe Poppy one for that. While she's swanning about the halls, lording it over her minions, I sneak past hoping that no one will guess we're related. As long as I remain a nonentity I'm probably safe. As far as anyone knows I'm Bethany 'you know, the swotty one who always sits at the front' Greenwood and it doesn't remind them much of 'wouldn't you just die to be?' Poppy.

I even tried to make my mother enrol me under her maiden name instead of 'Greenwood', just so no one would guess Poppy was my cousin. More fool me – I needn't have worried. Not even Louise, my best friend, has ever noticed any similarity between us. Poppy simply rules that school and I'm about as noticeable as carpet fluff.

I hugged my painting tighter and hoped that I'd be able to survive this vacation without dying from Poppy over-exposure. Strangely enough, it seemed to help. My mother had looked at me narrowly when I told her I wanted to take the painting with me but the fight I had expected hadn't materialized. Instead she had said,

'I don't suppose it'll be much of a problem,' and found me some brown paper to wrap it up in. Relieved, I'd tried to be especially helpful with the preparations for her trip. I didn't think I could have faced leaving the painting behind. I look at it every night before I go to sleep and I think I've even started dreaming about it. I don't care that it isn't valuable. My father wanted me to have it and it must have meant something to him.

The car came to a halt and my stepfather turned off the engine with a sigh of contentment. While I climbed awkwardly out of the car, he and my mother gazed at the house with a kind of distant pride. They do this every time they visit and it's inevitably followed by a conversation on the way home in the car about what generous hosts my uncle and aunt are. Since I was being inflicted upon that hospitality I wasn't quite as misty-eyed about it but I admit that, were it not for Poppy, I'd find Camomile House an attractive prospect as well.

The house is large and has been added to over the years so it rambles in all directions. I think my aunt and uncle originally intended to have lots of children but either they couldn't or they decided one Poppy was enough. But the house is large enough for a horde of them. It has all of the interesting character features that parents rave about: a little staircase that you get to through a cupboard and twisty, turrety bits that make it look like a children's book illustration. There's a stable block at the back which my uncle and aunt intend to convert properly some day. My father spent the summer after the divorce living in it. I have vague memories of visiting him there and being jealous of Poppy who got to live with my father when I didn't.

My mother doesn't seem to find visiting Camomile House socially awkward but that's mostly to do with Emily. She and my mother are friends from way back and my mother sometimes says, 'Emily is the only person who has any comprehension of how difficult it was to be married to someone like your father.' But really my uncle Sylvester isn't anything like my father.

It was Sylvester who opened the door to us and I thought he was looking better than he did at the will-reading. But my father's death had marked him, and his white hair always makes him look older than he is anyway. He shook hands with David and kissed my mother on the cheek before turning to me.

'I'm looking forward to having you stay with us, Bethany,' he said warmly. 'It seems like a long while since we've spent any time with you.'

I tried to smile back and mumbled some kind of thank you but was saved from having to make any more conversation by the appearance of my aunt Emily, who set about organizing us. David and Sylvester were packed off to the library to talk about books and my mother and I were settled down in the kitchen, where my aunt broke off from doing complicated things with the Aga to pour herself and my mother drinks.

'Lunch is in an hour and a half,' my aunt explained to us. 'I've had to put things back a bit because it's just been one of those days for some reason. Sylvester found a dead crow in the drawing-room fireplace.' My mother made the standard offers of help and my aunt smiled at her sunnily. 'There's no need,' she confided in us. 'Everything's under control but I have to sit here and look attentively at things to make sure it stays that way.' She turned to me and suggested, 'Why don't you take your things up and get settled, Bethany? Sylvester will bring your cases up later but you can start to move in. We've given you the L-shaped room again.'

I agreed as positively as I could, since it wasn't as if I had much option, and picked up my painting awkwardly. My aunt gave it a look and then frowned unexpectedly.

'You don't mind, do you, Emily?' my mother asked, catching the look. 'She seems to have become quite attached to it.'

'No, that's all right,' Emily said quickly. 'It's no problem, Beth. Hang it wherever you want.' But once I'd left the room I heard her say something else in a voice too low for me to hear and I knew she wasn't entirely happy about it.

I wandered slowly upstairs and found that the L-shaped room had been made up for me. A large vase of flowers sat on my bedside table and, for a mercy, didn't appear to contain any wildflowers of any description. I dumped my shoulder bag on one of the beds and unwrapped my painting. There was a suitable nail on the wall facing the bed and I removed a framed print of Corfe Castle to make room for it. Once I had put it up carefully, I sat and faced it. The print was still leaning against the wall and the comparison made the castle my father had painted look even stranger. It was almost as if he'd forgotten how to draw; the shadows and colours were all right but the shapes looked sketched in and there was no detailing on any of them, which made the castle look flat and two-dimensional.

It was then I heard a knock and turned to see Poppy lolling in the open doorway looking like a poster child for the MTV Generation. She was wearing faded blue jeans and an immense white shirt and had tied her red hair into two short braids. She would have looked about ten years old if she hadn't been wearing make-up. She half-smiled at me, which became a look of complete glee when she saw what I was doing.

'You brought the painting!' she said, coming in uninvited to stand almost in front of me and look at it. 'Excellent. Do my parents know?'

'Your mother said it wasn't a problem,' I told her, not giving away that it had seemed as if it might be.

Poppy raised her eyebrows at me as if she gravely doubted it but all she said was, 'You missed all the exams.'

'I know,' I said. 'What were they like?'

'*Très* tedious,' she said, flipping a hand dismissively. 'Don't bother revising. But your French teacher sent you some work and your friend . . .' she paused and wrinkled her nose thoughtfully, '. . . Louise? She sent you a letter.'

'She gave it to you?' I said stupidly, and Poppy gave me a 'well, obviously' look. I blushed, realizing that she had already managed to wrong-foot me within five minutes of conversation. 'I didn't realize you knew her.'

'I don't,' Poppy said, flicking her eyes at me. 'But she knew me and someone must have told her I was your cousin. The letter's in my room, do you want it?'

'Yeah, thanks,' I said getting up and following her, trying to disguise the fact I was seething. My absenteeism had obviously undone all my hard work spent disassociating myself from Poppy, and Louise would almost certainly be angry with me for not telling her. I trailed after Poppy into her room and immediately determined that I wouldn't comment on it. Last year Poppy's bedroom was purple and blue with white muslin curtains hanging from her four-poster bed. Now it looked like 'Hello Visits the Addams Family in their Beautiful Showplace Home'. The walls were black, the floorboards were black, the muslin curtains were black and had acquired huge claw-mark rips and tears. Only one wall out of the four was still purple and the furniture had been dragged back from the wall and covered with black velvet, whether as dust covers or part of the gothic décor wasn't clear, ready for Poppy to paint it. My cousin was obviously preparing for a no-holds-barred bout of 'Let's Wind Up The Parents'.

I shuddered inwardly while Poppy unearthed a tiny black backpack from the gloom and produced a pile of badly photocopied sheets of paper and a red envelope.

'Do you want to read it now?' she asked. 'My mother said I should take you for a walk, by the way.'

The only thing that makes staying with Poppy halfway bearable is that she doesn't let her parents force us together. Poppy lies to my aunt and uncle as easily as breathing about all the social activities we've been sharing together when in reality I've been reading a book while she flirts with boys. Either she realizes that I cordially hate her or she just doesn't want to spend time with me any more than I do with her. But she does cover for me with her parents when she could easily dump me in trouble with mine by complaining that I don't like her. It's not a great help but it is practically the only time I've seen Poppy go out of her way to help me out. Normally I would have colluded, but I didn't want to read the letter right away, not while I had to be with Poppy. And I didn't want to risk my mother accusing me of not trying with her, so I said:

'I don't mind going for a walk. Where did Emily say we should go?'

Poppy shrugged. 'We may as well go to the tree house,' she said. 'At least there are books.'

We spent the rest of the time before lunch there. Poppy's tree house is a custom-built kids' fantasy bought for her eighth birthday. It's up in a big oak tree and has more mod cons than some council flats. There are two platforms; one is about twenty square foot and supports a small house, which has bookshelves and built-in cupboards and a hatchway in the floor through which you can let down a ladder. For some unknown reason the house also has electricity and Poppy has acquired a fridge from somewhere which is inside one of the cupboards. A spiral staircase leads out of the room and then extends further up the tree to a second platform, which is half the size of the first and has only a low railing around it. When Poppy and I were young enough to be almost friends we played here and I know that Poppy sleeps here sometimes because there's a hammock next to the top platform. I swear her parents don't seem to have considered that she could break her neck some day.

The only other good thing about staying with Poppy is that she has reasonable books. The tree house's current selection is a bizarre collection of Wiccan magic books and everything ever published by Penguin Classics. That allows quite a wide range of choice and I had reread the first part of *Stalky and Co* when the bell went for lunch. As we walked back in Poppy said, 'I can't stand that book. Have you noticed how the characters always accept the just criticisms of their elders?'

Taken by surprise, I laughed and found myself saying, 'What about the way the headmaster always knows the true story?'

Poppy grinned at me as we walked into the house and said in a lower voice, 'If he's anything like teachers at Ashmount, he just looks for the obvious culprit.'

Which would be you, I thought to myself. I don't think there can be anyone in the entire school who doesn't know that Poppy and her friends break out of school at least once a week to go to a nightclub somewhere in town.

CHAPTER FIVE

~❀~

No, no, go not to Lethe, neither twist
Wolf's-bane, tight-rooted, for its poisonous wine;
Nor suffer thy pale forehead to be kissed
By nightshade, ruby grape of Proserpine . . .
For shade to shade will come too drowsily,
And drown the wakeful anguish of the soul.
—John Keats

The Book of Lies
Poppy's Book

I sometimes think that Bethany might be OK to hang out with if she wasn't so programmed by her mother to be Little Miss Normality. When we went inside for lunch I said something about school and she shot me a look halfway between envy and disgust, which sums up her attitude to me nicely.

My mother had prepared an elaborate meal designed to lubricate conversation and leave the guests sated and slow of mind. She chatted affably to Bethany's mother and stepfather about their trip while my father talked to Bethany about books. Beth didn't talk much and played with her food dismally. I'm not sure if it was just misery because she's on a fairly permanent diet. I, on the other hand, am blessed with a fast metabolism and I loaded my plate high enough to escape the conversation entirely.

It wasn't until halfway through second helpings that anyone mentioned Felix. David asked my father how long Felix's house would be kept on.

'It's only a minor matter,' he said, darting an apologetic glance at Bethany. 'But Beth has various belongings there that will need collecting.'

Typically, no one mentioned that Uncle Felix had almost certainly left Bethany all of his estate; just as at the will-reading the issue of money was politely glossed over. But the introduction of Felix into the conversation threw a blanket of tension over the company and I could feel my parents meeting each other's eyes in silent collusion before my father nodded and reached to pat Bethany's wrist.

'No, I completely understand,' he said, laying aside the piece of meat he had speared with his fork. 'It is a little difficult, though. My brother and I are co-trustees of the estate and various legal arrangements will have to wait until I can contact him. However, Felix owned the house outright and the utilities are paid through to the end of the year so there shouldn't be any dramatic changes.'

I closed my eyes for a moment when he had finished speaking to gain some distance. The air was thick with emotion. Even when I'm furious with my parents I can't ignore their misery and, *my*, it had taken an effort of will for my father to deliver that speech with any pretence of normality. David was radiating awkwardness at introducing the subject and Bethany was sunk into a depression so deep I could feel it dragging the rest of us into that same black whirlpool of despair. My mother and Cecy changed the subject of conversation with a skilful double-pronged manoeuvre, which was all the more technically excellent for its pretence of being completely natural.

There are pictures of my father and Felix with my mother and Cecy. The brothers are wearing identical secretive smiles and the women are perfectly poised with 'cats who've got the cream' expressions. When I see them at their dual-flanking conversational attacks I remember that photograph and wonder how many times they have worked together to circumvent awkwardnesses.

Bethany didn't notice any undercurrents to the conversation. Ever since Felix's name was first mentioned she had been looking bleakly down at her almost untouched plate of food. It wasn't until the subject was changed that she looked up. I flicked my eyes away quickly so that she wouldn't see that I had been watching her and took advantage of the artificial joviality to pour myself another glass of wine without my mother noticing.

It was at that moment that I suddenly knew there was something important about to happen. I was half-standing even before my mother. We met each other's eyes at the exact moment a car crunched on the gravel outside and our premature reaction was concealed by a general motion towards the window.

'It appears to be a taxi,' David said, since he was closest to the window.

'I wonder who it could be,' my mother said, joining him there and simulating a perplexed look.

'Danaan,' said my father with an unshakeable conviction, and stood up with a sudden vigour.

CHAPTER SIX

⮜⮞

Is there any peace
In ever climbing up the climbing wave?
All things have rest, and ripen toward the grave
In silence; ripen, fall and cease:
Give us long rest or death, dark death, or dreamful ease.
—Alfred Lord Tennyson

The Book of Secrets
Rivalaun's Book

We found a taxi at the station and Danaan calmly gave the driver directions with his usual lack of concern for our rapid changes of paradigm. The vehicle was uncomfortably enclosing but we drove with the windows open and, even though the air was cold, the sun shone palely from behind the clouds.

Danaan sat beside the driver and showed increasing signs of life as he engaged him in conversation about sports. Listening to them it became clear to me that this was a world my father had visited before. Danaan is capable of gaining information from people that they would swear he must have known already. But I stand outside the spell cast by his words and know his tricks well enough to see he wasn't using them. It has happened only occasionally on our travels that Danaan revisits a world, and even then he is secretive about his history there. This time I knew some of that history already and I was intrigued by the idea that Danaan had maintained some kind of connection with the family that awaited us.

That impression was vividly reinforced when we arrived at our destination. The taxi turned off the main road and approached a gated wall. As it did so, I had the unmistakable impression of power. There were three different magics worked on the entrances to the house, lying in layers and blending in and out of each other. The first was overwhelming. Like the charisma Danaan exudes when he tells his stories, I could sense it. But although there was a taste of him in this, it wove itself more subtly through the grounds ahead, giving no indication of its source.

The gates themselves were warded with a visible witchmark: a simple but well-worked little charm intended to welcome friends and discourage felons. It was not dissimilar to wardings used by the people in the village and indicated a practical and less overbearing use of magic.

The third enchantment assailed us just as we passed the gate, crashing into my consciousness without subtlety or restraint. It was woven into the wildflowers that lined the banks with an airy disregard for the difficulty of such a working and screamed 'witch' as the other two had not.

Magic surrounded us, but the taxi-driver gave no indication that he heeded it and drove up the stony path without ceasing his monologue on the iniquities of the off-side rule. At any other time I might have been interested in what he was saying but, as we neared the house, I was wound tight with excitement. The tranquillity of the location, with its aura of mixed magics, was seducing me with the sense of coming home.

The double doors of the house opened as the taxi drew to a halt.

'Looks like you're expected,' said the driver as Danaan swung open his door.

'Seems so,' Danaan said affably, and I thought to myself that, with this much magic floating around, it would have been a wonder if we hadn't been.

As we got out of the taxi I realized that Danaan's assurance had misled me. There was a group of people coming out of the door of the house that I knew no more about than their names and I hung back while my father stepped forward to greet them.

I knew which of the strangers was my uncle, even before Danaan greeted him. A tall, imposing figure with silver-white hair and eagle eyes. I felt certain he was the source of the flow of power I had sensed at the gates. He and Danaan clasped hands silently and then stood still in a silent communion of grief while the others crowded out of the house behind them. The woman who moved forward to join them I felt certain must be my aunt Emily by the way she gathered all of us together with her words.

'Daniel, it's good to see you. And this is the perfect time for you to arrive.'

Glancing about at the rest of the family, I was distracted from noticing her unusual rendition of my father's name by thinking that it didn't look much like the perfect time. The other woman, whom I tentatively identified as Cecily, was watching Danaan with mistrustful, narrowed eyes. Almost unconsciously, she was resting her hands protectively on the shoulders of a young girl. She, I decided, was probably my cousin Bethany. When I looked at her she blushed and ducked her head, causing her long brown hair to swing forward, hiding her expression. Another man, a stranger, stood further back; seemingly wondering, as I was, what his role here should be. Danaan was clearly having his usual effect on strangers, leaving them uncertain, fascinated and enchanted despite themselves.

But one of the assembled company was watching the others as I was, set apart from them by the fact that she wasn't participating in their group reaction. Red-headed, attractive and with an aura of wild magic, she was watching Danaan with an expression of unholy glee. This was such an unusual response to my father that I stared at her in turn until she noticed and looked back at me. Instantly her face changed, as if shutters had closed over her eyes and, caught between a calculating wariness and an easy complicity, she stared back at me. Secrets abounded around me and the tension didn't break until Danaan stepped back and said:

'I came as soon as I could.'

He was looking at my uncle when he spoke. But it was my aunt Emily who answered him.

'We're very grateful that you did,' she replied, and was already gathering me in with a warm smile as she added, 'And this must be . . .'

'My son,' Danaan filled in the blank helpfully. 'Rivalaun.'

'What a beautiful name,' Emily said smoothly. 'From the Mabinogion, isn't it?' She came to me with an affection that her social demeanour couldn't disguise. 'Rivalaun, these are your cousins: Bethany and Poppy.'

Bethany half-smiled at me from behind her curtain of hair but Poppy launched herself at me like a missile and I had to adjust my balance quickly to catch her. She beamed up at me from under my arm and said ingenuously, 'Where have you come from, Rivalaun?'

Everybody suddenly started talking at once and my aunt Emily took advantage of the occasion to bustle us inside. Amid offers of food and drink, the company began to adjust to each other and within a short space of time Danaan had been swept off by Emily, and Bethany's parents were returning to the dining room with Sylver to continue the meal we had obviously interrupted. Bethany followed them, deliberately ignoring me and Poppy, and as soon as she was out of earshot Poppy turned to me quickly and seriously to say:

'We have about two minutes before my mother and father come back and start lying to us all. Will you meet me later and tell me the truth?'

I didn't need to consider my reply.

'I'll trade you,' I told her. 'My secrets for yours.'

~¢~

Though I am young, and cannot tell,
Either what Death or Love is, well,
Yet I have heard they both bear darts,
And both do aim at human hearts.
　　　　　　　　　　—Ben Jonson

The Book of Dreams
Bethany's Book

Poppy must have ears like a cat. One moment she was sloshing wine into her glass, the next she was practically racing her father to answer the door. I heard Emily say 'Poppy!' and then she quickly followed them out, leaving the rest of us looking at each other.

'And Danaan would be . . .?' asked David with some amusement.

'Daniel,' my mother frowned. 'The missing Greenwood brother. I haven't seen him for years. Not since I married Felix.'

'And I gather there was some tension?' David raised his eyebrows at her tone.

My mother looked at us both and then shook her head.

'Words fail me,' she said. 'They really do. Let's just say that this is typical Daniel. Nothing about him is ever predictable.' Then, putting her hand on my shoulder, she guided me towards the door. 'Come on, Beth,' she said. 'We'd better go and show the flag.'

We reached the front door just in time to see two people getting out of a cab and, as they did so, I froze in my tracks. My uncle Daniel would have been enough of a shock on his own. His features were sharper than my father's but other than that the similarity was eerie. They could have been textbook illustrations on genetically inherited traits. But, embarrassing as it is to admit, it wasn't Daniel who made my legs turn to stone. It was the boy with him.

Just for the record, I'm not normally the type to fall for a pretty face. Growing up in the same family as Poppy has provided me with a crash course on how deceptive appearances can be. But that doesn't mean I'm blind either, and there are some things you just can't ignore. For example, your legs suddenly not working while you forget how to breathe. He was stunning. Dressed in shapeless woollen clothes with silver-blond hair spilling all over his shoulders and leaf-green eyes meeting ours warily. He looked like nothing I've ever seen before and I blushed when he looked directly at me. But he barely noticed. While Daniel and Sylvester hugged each other he was watching us all – but it was Poppy his eyes fixed on.

I should have known that the first boy I was attracted to would be swept up by Poppy within seconds of meeting him. Barely had we been introduced when she hurled herself into his arms. Then, as we went back into the house, she dragged him aside to whisper with her in the hallway. Luckily, my aunt Emily is wise to Poppy's tricks and hustled them both into the dining room where she started serving a third helping of lunch. But that didn't stop them sitting next to each other. I stared down at my plate and contemplated Poppy's gory death. Her flirting was obvious even by her standards and I was almost certain they were already holding hands under the table.

This was quickly becoming the most excruciatingly uncomfortable social gathering it has ever been my misfortune to attend and I've had plenty of experience. I sat silently through my new uncle's apologies for his sudden arrival and Emily's explanation that Daniel had been working abroad in a village without any standard communication lines. I continued to sit there glumly when three different kinds of pudding were presented and Daniel declined the offer of a guest room in favour of the privacy of the stable block. I went obediently with everyone else into the living room for coffee and watched Poppy foil her parents' attempts to separate her and Rivalaun. They sat together on one sofa and I saw my aunt Emily keeping a discreet watch over them as they whispered together.

When we finished coffee my mother and David made noises of departure and everyone stood up. While I said goodbye to them I saw my aunt Emily draw Daniel aside and say something to him quietly. My mother released me from an unusually tight hug and said:

'Take care, Beth. Don't worry too much about school work. Try and have some fun, OK?'

'We'll take care of her, Cecy,' my uncle Sylvester assured her and shook hands formally.

'I'll come and see you out,' Emily added. 'I'm taking

40

Daniel and Rivalaun to get settled in the stable block.'
She glanced back at Poppy and said, 'Why don't you
help Beth unpack, darling?'

Poppy smiled sweetly at us all.

'I'd love to,' she lied easily. 'But I haven't finished
painting my room yet. Why don't we give Beth and
Rivalaun a chance to get settled and then we can all go
out riding tomorrow?'

Before I had time to say anything the plan had been
seconded and any protests I might have made were
lost in the general exodus. I retreated upstairs into the
L-shaped room and sat down glumly on my bed. My
painting was hanging where I had placed it and I tried
to focus on the castle through prickling tears.

I'm angry with my mother for leaving me here and
with David for making her go. I'm furious with my
uncle and aunt for making me spend time with Poppy
and for having such a vain, manipulative little witch for
a daughter. I loathe Poppy for getting everything she
wants and Rivalaun for not seeing through her, and I
hate my father for dying and letting all of this happen.

~c~

Soundlessly collateral and incompatible:
World is suddener than we fancy it.
—Louis MacNeice

The Book of Lies
Poppy's Book

My parents attempted to counteract the effect of this afternoon by casting a blanket of dullness over the evening. Beth didn't come out of her room for dinner and Danaan and Rivalaun stayed in the stable block all evening, so it was just the three of us. As we ate I counted the times my parents lied to me but lost track wondering if the confusion over names counted as a real lie or a misdirection.

My father styles himself Sylvester Greenwood on his books. But in old pictures, and sometimes when my mother doesn't realize I'm there, he's always called Sylver. My mother's endless repetitions of Daniel this and Daniel that didn't do much to disguise the fact that his son apparently knows him only as Danaan. And Rivalaun . . . I wonder if my mother is going to start calling him Robbie or Ryan before the week is out?

But the lies were coming so thick and fast I don't know if I could have kept track anyway. The only positive thing about dinner was that it helped me make a list of all the things I have to ask Rivalaun about. My parents were actually quite helpful about that. I already wondered where on earth they'd been living up until now but without the skilful concealments this evening I wouldn't have known to ask about half a dozen other things.

I think my father might have realized that I saw through their lies because halfway through dinner he changed the subject and the conversation entered the realms of erudition as my parents dissected Proust. I can never make up my mind if they do this to encourage me academically or to shut me out completely, but they gave me their full attention when I left the table.

'What are your plans for this evening, Poppy?' my mother asked innocently. 'More work on the bat cave?'

I ground my teeth but I knew if I objected I'd be in for another lecture on how depressing it is to live in a black room, so I let it pass.

'I'm going out to the tree house,' I told her.

'Well, don't bother your uncle,' she told me. 'Or your cousin. They've had a long journey and need their rest.'

'I won't,' I told her and she must have believed me because she nodded with satisfaction and let me go.

Later, in my hammock, I watched the light coming from the windows of the stable block and thought to myself that there wouldn't have been much point. When Danaan (or Daniel, whatever) arrived I hoped we'd see sparks. But it looks like he's joining in the popular myth that our family is normal. I just hope he doesn't manage to programme Rivalaun to think the same. I know we made a bargain but I don't put much faith in the reliability of other people.

Bethany's lights are still on as well. I can just guess what she's doing. She's staring at that painting and crying. I think her parents are crueller than mine. How can they allow her to believe everything's normal when she's this unhappy? There must be something they could do to make her happier if only they didn't care so much about their precious secrets.

It's starry tonight and I can feel myself getting sleepy. Much though I hate to admit it, my mother's right about my room. It is depressing. But since that's the point, what does it matter? Out here at least everything I can see is real. Inside everything's so fake that it doesn't matter which of the lies you embrace. It's easier to remember that nothing is true if you're acting all the time. Only problem is . . . how do you know where the act stops and the truth begins?

CHAPTER NINE

~❦~

I have come to the borders of sleep,
The unfathomable deep
Forest where all must lose
Their way, however straight,
Or winding, soon or late;
They cannot choose.
　　　　　　　—Edward Thomas

~ *In Dreamland* ~

Bethany is walking along a narrow street. On either side of her there are houses, but without looking at them she knows that they are empty. The street widens out and ahead of her she sees the castle. The drawbridge is down and the gates are open. The only movement is the thick black water in the moat reflecting the grey starless sky. It doesn't move like water but like oil. Thick and viscous.

Now she is standing on the drawbridge looking down. At first she can't see her reflection but when she concentrates a face appears. But the face is Poppy's.

'I'm not Poppy,' she says out loud and the waters blur and ripple, obliterating the face and leaving only the blank grey surface of the moat.

She shivers and looks up at the castle. Close to, it looks menacing and she's not sure she wants to go in.

'But I have to,' she says to herself and walks inside.

*

Poppy stands at the edge of the battlements looking down. She can see that the castle is on a hill and around are gardens, giving way to a tangled forest. The shapes are like cardboard cut-outs, no reality to anything. A figure walks up to the draw-bridge and then moves out of sight somewhere down below.

'Was that Bethany?' she asks, and kneels on the edge of the parapet to look down.

'Careful.' A hand takes her arm. 'If you fall you'll wake up.'

She turns abruptly and now she is standing on the battlements. A boy is looking at her. He has black hair and white skin, like an old photograph. His eyes are black and she can see the grey sky reflected in them, clouds scudding across them as if in a high wind. But the air is dead still.

'What do you care?' she asks. 'Who are you?'

He looks away.

'Just a dream,' he says.

Rivalaun is lost in the forest. The trees close in from all directions. He suspects there is no point in walking in any direction but he pushes through them regardless. He knows he is dreaming but he can't wake up.

'The land remembers,' a voice says. 'In you it stakes its claim.'

He looks around carefully but cannot see the speaker. Just when he has stopped looking, a trick of the light catches his eye and he sees that the colours in front of him which seemed to be just forest make up the shape of a person. The air ripples like water and then he can see a figure clearly. He wears fluttering grey robes and his hair coils around his head like white smoke.

'Who are you?' he asks.

The figure shakes its head and its hair floats in the non-existent wind.

'You should know better than to ask that,' it says and then all at once blows away into nothingness.

Bethany is walking along a long gallery. There are paintings on the walls but she can't see them properly. A boy is walking beside her. He is wearing black.

'Are these my father's paintings?' she asks.

'I thought they were mine,' he says.

They stop and look at a painting together. Bethany can make out the details now. Her father and Sylvester and Daniel are in it. All three are smiling but black shadows reach out from the corners of the painting to coil around their wrists.

'What's that?' Bethany asks.

The shadows are coiling out of the painting now and reaching towards her. She backs away. But the boy doesn't move.

'You can't escape it,' he says sadly. 'It's part of you.'

There are buildings ahead. A fortified hill town with a castle at the centre. He can see a figure standing at the very top looking over the battlements. He can see bright red hair. He waves but she doesn't see him.

'She can't see you,' a voice says. A boy is standing in the road ahead. 'You're not part of her dream.'

'But I am,' Rivalaun replies. 'We're here together.'

The boy shakes his head.

'You're mistaken,' he tells Rivalaun. 'Here everyone is alone.'

'Someone's looking for you,' the boy says. 'Look.'

Poppy looks but she can only see the forest, green and black shadows merging in and out of each other.

'I can't see anything,' she says. 'Why should I believe you?'

'I can't lie,' he tells her. 'Not to you.'

'Now I know you're lying,' Poppy replies. 'Everyone lies to me.' And she steps off the balcony and falls.

There is a wrench and Bethany is standing outside the castle.

'There's not much time,' the boy says.

'How do you know?' Bethany asks him.

'Close your eyes if you don't believe me,' he says sadly and Bethany shuts her eyes.

'They've both gone now,' the boy says.

'How do I know they were ever really here?' Rivalaun asks.

'You don't,' he replies and Rivalaun wakes up.

CHAPTER TEN

One foot in Eden still, I stand
And look across the other land.
The world's great day is growing late,
Yet strange these fields that we have planted
So long with crops of love and hate.
> —Edwin Muir

The Book of Lies
Poppy's Book

I woke up disorientated and struggled out of sleep, with the sense of surfacing from a suffocating ocean of dreams. I had fallen out of my dream. I still remember the sudden lurch out of sleep to realize that I was falling in reality, the hammock twisting out of reach as if the world had decided to cast me loose, and I was forced to twist frantically, my fingers forming a death-grip on the hammock's ropes.

In moments the rocking hammock stilled and I lowered myself to the platform carefully, my heart pounding as if I had been running a race and my skin clammy with fear as I stood there shaking. Disgusted with myself, I dug my nails hard into my palms and breathed a long shaky breath as I forced myself to regain control. Blood was hammering in my ears and I heard myself say, 'I won't let you . . .' before the tremors stopped and I was myself again.

Calm now, I climbed back out of the tree and, when I stood on the ground, glanced up at it frowning. 'That was not good,' I said thoughtfully and went back into the house.

I met my mother in my room. I hate it when she does that. Has she no sense of privacy? Why do parents seem to think that their children's lives are somehow less private than those of strangers? It's within families that we need a personal space most of all. But I have no private space except inside my head. My parents try to invade everything else and I wish them joy of it.

'Can I help you?' I asked freezingly.

She looked at me with a sudden shock and something that for a second looked like worry. Then she smiled with that patronizing tolerance that parents are so good at and said:

'Are you preparing for a Black Mass, Poppy? We could hire decorators and come up with something a little less . . . oppressive.'

'Thank you, no,' I told her, looking for my towels so I could go and shower the fear off myself.

'Is that wall going to be black as well?' she asked, refusing to leave it alone, and glancing at the one wall I hadn't painted yet.

I spun with a savagery that surprised even me and, realizing that I was still not completely in control of myself, forced myself to speak calmly. I won't let my parents get a rise out of me. I refuse to.

'Unless you have a better idea?' I said lightly and then suddenly found myself grinning as I had an idea myself. 'Then again, maybe not.'

My mother didn't notice my distraction. Not really interested in my reply, she said, 'Are you going to shower now? I came to tell you we can drive you children to the stables in about an hour and a half.'

'Wonderful,' I said, finally finding a towel hiding under one of the dust sheets. 'That will give you adults a chance to catch up on news,' I added sarcastically as I left the room.

Pleased with myself at that comeback, I grinned all the way to the bathroom. But once inside I got more serious and, as the water sluiced the terrors of the night down the drain, I thought about my idea for that blank wall. The difficulty would be getting hold of the template for what I had decided to do. But even that wasn't impossible. If everything else failed I could always steal it.

I met Bethany on my way out of the bathroom and was struck by how awful she looked. Well, no one is at their best all mussed and sleepy but Bethany looked really bad. Her eyes were bloodshot and her skin looked grimy with shadows. She actually flinched when she saw me as if I was some horrible thing she was unprepared to meet with her guard down and I was surprised to find myself feeling hurt.

'Morning,' I said quickly and walked past her into my room. Why should I care what Bethany thinks of me? She's a sad, dull, nothing person who no one even knows exists. If she wasn't my cousin *I* wouldn't even know she existed.

I really wasn't on form today, I decided as I sat down at my dressing table, and I had to get myself into shape quickly. I had to be clever when I talked to Rivalaun,

51

and there's nothing worse than trying to ride in a bad mood. Especially with novices. My heart sank as I remembered that my mother still didn't know that Beth is a hopeless rider. I've seen her at school and it's embarrassing. Like a sack of potatoes sitting on the horse, as if she wanted to apologize to it for being there. This could be awful, especially if we were riding alone. Beth hating me and falling off her horse all the time while I tried to talk to Rivalaun. Well, maybe I could try a little practical magic, I decided, and brushed my hair extra fiercely to impress my personality on the day. I looked into my own eyes in the mirror and concentrated. I could feel my own power, lying beneath my skin, a presence that was always with me. It was like a hidden pool deep inside; a wellspring of magic that longed to flow out into the world, fountaining into reality. It is the source of my unintentional charisma and now I reached for it. I drew on its power until I felt myself glowing with it: the shining source of my power.

I found my riding clothes still in my school trunk but had to search for my black hacking jacket. When I was looking for it I heard my mother ringing the bell for breakfast just like at school and had to hurry to be ready in time. I checked myself carefully in the mirror before going downstairs and decided I was satisfied with my appearance. No trace remained of the frantic animal I had been when I woke up. I put on the white poppy necklace Felix had given me and tucked it under my shirt to be a good-luck charm. 'That ought to sort today out,' I told myself and went downstairs for breakfast.

~•~

Why should I blame her that she filled my days
With misery . . .
Why, what could she have done, being what she is?
Was there another Troy for her to burn?
—W. B. Yeats

The Book of Dreams
Bethany's Book

I knew today was going to be awful as soon as I woke up and the awfulness seemed to have centred itself on Poppy. I know she was in my dreams last night as well. It seems so *unfair* that I can't even get away from her when I'm asleep. She was coming out of the bathroom as I went in, and I had to shower in a cloud of Poppy-scented steam. All white musky perfume and orange-blossom shower-gel. I had the feeling that I was washing her into and under my skin. Horrible thought. As if Poppy was some kind of disease you could catch.

I felt bedraggled and achy from having cried myself to sleep last night. The water seemed to wash out of me any energy I might have had and I trailed downstairs feeling like something the cat had brought in. When I got into the kitchen the first thing Emily said to me was, 'Beth, you look really tired. Didn't you sleep well?' Right in front of Rivalaun who was sitting at the table drinking coffee and looking amazing in riding clothes he had managed to find somewhere. I had completely forgotten that we were supposed to be going riding today. Sylvester had glanced up from his newspaper to join in with the general Bethany critique and was looking at my jeans askance.

'Will you be all right to ride today?' he asked with concern and, relieved, I was about to say, 'Maybe, I'd better not,' when Emily contradicted him.

'Don't be silly,' she said. 'Fresh air will do her good. Remember how much it helped Poppy when she was ill, two years ago?'

Foiled by Poppy's wretched love of horses, I sat down at the table and tried to drink a glass of orange juice without feeling as if I was going to throw up. Daniel appeared as I was declining cereal and toast and declared that he could eat a horse. He was promptly offered a banquet of choices before he settled on bacon sandwiches.

'Much rather eat a horse than ride one,' I mumbled to myself. But the only one who heard me was Rivalaun, who slanted a sideways glance at me and smiled as if we shared a secret. That cheered me up for all of half a second before Poppy came bouncing in and I lost his attention for good.

Ugh. That's all I can say. Just uggghh. Poppy, in cream riding clothes and a jacket that *anyone* could tell was one she'd worn in competitions and probably won prizes in as well. Poppy, with her red hair in sickening kiddie bunches that were probably what you were *supposed* to wear under a hard hat. Poppy, bouncing in and glowing with life and grabbing Rivalaun's cup of coffee because she 'just couldn't wait' for her own.

Poppy, giggling as he ruffled her hair and then tickled her, trying to get it back. Why is she always the centre of attention when she comes into a room? Why is my life so tormented with bloody Poppy everywhere?

All I wanted to do was go back to bed and pull the covers over my head, but soon Emily was hustling and bustling us so that we'd get to the stables in time. I managed to get out of breakfast but Poppy ate a bacon sandwich as if it were the nicest thing she'd ever tasted and drank three cups of coffee, getting steadily more hyper every second. Emily was driving us and presented me with a hard hat of Poppy's to wear. I held it awkwardly on my lap in the back seat of the green Range Rover. Rivalaun sat up front in his position as guest and carried out a polite conversation with Emily about, of all things, botany. Meanwhile, Poppy, next to me, stared out of the window with the glazed expression of someone who wished they were wearing a Walkman.

The drive ended all too quickly and Emily pulled up in the front yard of what must be the most pretentious stables in the universe. It looked like something out of a doll's house catalogue, complete with country women in wellington boots and a group of teenage girls hanging about the horses who flicked their eyes at Rivalaun when we got out of the car. To my horror they all seemed to know Poppy and when she got out they rushed over to greet her. I lost her in the swarm and Emily disappeared off somewhere to arrange horses.

Poppy actually has her own horse. Hell, she probably has two or three. And something ominous had been said by my mother about Emily hiring a horse for me. Rivalaun and I were left out of the arranging, however, and stood uncomfortably while we waited to be told where to go. We drifted over to the stalls and looked at horses.

'Do you really not like riding?' he asked me quietly and I blushed.

'It's OK, I suppose,' I said, embarrassed and not wanting to seem ungrateful. 'Do you ride much?'

'I have ridden,' he said carefully. 'But not recently. Is Poppy very good?'

My heart sank at the thought that he was interested in her and I said sharply, 'Of course she is. Poppy's good at everything.'

A tall, horsey-looking woman came up to us then and looked at me measuringly.

'You're Beth, right?' she said and didn't wait for my confirmation. 'I expect you'll want something quiet.'

'Yeah, thanks,' I said, wishing for the first time I could say, 'No, actually, nothing too tame,' and was led up to a brownish, dull-looking horse with the name 'Sandy' over its stall.

'This will be yours then,' the woman told me. 'I'll send someone to help you get kitted up.' I looked at the horse and thought it looked as excited to be stuck with me as I was to be stuck with it.

Poppy's horse is called Claret and she has it shipped up to school every term so she can ride it there. I've never actually seen her currying it or mucking it out or any of the other things that people who love horses are supposed to do, but then her crowd of hangers-on probably does that for her. The group of girls she'd attached herself to knew all about it, naturally, and fussed over her and her horse jealously while a bored-seeming man came out to help me with saddles and tack and looked at me like an idiot while I failed two times running to actually get up on the damned thing.

Rivalaun's horse was white with greyish blotches and it looked as if the stable woman had decided he was the kind of rider I wasn't because it kept dancing about. But Rivalaun had blatantly lied about how much of a rider he was because he got on it in one smooth motion and it settled down in seconds. Mine dismally trooped out to join them and I hoped against hope it was going in that direction because I was telling it to.

'You all look pretty settled,' Emily said with a pleased smile. 'I'll be back to collect you at two, OK, Poppy?'

'OK,' Poppy agreed and swung up on to her horse as if she did it every day.

The Range Rover disappeared through the gate and I wondered what we were supposed to be doing now. The horsey woman knew, of course, and came over to tell us.

'I have to give a lesson now but you'll be all right on your own, won't you?' she said, looking at Poppy.

'We'll be fine, Angela,' Poppy said sweetly. 'I thought we'd take the path to the stream.'

'Good choice,' the woman said. 'A nice easy ride.' And I'm sure she looked at me as she said it. Mercifully, she took herself and the horde of giggling girls off with her and Poppy turned her horse towards a side gate which led into an open common with trees in the distance.

CHAPTER TWELVE

~◖~

In the uncertain hour before the morning
Near the ending of interminable night
At the recurrent end of the unending
　　　　　　　—T. S. Eliot

The Book of Secrets
Rivalaun's Book

This is what it's like to have a family. I'd walked with them in dreams all night and in the morning I could feel their presence in the grounds of the house. Danaan had already disappeared somewhere when I woke up, but I had the impression he'd only just left. I sat up and looked around, taking in our surroundings. This was the place where Danaan had requested to stay: a long loft space above the stalls of the unused stable, empty except for two wooden beds. The loft was clean and bare but below in the stables I could smell musty hay and old dust.

In the long, light room of pale wood I could see that Danaan's bed had been made neatly and on it he had left a set of clothes in my size that I identified tentatively as riding wear. They were brown and fitted almost perfectly and on the dark coat that accompanied them I found a piece of cloth sewn inside with the name 'S. Greenwood' written on it.

Familiar with having to explore strange places alone,

58

I found my way to the kitchen through the small herb garden that separated it from the stable block. Emily was there making a hot drink that I could smell from the garden. When she saw me in the doorway she smiled instantly and said:

'Rivalaun, come in. Would you like some coffee?' I accepted instantly, pleased to be welcomed, but was instantly baffled when she asked, 'Do you take milk, or sugar?'

'I don't know,' I confessed, feeling awkward. Poppy's remarks yesterday had warned me to expect secrets and the conversation over lunch had disturbed me. I could tell that Danaan and my presence was being explained away by some terms I didn't recognize and I was unsure of what I was supposed to know about this world. 'I've never had coffee before,' I said carefully, deciding that some measure of honesty must be acceptable.

Emily glanced over at me, her expression serious for a moment. Then she smiled. 'Try it black then,' she said. 'If you decide you'd like it sweeter there's milk and sugar on the table, or cream as well if you'd like.'

'How do you take it?' I asked, accepting the cup she gave me.

'Black with cinnamon,' she said easily. 'But I'm abstaining at the moment. It's a stimulant and it can make my nerves a little too sharp.'

I sipped the hot liquid and it was rich and bitter. I held it in my hands while I listened and thought to myself, 'I can do this.' I'm used to learning the rules for the societies I find myself in. This was no harder, just more important to me. I wanted these people to accept me with an intensity that was almost frightening.

'Daniel is having a shower,' Emily was saying. 'And your uncle Sylvester will be down in a moment. Poppy and Beth are probably squabbling over the other bathroom.' She looked at me expectantly as she added, 'I see you found the riding clothes.'

'Yes, thank you,' I told her. 'Do they belong to my uncle . . . Sylvester?' I chose the name carefully and was rewarded with a smile.

'Yes. He doesn't ride so much now but we thought you might be about the right size. You know you look very much like him when he was younger?'

I pondered that thought as I sat at the table and felt a glow of pleasure which increased as Sylver himself arrived and offered to share a newspaper with me. But I found myself increasingly anxious to see Poppy. The explanations she promised looked all the more urgent since Danaan seemed determined to leave me to find my own way. I drank my cup of coffee and read the newspaper curiously. While I was learning about this family I had to remember I needed to learn about this world as well. The dreams of the night seemed spun through the morning like sunlight and the house seemed to glow with warmth and friendship as I sat in the huge kitchen with its stacks of shining brass and smells of dried flowers and herbs. It took the arrival of Bethany to remind me that this family had been recently touched by a tragedy that I took no part in.

Bethany entered the kitchen with the lethargy of depression and I felt the web of relationships around me growing tense with unspoken thoughts. Sylver and Emily reached out to gather her into their communion, but even I could see that her grief made her unreachable. Bethany was awake enough to see the way she was being manipulated because it seemed as if she resented it. When Danaan entered unexpectedly cheerfully and fell into conversation with Sylver, she said to herself, 'I'd rather eat a horse than ride one.' I smiled at her, hoping she would say something else, but before she could, Poppy came into the room and all the currents of magic I had sensed in the early morning intensified. I could feel them swirling about her and even though everyone pretended they couldn't sense it, Poppy was the focus of everyone's attention. Everyone except Danaan, who watched me as Poppy and I teased each other with an enigmatic smile.

The plan for the morning had been pre-arranged according to some schema I was just beginning to comprehend. The adults would remain at the house and discuss things more honestly than they had been able to in the presence of Cecily and her second husband, the outsiders, yesterday. Meanwhile, we children would be sent out to socialize together. Poppy, the wild element, would be contained by Bethany's shyness and grief. It had been well done and Poppy and I were both playing along. But the looks she shot me indicated that the pretence would last only as long as it took to get out of the eye of the adults.

I tried to speak to Bethany again later, at the stables, but managed to offend her in some way and didn't get much response. I was beginning to guess that there was more to her abstraction than just grief and was relieved when we took the horses out on to a grassy sloping hillside and headed towards a small wood.

Bethany was not a good rider, but she kept up with me as Poppy led us on to a path she seemed to recognize. I glanced across at her. She had swung her hair forward, looking fixedly at the ears of her horse. I took the point and watched Poppy instead, racing ahead of us and setting her horse caracoling.

At that point I understood something I should have known earlier. The dreams last night had been some kind of warning. Poppy, suddenly set free from her family, was energizing the air around her. Bethany was churning up those same currents of energy with grief and I could feel the charge of magic sparking in the atmosphere around me.

~❦~

God! of whom music
And song and blood are pure,
The day is never darkened
That had thee here obscure.
—George Meredith

The Book of Lies
Poppy's Book

I forget sometimes what it's like to be free. The morning had been peppered with incident and other people's personalities clashing against mine. Meeting the Riding Club at the stables was like being transported back to school and, even while I was watching the girls fawn about me, I realized how bored I get of it all. When I was younger I really exulted in that kind of worship. Now a sense of dissatisfaction seems to permeate my life and I wanted to ride away and leave Rivalaun and Bethany behind me.

Of course, it was impossible. The day had to be faced and, with the promise of uncovering secrets ahead, I reined Claret in and cantered back to my cousins.

'Do you realize that the air is fizzing around you?' Rivalaun asked when I pulled up next to him.

'Of course,' I laughed at him. 'Now tell me something I didn't know.'

'I can't.' He looked across at me seriously. 'I don't know what you don't know.'

'That's our family down to the ground,' I said idly, my gaze drifting over to Bethany. 'Secrets and lies and no one knowing who they are.'

Bethany looked up and shot me a look of furious contempt.

'Where are we supposed to be riding to, Poppy?' she asked coldly. 'Since this is your idea?'

'This track leads up to the woods and through them to the stream,' I told her. 'Then it curves back to here, coming back along the roadside.'

Bethany nodded and Rivalaun and I stayed silent for a moment. This was going to be harder than I'd thought. Bethany hadn't been this antagonistic when she arrived yesterday morning but she was practically fuming with silent enmity now.

That gave me a thought and I asked her, 'What did you dream about last night, Beth?'

She jumped and her horse whickered nervously under her. I could see what Rivalaun meant about the air fizzing. The three of us together were an explosive combination and even a horse as calm as Sandy could sense it.

'None of your business, Poppy Greenwood,' she snapped. 'Why don't you ask Rivalaun what he dreamed?' Then she kicked her horse roughly and showed us she knew enough about riding to urge it into a trot as she moved out ahead of us. Rivalaun started his horse walking after her and Claret and I fell alongside.

'What did you dream about, Rivalaun?' I asked softly.

'About you,' he said, and ahead of me I saw Bethany goad her horse into a canter and head quickly uphill.

Now let's just hope she doesn't break her silly neck, I thought, and ignored her.

'About me?' I asked curiously.

'Yes. There was a forest, and then later a castle. I saw you standing at the battlements and waved, but you couldn't see me.'

A shiver went through me.

'Now isn't that curious?' I said slowly. 'I wonder why I couldn't see you.'

Green eyes met mine with sudden interest.

'Then you were there?' he said.

'Yes, I was there,' I said. 'And so was Bethany. I saw her at the drawbridge. And I bet she saw one of us too.'

'If she did, she doesn't seem willing to admit to it,' Rivalaun said testily, looking up at where Bethany was already at the edge of the woods.

'That's Beth for you,' I said with a shrug. 'Little Miss Normality. Her parents have really done a number on her.'

'And yours haven't?' Rivalaun said dryly, suddenly making me angry.

'Yes, obviously!' I hissed and he looked alarmed.

'Sorry,' he said instantly. 'Don't be offended. Please? It's not as if I'm familiar with my father's secrets.'

'OK, then,' I said. Then later, 'No, I'm sorry, too. They just set me on edge. And I'm not planning on sticking around for it much longer.'

'You're leaving?' Rivalaun looked alarmed at that and I grinned at him.

'Well, not right now. It's pretty hard for a

sixteen-year-old to run off in this world. Even if they do have . . . unusual resources.'

'I have a feeling you'd find a way,' he replied, but then added, 'How did you know I come from a different world?'

With that we were away. The life Rivalaun described when I asked him was as unlike the pale, polite version my mother had offered us yesterday as something could possibly be. I was almost sick with envy as he told me about wandering from world to world, changing dimensions as easily as taking a bus, living in a web of stories and storytelling. But after a while I realized that he was telling me something else as well. All of his stories were unconnected fragments he didn't understand how to fit together. Even while living the life that I knew was true and real his father had managed to keep him as much in the dark as mine had with me.

'I don't know anything, really,' he kept telling me. 'I sense magic and power and all kinds of other things. But I don't know what they are and I don't know why I feel them. I've been to other worlds, like yours, where everything like that was hidden. But, trust me, seeing it in front of you doesn't make it any more comprehensible. You're a witch to begin with. I'm not sure I am.'

What he was saying made me less sure than ever before that I was a witch. The one thing I knew for certain seemed to be slipping away from me. Rivalaun's secrets only seemed to inspire more questions.

'There's so much we don't know,' I said angrily, and Rivalaun nodded.

'And they don't tell us the answers,' he added.

I thought of my dream and said slowly, 'I can think of a way to find out the truth.' He looked at me for a long considering moment before finally asking:

'How can I help?'

CHAPTER FOURTEEN

~❦~

The glories of our blood and state
Are shadows, not substantial things;
There is no armour against fate.
—James Shirley

The Book of Dreams
Bethany's Book

I have to wonder if this is going to be the pattern of my entire life. Will I always, whatever I do, be under the shadow of Poppy? It's not an exaggeration. Living in this house is like being possessed because there's nothing here that Poppy doesn't seem to have completely under her thumb. It's not even just here – there's no space anywhere that Poppy hasn't staked out and marked as hers.

Last night I read the letter that Louise sent me care of Poppy and I decided I'm never going back to Ashmount. Never. Louise is supposedly my best friend at that sickening school. When we reached the fifth form we chose to share a room together. We're right up in the attics with the other loners and the people who came low on the room ballot. Poppy came first and she and Awful Alys, and Scottish Siona who wears her own plaid instead of a regulation kilt, share a three-bedroom set with a living area that's known as the Conference Suite. The head girl used to get it until they added it to the ballot because of some unusual notion of fairness. I myself heard our history teacher say it was inevitable that Poppy would end up in it, 'since everyone knows she'll be head girl'. How is that even possible? How can everyone love that devious snake–girl so much?

The letter was a classic example of how sneaky she is. I thought Louise would be cross that I'd kept Poppy being my cousin a secret, because I thought she hated the sly, cliquey little witch as much as I do. But it seems I was wrong. She said they'd told her at the office that Poppy was taking my coursework home because she's my cousin. Louise was thrilled. She said she'd spoken to Poppy about me and that Poppy had been so NICE. That Poppy and Alys and Siona had invited her into their set and that Poppy had given her the paper she was writing this letter on. That they'd said she should come and sit with them at lunch sometime. How awful is that? How incredibly unbelievably horrible is it that your best friend can get captured by your worst enemy? And that she should think you'd be PLEASED!

Today, all I could think of when we were out riding was how bloody unfair it is that Poppy should get everything so easily. Why couldn't I, just once, have the chances she does? Her parents are crazy about her; Rivalaun blatantly adores her . . . I'd actually heard him say he'd dreamed about her last night. I was livid. Admittedly, I'd dreamed about her as well, but what reason could he have? I've had to put up with her for years. He only met her yesterday.

I could see that the summer of rain cooped up in the

house with Poppy that I'd been dreading could easily become an even worse summer with Poppy and Rivalaun falling in love in the sunshine and me tagging after them like an unwanted puppy. Followed by going back to Ashmount and having Louise tell me how nice Poppy was when you got to know her. At that point I tried to encourage my horse to move off the path.

It didn't want to. It knew exactly what it should be doing and that was following Poppy's plan about where we should go. The plan had probably been cooked up by her and that horrible Angela woman back at the stables. It was probably on a list of 'Rides to Take with Your Boyfriend and Your Dim Cousin Who Can't Ride for Toffee'. She had probably discussed it with those giggling girls who had formed an instant clique the second Poppy had entered. I told the horse this. I pleaded with it.

'Come on, Sandy. You must have some kind of sympathy for me. It's not like you're the star horse in the stables. I bet everyone pets bloody Claret all the time.' I tried to point its head off at a smaller track leading into the woods away from the one Poppy had described. I kicked its side hopefully and said, 'Come on, Sandy,' again until finally it moved on to the path I wanted, shook its head a couple of times and walked on.

I felt better already. When I found that the track ended in a small clearing I couldn't have been happier. Sandy stopped walking and I climbed off. I tied its reins as well as I could to a suitable tree and it seemed reasonably happy to stand there. Then I sat down under a tree and took out this journal.

Let them ride about for hours together since they seem so happy. I don't care anyway. I'm obviously not supposed to be happy. I'm the extra in a story all about Poppy.

CHAPTER FIFTEEN

~⟨~

Hence, viper thoughts, that coil around my mind,
  Reality's dark dream!
I turn from you, and listen to the wind,
  Which long has raved unnoticed.
                    —Samuel Taylor Coleridge

~ *In Dreamland* ~

'It's not, you know.'

The forest is deeper and greener here and shadows flit through it. Up above there is a night with no stars. Bethany is standing facing a boy wearing black. His face is pale and his eyes are dark grey and he looks like a black-and-white photograph.

'What's not?' she asks him.

'It's not Poppy's story,' he tells her. 'It could be yours.'

'What could be mine?' Bethany asks.

'The story. It's your dream, isn't it?'

For the first time Bethany looks around her properly.

'This is the forest from my dream, isn't it?' she says. 'Can I get to the castle from here?'

There is no answer and she realizes the boy has disappeared. But the clearing seems lighter somehow and she can see she is carrying her journal. A path has opened out of the clearing and she walks towards it. Even though the trees on either side are wound with brambles and the earth is a tangle of nettles on either side, the path is smooth and grassy beneath her feet. Ahead of her she can see it stretching ahead in a long tunnel of greenery.

There is light ahead and Bethany heads towards it. Suddenly she finds herself out of the forest and on a high hillside. What seems to be an impenetrable void of darkness is ahead of her, but beyond that chasm is another hillside and on it the castle her father painted.

'Can't I just go to the castle?' she asks herself but the scene doesn't change. 'Wasn't it nearer before?' she asks again, looking closer.

'The landscape of dreams is vast,' a voice says softly. 'You cannot cross it in a single night.' Bethany turns, expecting to see the boy and the forest behind her.

Instead, there is a long, bleak scrubland stretching into infinity, with mists coiling up from the cold ground.

'What is this?' she demands, feeling frightened. 'This isn't my dream.'

'You can't own dreams, child,' the voice says and a figure appears out of the mists. Smoke curls into the shape of fluttering robes and the air starts to ripple as if from a heat haze. Bethany can see pale purple eyes, the shape of a face, and a swirl of white smoke makes up a cloud of hair.

'Why not?' she demands, trying to stay calm.

'Dreams own you,' the figure tells her and swirls back into the mists.

Bethany is back on the edge of the forest. The maze stretches ahead of her. The bushes and brambles have wound themselves into a tangled thicket of hedges and she cannot trace a path through the maze.

73

'Why do I still have this?' she asks.

No one answers her question and she opens the book. She can read her own lines of handwriting. The last words are: 'I'm the extra in a story all about Poppy.'

She carefully turns to the back of the book and writes, with a pen that has appeared in her hand:

'What happens to the dream when the dreamer wakes up?'

~⁓~

Man is the shuttle, to whose winding quest
And passage through these looms
God ordered motion, but ordained no rest.
                    —Henry Vaughan

The Book of Secrets
Rivalaun's Book

My sense of coming home stabilized that afternoon. Despite everything that happened later, I realized during that ride with Poppy that this was where I wanted to be. This place, this family, this world gave me an idea of who I was, or rather who I might become. In my wanderings with Danaan nothing has ever been fixed or certain. Here I knew what questions might be answerable and for the first time I had an interest in the story we were creating.

I thought about Marten, the villager who gave me this book, and of how simply and easily he had passed out of my life. I thought about other friendships that had disappeared and of ones that might have been and I wondered how I had ever accepted such a transient life as natural.

Riding with Poppy, I felt a part of something. I had secrets of my own now and with them I had acquired a power to make decisions. Ever since I had arrived Poppy had been forcing that upon me, demanding that

75

I make choices. And I had made them instantly, with a feeling of liberation every time.

I enjoyed being with her, even if I wasn't sure yet how much I liked her. She strikes me as dangerous. Not because she is, but because she wants to be. Poppy's reaction to secrets is anger. She wants to know everything and, kept in the dark, she wants to throw everything into disarray. I like her parents: my secretive uncle Sylver and my kind, clever aunt Emily. I even like Cecily, Bethany's mother, who was wise enough to mistrust Danaan and his stories yesterday. I didn't want to side with Poppy against them but I did have reasons for wanting answers myself.

Poppy and I agreed that the dreams we were having were important. And I agreed with her that it seems unreasonable that her parents should refuse to discuss any form of magic with her.

'Even if your ideas are all wrong,' I told her incredulously, 'I still can't believe they make fun of you for having them.' I've met magic-users before in the past and they have often been secretive, strange individuals, but in every world they've had their own community. It sounded strange that Poppy genuinely knew nothing about this. From what she was telling me, there was no organized idea even of what magic was in her world. But she was bitterly angry to hear what little I knew of our travels between realities.

'Can you make the shift yourself?' she asked me immediately. Poppy has a natural talent for asking the one question you'd rather not answer.

'No,' I told her, lying. I've been travelling with Danaan for long enough now. Not all worlds are isolated like this one and Danaan's story-telling has taught me a lot one way or another. I haven't tried to make the shift myself but I'm fairly certain I know how to manage it. Although Poppy had told me she wanted to leave here, I wasn't about to provide her with a nice easy way of doing it just yet.

I'm not certain she believed me, but it was then that we came past the stream in the woods and I realized that Bethany was nowhere in sight. Poppy had planned that we could stop here and talk but now we continued on down the path until the stables were in sight.

'She couldn't have come back this way,' Poppy said decisively. 'She'd end up at the stables in no time and then she'd look stupid on her own. She wouldn't have walked back on her own and . . . no, it's impossible.'

'She must still be in the woods then,' I replied and Poppy rolled her eyes.

'I bet she's gone off on another path,' she said. 'This is so typical of Bethany. She's always wandering off like this. You can't take her anywhere without her slipping off somewhere to read a book or daydream.'

'She's got a reason to want privacy,' I said awkwardly as we headed back up the hill. Poppy looked surprised and I clarified: 'Her father dying.'

'You think this is about that?' Poppy frowned. 'Well, it could be, I suppose. But I suspect it's because she loathes me with a passion.'

'She does?' I hadn't realized this but when she said it a lot of things made sense. 'Why?'

Poppy laughed at this and became quite vocal on the subject of Bethany. She's got a way with words that reminds me of Danaan. It's the way she writes a completely convincing reality on to everything and then tells me not to believe it.

'I can't tell you anything about Bethany,' I remember her saying. 'Anything I say she'll twist to make it sound as if I'm intentionally disrespecting her. I can't say anything to her she doesn't take as something negative. She simply doesn't credit me with the ability to be nice or honest.' Then she started laughing again. 'The problem is I think she might be right.'

'That you can't be honest or nice?'

'Exactly. I don't think I've got enough experience with honesty to know what it is.'

'What does Bethany think you do that's so evil and treacherous?'

'Everything,' she responded instantly, but as we continued back into the forest she proceeded to give me some examples. 'Witchcraft,' she said. 'She thinks I'm a fake.'

'Hasn't been established,' I insisted. 'We don't know what she thinks about that, we haven't asked her. And the situation is complicated because in your world it's entirely possible that she has no reason to believe that you're not.'

'OK, then, school. She has a problem with me there.'

'Why?'

She sighed at me and slanted me a look through considering hazel eyes.

'You're being deliberately obtuse, Rivalaun. Beth doesn't like my image. She doesn't like the way I'm popular and clever and don't have to work for anything. She's jealous and she thinks it's sickening.'

'But there's more to you than just an image, isn't there?' I pointed out.

'I think so,' she laughed. 'Beth doesn't.'

It was at that point in the conversation that we started to get seriously worried about Bethany. 'It's nearly one-thirty,' Poppy said. 'If we don't find her soon we'll be late back to the stables.' The wood wasn't all that big compared to others I've seen but it diverged into a number of smaller tracks, according to Poppy, and I had the thought that with all this magic floating around there might be other dangers we didn't know about.

'That's why this is so stupid,' Poppy said, beginning to get seriously annoyed. 'If Beth could be a sane human being just for one day we could have talked about all of this and made some sense of things. But instead she has to get the hump and go wandering off to sulk.'

'I can see why the two of you don't get along now,' I told her. 'Do you hate her as well?'

Poppy shot me a dangerous look and I realized how quickly she loses her temper.

'Don't be stupid,' she said shortly. 'I'm freaked about her now. I can't discuss it properly. And if she breaks her silly little neck I'm going to kill her.'

Although what she said was completely contradict-ory, I took her point.

~⟨⟩~

Between the suffering and the will,
Which torture where they cannot kill;
And the inexorable Heaven,
And the deaf tyranny of Fate,
The ruling principle of Hate.

—Lord Byron

The Book of Lies
Poppy's Book

I couldn't believe it when we finally found Bethany. I had wondered if I would find that she'd been thrown off her horse, or broken her ankle, or got into some kind of legitimate difficulty. Then at least I would have been able to calm down and do something about it. As it was, however, we found her asleep in a clearing about five minutes off the main path and I was furious enough to spit.

Rivalaun jumped off his horse and went over to wake her − possibly because he sensed I was angry enough to kick her, or let Claret do it for me. She woke up quickly enough when he touched her and sat up sharply as if she'd been electrocuted.

'What's going on?' she said nervously as he reached down to help her to her feet.

'We had to look for you,' he said. 'It's time to go back to the stables.'

'Damn right it is,' I added. And then continued, with a malicious joy in the fact that the argument that had been threatening all day was finally upon us, 'Are you quite finished being a sulky brat now, or should we wait around a bit longer?'

'Oh, shut up, Poppy,' Bethany said in a bored but prepared voice, as if she'd been wanting to say it for a long time. 'I don't care what you think.'

'Should I be impressed by that statement?' I asked her sarcastically. 'Or shall I dismiss it as a truly pathetic attempt to make yourself look clever and try not to laugh while you haul yourself on to your horse?'

She had been heading towards Sandy but now she stopped dead in her tracks and looked as if she was either going to cry or try to kill me. At that point, Rivalaun intervened.

'Both of you, stop it,' he said. 'I don't want to be here all day while you two trade insults. Let's just go and you can argue about it later.' He turned to Beth and asked in a quieter voice, 'Do you need a hand to get up?'

'No,' she muttered and then proceeded to prove herself a liar by failing to manage it twice running. Rivalaun looked fiercely at me as if warning me not to laugh. I arched an eyebrow at him, deadpan, and he had to fight not to laugh himself.

'Stop baiting her, Poppy,' he said quietly instead. 'I have to live with you both.'

'Oh, let's just go,' I said, seeing that Beth had managed to mount. 'If we're quick we may not be more than fifteen minutes late.'

*

Whether or not Beth took that as a reason to delay or she genuinely couldn't coax more than a trot out of Sandy, we didn't get back until half-two and I could see trouble brewing ahead. Angela was waiting in the stableyard when we came through the gates and my mother was next to her. Her worried expression changed to annoyance when she saw we were all OK.

'Where were you?' she demanded instantly.

I decided telling the truth would only result in a truly ugly argument and somehow didn't really want to start it all off again.

'I'm sorry,' I said, focusing on Angela, not my mother – partly because I knew Emily was mainly worried we'd insulted the stables and partly because I know she doubts everything I say. 'Bethany took a tumble coming over that rough patch of ground at the edge of the common, the one we petitioned about last year? And her falling spooked Claret and it took me longer than it should have to get him back under control. I'm really very sorry but everyone's OK, horses too.' I knew I had them before I'd finished speaking. A perfectly constructed, believable lie. Rivalaun came up behind me then and I hoped he'd have the sense not to elaborate too much. But he only said:

'And apart from that the ride was wonderful. I enjoyed myself so much!'

Angela was already content but it was Rivalaun who melted my mother and they beamed at us all.

'Well, all's well that ends well,' Angela said. 'Glad you had a good day of it.'

'Nothing sprained, Beth?' my mother said, checking her over by eye. 'You look all right from here.'

82

'She looks fine to me,' said Angela. 'Looks like a bit of rough riding's what it takes to put some colour in her cheeks. Will you be back next week, Poppy?'

'Of course.' I patted Claret's neck affectionately. 'Maybe go to the field next time and try some jumps, if that's OK.'

'Anything you like, my love,' Angela said, and shook hands with my mother before coming to see to the horses.

Rivalaun refused the front seat in my favour by claiming he'd like to sit next to Beth. Whether it was his intention to keep us apart or he said it because he actually wanted to talk to her, he got little out of it. She either ignored him or muttered monosyllables in response to his remarks the whole trip back. I could hear them behind me while I listened with one ear to my mother and embroidered a little more on to my earlier lie. Mainly I talked about Claret. A nice easy subject and one with lots of opportunities for discussion. I have a pony as well and another horse on loan from a friend who's in America and stabling is becoming an issue.

'We still haven't got around to converting the stable block, and Rivalaun and Daniel are only using the loft,' my mother said. 'I'll speak to Sylvester about stabling them at home. What's Siona's horse like? At all suitable for Beth?'

'Um . . . no,' I said, trying hard not to laugh at the thought. 'Gigolo isn't really suitable for anyone except an experienced rider. He's a bit high-spirited. But, apart from the fall, Beth was fine today on Sandy.' I thought for a minute. 'Rivalaun could probably handle Gigi though. He's very good.'

'Are you?' My mother caught Rivalaun's eyes in the mirror. 'I thought you might be. You have that look.' She smiled to herself and I saw that Rivalaun had made a bigger hit with Emily than I'd realized. She seemed quite easy and comfortable with him.

We were late for lunch, naturally. But it was only a light meal: salad and some leftover chicken from yesterday. My father and Danaan were not in evidence and my mother said they'd had lunch and were in my father's study and not to be disturbed. She was distracted herself by plans for a benefit dinner she's organizing next week and left us to ourselves in the kitchen. A recipe for disaster if ever I heard one.

Bethany made it clear in five minutes that she wasn't going to talk to me and Rivalaun decided to confine his conversation entirely to food. I put on the radio so at least we'd have something to listen to and found myself explaining the rules of football to Rivalaun. We were at least keeping up an appearance of sociability when my mother returned.

'What are your plans for this afternoon?' she asked us.

'I'd like to explore the grounds,' Rivalaun said. 'Would that be all right?'

'I'll just stay in my room,' Beth said, and my mother frowned at her.

'Don't do that,' she said seriously. 'Go for a walk with Rivalaun.'

'And I'll finish painting my room,' I said calmly. I

was bored of being with Beth and her fuming resentment. If I was going to be seethed at and glared at all summer, I thought, I might as well have a reason to deserve it. And I could see a nice neat way of combining several objectives at once.

My mother obviously decided that was a safe enough pursuit that she didn't need to comment, and took herself off again.

'Any suggestions as to where we should go, Poppy?' Rivalaun asked.

I punished him for being so mundane earlier by saying lightly, 'Why? So Beth can work out its direct opposite and do that instead?' I stood up and headed for the back staircase. 'I'd suggest you confine your explorations to the house and grounds though. There are more places to get lost.'

≈≈

Sick-hearted, weary — so I took a whim
To stray away into these forests drear . . .
And I have told thee all thou mayest hear.
                                    —John Keats

The Book of Dreams
Bethany's Book

I don't think I've ever been as embarrassed as I was that afternoon. I woke up to find Rivalaun bending over me and Poppy glowering from across the clearing. I hadn't meant to fall asleep at all, just to keep out of the way until it was time to go back. But I was too embarrassed to say so.

Poppy made me feel about five inches tall and I had a feeling that Rivalaun, even though he was being nice, agreed with her. Worst of all, I've been planning for months what I'd say if Poppy ever got at me directly instead of just sneaking about, but when I told her I didn't care what she thought she just laughed at me. Feeling silly and childish I followed the other two back to the stables and watched as Poppy and Rivalaun told lies about me delaying them by falling off my horse. I suppose it didn't make much difference to the stable woman, who obviously already thought I was a moron, but it was maddening to see how easily everyone accepted it as true.

Feeling stupid and angry doesn't do much for my conversation and I sat silently on the drive home and through lunch, hoping it wouldn't be long before I could escape somewhere off on my own. But my plans were foiled by Rivalaun saying he'd like to explore and Poppy using her catch-all excuse of painting to disappear herself.

Yesterday I'd have been thrilled to be going for a walk with Rivalaun but today I was too embarrassed to be pleased. He and Poppy were obviously thick as thieves and I was certain that if I said anything about her he'd instantly take her side. So we walked in silence through the grounds until Rivalaun finally said:

'Bethany? Would you tell me about your father?'

I turned and stared at him. It was not at all what I had been expecting him to say. Not what I had been expecting anyone to say. It wasn't even two months since my father's death, but during that time everyone had avoided the subject. I had got so used to sympathetic touches and meaningful silences that having Rivalaun mention the subject stunned me and I felt tears start.

Misinterpreting my silence he frowned at my expression and shook his head quickly. 'You don't have to talk about it,' he said. 'I'd just . . . like to know what he was like.'

'It's OK.' I sat down under the trees so I didn't have to look at him. 'At least,' I continued, trying to explain. 'It's not OK. But I can talk about it. I'd like to talk about him.'

'Please,' he said and sat down next to me. I looked

up, blinking away the water from my eyes, and tried to smile.

'He was wonderful,' I told him. 'Not just because he was my father. I mean, after the divorce I didn't live with him so we had to do other things together. But . . . that didn't matter so much because when I was with him it was easy to forget sad things. He was always so happy himself. Everything seemed to go right for him.' I thought a little more. 'And he made other people happy as well. There were always people with him. Artist friends and critics and just people he'd met. He worked in private but there were always people there in the flat. And they'd all be so interesting, talking about things and having ideas and when he was there it was like an extra light inspiring them all. And I never felt left out because it made me feel special being a part of it and he'd never forget I was there. He made me feel a part of it all. Of all the specialness.'

It wasn't until Rivalaun cautiously put his arm around my shoulders that I realized I was crying properly. I looked up at him through my hair and said, 'It feels awful to miss him so much because he made me promise I wouldn't. When he knew he was dying he told me that I shouldn't be sorry for him because he'd had so much in life. He made me promise I'd live for him when he wasn't there. He wanted me to be happy.'

'But you're not happy,' Rivalaun said quietly and I shook my head.

'No,' I said. 'I don't mean to wallow in grief, I'm not trying to punish myself. I just . . . ever since he died. I haven't felt happy.'

'I'm sorry,' he said and stroked my hair almost

absent-mindedly. 'I'm especially sorry because I am happy. I feel so at home here with this family. And I don't like feeling that my contentment comes at the expense of yours.'

I tried to understand what he was telling me and pushed the hair out of my face so that I could see him better. As I did, he handed me a handkerchief and gave me one of those sideways smiles and suddenly I felt better. Better enough to say:

'I'm sorry you got caught between me and Poppy today.'

He laughed and I found myself smiling back.

'It's all right,' he said. 'I don't really mind because you're both so new to me. But I don't want to end up taking sides.'

I looked at him carefully, wondering if I dared ask what I really wanted to know.

'You like her, don't you?' I said finally, hoping he would understand what I meant.

'I'm not sure that "liking" is an emotion that can properly be applied to Poppy,' he said thoughtfully. 'She's fascinating and I enjoy being with her. I don't know her well enough to say that I like her. But I feel close to her.'

My heart sank. It sounded as if he was well on the way to falling in love with Poppy and I liked him too much for that to be easy for me. But I realized then that even if he did love Poppy, it didn't have to be hell on earth for me. Rivalaun is so easy to be with that maybe we can be friends in spite of this.

'Thanks for letting me talk about my father,' I said eventually and he nodded.

'Thank you for sharing him with me,' he said and, standing up, reached down to help me to my feet. 'It helps me to understand this family. Knowing what's been lost.'

'I wish you could have met him,' I said and meant it.

'So do I,' he said and I believed him.

CHAPTER NINETEEN

〜❮〜

Must helpless man, in ignorance sedate,
Roll darkling down the torrent of his fate?
Must no dislike alarm, no wishes rise,
No cries attempt the mercies of the skies?
—Samuel Johnson

The Book of Secrets
Rivalaun's Book

Together, Bethany and Poppy are an accident waiting to happen. All the lines of force become jagged and the atmosphere is raw with pain and anger. When they are apart from each other everything relaxes and conversation becomes simple again. It seems twisted that the adults invariably ignore their obvious antipathy.

Talking properly to Bethany for the first time made me realize how similar they are. Even though the two of them are surrounded by people, they're both still so separate from everything. I could almost feel more sorry for Poppy than for Bethany. At least Bethany's had that sense of belonging that I feel now. Poppy's like Danaan. She's so enmeshed in a web of truth and lies that it's difficult to connect with a real person at the centre of it all.

I felt anger on behalf of them both and, during my walk with Bethany, tried to think about how they were affecting me. No matter how hard I tried to stay out of their problems with each other and with the rest of the family, I felt certain I would end up taking sides against someone. I had already promised Poppy I would help her in her search for the truth. That afternoon I silently promised Bethany that I would be her friend. But I still had no idea what I was letting myself in for and when we headed back towards the house I told Bethany, reluctantly, that I had to find my father. She nodded and gave me a shy smile as she added:

'It's been nice talking to you.'

I found Danaan outside the stable block smoking a pipe in the weak sunshine. He looked up with a quizzical expression as I approached, and invited me to sit down with a wave of his hand. Even though he was still wearing the homespun clothing of the village, he seemed completely at one with his environment. It is his gift to appear to fit in so well. I watched him silently for a while as I wondered how to begin. Finally I spoke.

'I talked to Bethany about her father.'

A cloud crossed Danaan's face and he nodded.

'What did she say?' he asked.

'That when he died the light went out of her life,' I said, deliberately not taking the harshness out of my words. 'Why did you never tell me about him? Or any of them?'

'It's one story out of many,' Danaan said quietly. 'I gave you many others.'

'But this one is real!' I said angrily. 'This is personal. It involves me.'

'No.' Danaan shook his head. 'It's no more real than any other. All stories are true in the moment of telling.'

'But you never told me this one,' I said, trying to make sense of his words. 'There are fragments of it everywhere, but this story, your own story, you never told me.'

'This isn't my story.' He looked at me with some surprise. 'My story is the journey. I chose my own path. We all chose. Sylver, Felix and I. I never wanted to be bound to one world, or to one reality, one story.' He looked into the distance as he spoke and I was suddenly seized by the fear that he meant to be off again, to leave this world behind just as I was starting to find a place for myself in it.

'But what about me?' I asked. 'Where do I fit in? What's my role in your story?'

He smiled at me with affection and his eyes were alight with promise as he said to me, 'You're my son, Rivalaun. I've given you what gifts I have to offer. But your role in the story? You will have to find that out yourself. There are many paths the future takes, many courses of action open to you. The decision must be yours.'

'Was it always?' I asked, suddenly feeling dizzy with the freedom he was giving me. 'Aren't I bound to you?'

He laughed and said, 'Only by blood and your dreams.'

I thought for a while and then said slowly, 'All day I've been trying to ask the right questions. And I don't think I'm asking them now. So tell me, Danaan, when you made your own choices, you and your brothers, what did you choose and why?'

93

'Good question,' he said, approbation in his eyes. 'Why? We made the decisions our future demanded of us. Sylver chose wisdom. To understand and study reality. Felix chose art. To make an impression and shine in the eyes of the world. And I chose the story. To build bridges between worlds and between truth and lies.'

We sat there in silence for a long time after that as I considered what he had told me and he kept his thoughts to himself. I understood that Danaan's answers, cryptic and puzzling as they were, were the best ones he was capable of giving me. I didn't feel so cut off from the truth as I had with Poppy or as wary of intruding as I had with Beth. Instead, I saw possibilities opening ahead of me and understood for the first time why Danaan wandered the worlds as he did. Everything is an adventure to him and he progresses from story to story with a hunger for change and progression. Danaan hadn't hidden the truth from me, he'd told me to find my own and made finding it seem like an adventure.

CHAPTER TWENTY

~❧~

Some weigh their pleasure by their lust,
Their wisdom by their rage of will;
Their treasure is their only trust,
A cloaked craft their store of skill:
But all the pleasure that I find
Is to maintain a quiet mind.
                              —Sir Edward Dyer

The Book of Dreams
Bethany's Book

I went into the house with no real idea of what I would do next, and wandered towards the library. Books are given pride of place in Camomile House. They're everywhere, organized six ways from Sunday in every room. Cookery books in the kitchen, coffee-table books in the living room, books for guests in the spare rooms. But the library is a shrine to books in a way the rest of the house isn't. It's quiet in there. The long, high shelves are filled with orderly rows of bound volumes with titles stamped on them in gilt. They are regularly dusted and they gleam quietly to themselves in the dark room. When I was little I liked to climb up the library stairs and feel I was climbing up a mountain of books.

My uncle Sylvester's study opens off the library. He's a Professor of English Literature at Oxford and in his own field has a reputation as impressive as my father's. He wrote a book on Coleridge ten years ago called *Cain's Wilderness*, which was supposed to be ground-breaking. I tried to walk quietly past his door so as not to disturb him but I'd only been in the library for about five minutes when the door opened and he came out.

He looked troubled and at first he didn't see me. But when he did his expression lightened and he smiled at me kindly.

'Bethany!' he said, with pleasure in his voice. 'I didn't know you were out here. Would you like some tea?'

I said something about not wanting to disturb him but he brushed that aside and ushered me into his study, closing the door carefully behind himself and instantly creating a small island of peacefulness inside. He made tea quickly and meticulously from an impressively high-tech kettle over on one side of the room and gave me a cup and saucer as if he were bestowing a prize. He seated himself carefully in his desk chair and I faced him across the desk a little uncomfortably. I like my uncle, but he's always seemed a bit unworldly. My aunt Emily does all the family organization while Sylvester occupies an academic peak of excellence from a distance. But today he seemed determined to welcome me and, looking at me seriously, he asked:

'Did you have a good ride today?'

I remembered Poppy's lie about me falling off the horse and wondered if he had heard that story. But I couldn't bring myself to repeat it or to tell him what had really happened. Instead I said, 'I'm not really a very good rider,' and left it at that. He didn't challenge me.

'What would you like to do while you're here?' he asked instead. 'Cecily thinks you should have a proper holiday.'

The conversation with Rivalaun earlier had made me thoughtful and I answered honestly.

'I really would just rather spend some time by myself. I don't really feel able to have fun at the moment.'

He nodded and looked bleak.

'I understand,' he said in a low voice. Then he added, 'But you must have something to occupy your mind. Even if you don't feel ready for more strenuous forms of entertainment.' He smiled gently and I smiled back, feeling that he was an ally.

'Perhaps I could just read?' I said hopefully and he looked approving.

'That's a good idea,' he agreed. 'You're welcome to use the library and it would be nice to have you next door. We could have tea together.' Remembering my cup of tea, I sipped at it before saying anything. While I was drinking it he said quietly, 'Now Danaan's here we can make some of the arrangements David asked about yesterday. Would you like to go up to London with me at some point and discuss what you'd like to do with Felix's flat?'

'Yes,' I said quickly. And then, half-ashamed of myself for saying it, 'Does Poppy have to come?'

He looked at me for a long moment and I felt certain he was going to say something about me and Poppy and awaited his next remark with dread. But when it came, it was unexpected.

'I don't imagine so,' he said eventually. 'This is

something for us to do alone, I think?' The questioning note in his voice was gentle and I was reminded that he was coming to terms with his own grief. I smiled tremulously and gulped my tea.

'Yes,' I said finally. 'I'd like that.'

'Then that's how it will be,' he replied with a quiet assurance that comforted me.

We talked about other things for a while and then, inevitably, the conversation moved on to school. I can't think about Ashmount at the moment without dread. Much though it stings me to admit it, Poppy is Queen Bee at that school and whatever I do there I can't help but feel I'm struggling in her shadow. But I can't see my mother allowing me to leave. Not with GCSEs and then A-levels ahead.

'Bits of it are all right,' I said carefully in response to my uncle's questions. 'But I'm looking forward to leaving.'

'I think you'll do well at university, Bethany,' he told me. 'You may find the atmosphere more conducive to work. Have you considered a subject of study yet?'

'History, maybe,' I said. 'Or English. Those are my best subjects, anyway.'

'How about Classics?' he said. 'It's an excellent basis for thought.'

'I don't know much about Classics,' I said and he instantly began to educate me. I sat in my chair and listened while he told me about myths and philosophy and I found the rise and fall of his voice soothing. My father used to tell me about things with a passionate intensity, excited by everything he was interested in.

Sylvester talked quietly and seriously but I could see interest shining in his eyes as he explained things to me. I think he would be a good tutor. Even though my mind wandered during our conversation I felt as if I was soaking up knowledge from the river of his voice. It wasn't until the light faded outside and we could hardly see each other in the darkened room that I realized I'd been listening to him for hours and that all the unpleasantness of the morning had fallen away from me.

Emily came in then. She knocked lightly on the door before opening it in response to my uncle's 'Come!' and seemed surprised to see me at first. Then she smiled and turned on the soft lights, saying as she did so:

'Look at the two of you, plotting together in the dark. You must have been in here for hours!'

'Thank you, my love,' Sylvester said as she turned the lights up. 'I've been encouraging Bethany to consider a study of Classics and I fear I must have over-indulged myself in the pleasures of conversation.' He glanced at me with a smile.

'It's been fascinating,' I said honestly. 'I've had a love-ly afternoon.'

'Wonderful!' said Emily, beaming. 'But you must be half-starved. Come and have supper, both of you, and I can have my chance to promote a course of study. There's more than one option for someone with Bethany's gifts.'

We got up and were guided towards the dining room. But, as we left the study, Emily added to Sylvester in a lower voice, 'Poppy won't be joining us,

I'm afraid. We've had an argument and she's locked herself in her room.'

My ears pricked up at that but she didn't add anything and Sylvester said only, 'Oh dear, has she?' as if it was too common a thing to merit notice.

I wondered to myself what Poppy had done now but didn't dare ask, and we went into supper together.

CHAPTER TWENTY-ONE

~❦~

In fearless youth we tempt the heights of Arts,
While from the bounded level of our mind,
Short views we take, nor see the lengths behind,
But more advanced, behold with strange surprise
New distant scenes of endless science rise!
—Alexander Pope

The Book of Lies
Poppy's Book

I went upstairs in a rage that afternoon and had no compunction about stealing Bethany's painting. After her performance today I didn't see why I should accord her any consideration. She blatantly didn't give me any. I decided I may as well give her a real reason for her venom, and I had a use for the painting.

Once I was safely inside my room I sat down and studied it. Bethany has been hiding it jealously ever since the will-reading and this was the first time I had properly looked at it. The castle was definitely the one in my dream. I could see now why it looked so unreal. It was more an impression of castleness than a castle itself. But I could see the towering battlements where I had stood and then finally jumped from. The river that flowed past it was the same grey as the sky in my dream and like the grey eyes of the boy who had told me not to jump. In the distance, behind the castle,

I could see greenery. Trees tangled together in an unchartable maze and purple mountains rose steeply in the far distance with cloudy unreality.

Holding the painting in my hands I could *feel* its importance and I raised my hand to hold the poppy necklace at my throat. The necklace had the same quality of meaning as the painting; I knew I was on the edge of a discovery. The necklace hadn't protected me yet today and I silently exhorted it to work whatever magic it had now. Then, with no time to lose, I put the painting aside and dragged out my art materials from my wardrobe.

Art isn't my best subject at school. It's too personal. I do well at set pieces and I have a knack for caricatures, but my teachers tend to criticize me for a 'lack of feeling'. That makes me laugh. Surely they realize it's intentional? I'm not going to bleed my impressions on to a piece of paper to be pinned to a wall. They can content themselves with my straight As across the rest of the board and stop trying to force some kind of revelation from me. But sometimes I have tried to paint with meaning. In my studies of witchcraft I've occasionally had to draw, and hidden with this journal is a pack of tarot cards I designed myself. However I thought this would be harder. My uncle Felix was a great artist. Some of his paintings hang in the National Gallery and I've read books about him that struggle to capture the 'blazing truth' of his vision. I wondered how I was going to attempt to emulate him. An unusual concern for me, since I normally have no doubts of my own capacity to excel.

But, as it turned out, my concern was misplaced.

From the moment I took the first paintbrush in my hand I felt possessed by a power that was determined I should paint this picture. On the blank wall of my room I sketched out the blurred edges of the castle of dreams. And then, not properly conscious of my hand wielding the brush or of selecting and blending paints, I began to fill in the rest. I only had to glance once or twice at the painting. I felt as if I was drawing something already there on the walls of my room. Something that wanted to be there. Purple and grey and black. The colours blended and shifted and merged together to cast shadows across the mural. There was the castle, the river before it, behind it a tangle of forest and gardens and a maze of grey greenery. In the background the colours darkened further and the mountains formed an impenetrable stopping place at the back of the scene.

I worked for hours, not stopping for anything, until my fingers were cramped from holding the brush and my clothes and hair were spattered with paint. My hands were thick with it from where I had softened the edges with my fingertips, blending each element into the others. It wasn't until I had filled in the last space on the wall that I felt the spell lift from me and sat down suddenly on the floor to stare up at what I had created.

It wasn't the exact scene from the painting. Comparing the two I could see I had added details that were obscure in Felix's depiction and some of the angles were different. But the mural in its entirety captured the same mood as the painting, the same stark simplicity of dream imagery, and I knew I could never have painted so well without having first visited that place in my dreams.

As I was sitting there staring, feeling drained of energy as the possessing spirit left me, the door behind me opened and my mother came into the room. She was speaking as she entered but I can't remember what she was saying because a foot inside the door she froze, cut off in mid-sentence, as she stared at the mural. I looked up at her, not knowing what to say. In the action of painting I had worked off my fury, the tensions of the morning and the fear of the dawn earlier. I felt more like a magician than I ever had before. I had captured something miraculous and as my mother stood and stared I knew that she recognized it. For the first time she saw the power in me.

Then her gaze fell on Bethany's painting lying beside me and her eyes went dark with anger.

'Poppy!' she said sharply and fiercely. 'Did you steal this?'

A black fury overtook me then, giving me back the energy I had lost. I stood suddenly, my back to the mural, and faced her down.

'Yes, I did,' I said. 'So what?'

'Bethany is our *guest*!' she hissed at me. 'It's unforgivable that you should take this without her permission.' She picked up the painting quickly and held it in her arms. 'Especially something that has so much meaning for her.'

'So much meaning for HER?' My voice rose and I realized that all the anger I felt towards my parents for keeping me in the dark was cresting at this moment. 'What about its meaning for me? What about its meaning for this family? Bethany doesn't own what's in this painting. She doesn't even understand it. I do. And I claim it as my RIGHT!'

'You silly child,' my mother said in a tone of furious contempt. 'You have no idea of what you're talking about. I think it's time you gave up these infantile superstitions of yours, Poppy, and behaved like a human being for a change. Don't you have any common decency at all?'

'If I haven't, whose fault is that?' I said, glaring at her. 'I certainly don't seem to have any privacy. Get out of my room.'

She looked as if she was about to hit me. Then she turned and walked out, leaving the door open behind her. I followed her and slammed it behind her. Then I twisted the key furiously in the lock and kicked the door hard.

I tried to catch my breath and realized that I was sobbing. I fell on my bed, my breath clawing at my throat as I tried to breathe. But for a long time I couldn't and I turned my stereo on loud so no one could hear me crying.

~c~

Nor will he tell me for whose sake
He did me the delight,
Or spite,
But leaves me to inquire
In all my wild desire,
Of sleep again, who was his aid;
And sleep so guilty and afraid
As since he dares not come within my sight.

—Ben Jonson

The Book of Secrets
Rivalaun's Book

When it began to get dark outside, Danaan tapped out his pipe and stood up. Over in the main house lights glowed welcomingly and the smell of roasting meat wafted over enticingly from the kitchen.

'Time for supper, I think,' Danaan said and rested a hand lightly on my shoulder.

I stood and walked with him across the garden to the kitchen, where Emily was wiping down the wooden surfaces. When I offered to help she pointed me in the direction of the dining room and invited me to set the table there. As I carefully collected a stack of plates she said briefly:

'I'd just better tell Poppy we're eating soon. She's been upstairs painting all day, adding to the doom and gloom.' Danaan laughed and I didn't catch Emily's eye. I wanted to like my aunt but I couldn't feel comfortable with her attitude towards Poppy's behaviour.

As Emily headed up the back staircase, Danaan helped me carry plates and cutlery through to the dining room. Inside, he closed the curtains and turned up the lights enough to illuminate the table without chasing the shadows out of the room. Then he set out glasses and advised me of the correct way to lay the table. I had only just finished and was returning to the kitchen for napkins when I heard a door slam upstairs, followed by another banging noise, and looked up to see Emily at the top of the stairs. She was looking in the direction of the noise and her expression was one of such misery that I went quickly up the stairs to her.

'Is something wrong?' I asked, touching her shoulder.

She swallowed, forcing a tight smile.

'No, Rivalaun, thank you. Just Poppy acting up.' She gave a shaky laugh and then looked down at the object she was holding tightly in her arms. As she did so I heard a dissonant piece of music begin playing further back in the house. 'Oh, God,' Emily said softly. Then she said: 'Rivalaun, could you go and hang this in Bethany's room, please? I think I'm going to help Danaan open the wine.'

'Certainly,' I said, puzzled, and took the object from her, stepping back to allow her passage down the staircase.

★

Emily had been upset enough not to realize she'd used Danaan's real name and too upset to tell me where Bethany's room was. But only a few steps down the landing I found it. There were bags lying on one bed and the other bed was perfunctorily made up. Not wanting to intrude, I glanced down at the object I was supposed to hang for the first time.

It was a painting. A painting of the castle I had dreamed of. In the background was the forest in which I had seen the man made of mist. In the foreground a thick grey river flowed slowly past the castle gates. I sensed danger in the towering walls and buttresses of the castle, and menace in the torpid river. The whole painting resonated with power and I wondered what Emily had been doing with it. Then something made sense and I glanced automatically down the hall along which I could still hear the sound of Poppy's strange music playing.

I hung the painting on an obvious nail opposite the bed and promised myself that I would ask Bethany about its origins later. Then I went quickly and lightly down the stairs and into the dining room.

Everyone else was already there. Sylver was standing at the head of the table and courteously handing Bethany into a chair on his right. At the other end Emily was pouring glasses of wine. Her own stood half-empty in front of her. After I entered I had the sensation that everyone was looking at me, frozen in place. Then the impression left and I slid quietly into the remaining chair next to Bethany. Not wanting to mention replacing the painting in front of her, I looked over at Emily and gave her a reassuring smile as she handed me a brimming wine glass.

Poppy didn't join us all through supper. I loaded my plate with food and ate hungrily as the conversation flowed around me. Bethany seemed unusually cheerful that evening and, as the adults discussed literature, she made occasional comments and asked questions in a soft but easily audible voice. But, even though the food was excellent, the wine plentiful and the conversation pleasant, I worried about Poppy all through the meal. I could feel her like a taut string in the back of the house and in the back of my mind. But I couldn't sense her mood at all. She was closed off completely from us and I missed her vivacity.

It wasn't until we had finished a thick creamy confection of sugared pastry, cinnamon and apples that I dared mention Poppy. Bethany, Emily and I cleared the table while my father encouraged Sylver to share a cigar. As we came back to the dining room, I asked quietly:

'Should we take anything up to Poppy?'

'No,' Emily said. 'She can come down and get something if she's hungry. She's not imprisoned up there, no matter how much she might like to think of herself as a tragic heroine. She can come down any time she wants.' Her voice was strained with the effort of holding back anger and I dropped the subject.

~)(~

CHAPTER TWENTY-THREE

But how shall we this union well express?
Nought ties the soul; her subtlety is such,
She moves the body, which she doth possess,
Yet no part toucheth, but by virtue's touch.
—Sir John Davies

The Book of Dreams
Bethany's Book

Supper was delicious and I felt hungry for the first time in ages. Not having Poppy there was such a relief that I was able to talk comfortably as well. Daniel still unnerves me a little but I was beginning to feel almost at home with Emily and Sylvester. They're easier to be with than my mother in a lot of ways. But when I remember the way she hugged me tightly before she left I wish I'd tried to talk to her more about my father. I wonder if, privately, she misses him as well.

The only unpleasant thing about supper was that I could tell Rivalaun didn't feel the same way as me about Poppy's absence. He kept glancing at the door as if he expected her to arrive and, when we'd finished eating, he asked if he should take her anything. But Emily said no and he didn't say anything more. We all went through to the living room and Emily put on some quiet music. Rivalaun sat next to me on the sofa and flipped idly through my aunt and uncle's CD collection. It wasn't until the grown-ups were immersed in conversation that he looked across at me and said softly:

'Bethany, could I ask you something about your painting?'

'My painting?' I felt nervous when he mentioned it. 'How do you know about that?'

'I'd rather not say here,' he murmured, not properly meeting my eyes but watching the others instead. 'But I would like to talk to you. Could we go and look at it?'

I considered this for a while, but Rivalaun had been so kind today that I thought I owed him something. And even though I feel the painting is a personal thing, I didn't really want to say no.

'All right,' I said eventually. 'Now?'

'Wait just a moment,' he replied, still speaking quietly. 'Tell me first, are there any games you're good at?'

I blinked in surprise and he glanced at me with a quick smile.

'Anything at all,' he said in an undertone. 'Any kind of game.'

'Um . . . Scrabble?' I said uncertainly.

'What's that?'

'A board game,' I whispered, realizing that he didn't want us to be overheard. 'You put words together and score points.'

'Good,' he smiled to himself. 'Sounds very good, actually.' He went quiet for a while and then shifted a bit in his seat and cleared his throat. When Emily looked over at him he smiled again, winningly, and said, 'Is it all right if Bethany and I go and play Scrabble?'

'Of course!' Emily smiled back at us both. 'But you can play down here, if you want.'

'Oh, let them go and play,' Sylvester said. 'I'm sure we've subjected them to enough after-dinner conviviality.' But his tone was lightly teasing and I grinned at him spontaneously.

'No, it was great, really,' I said as I stood up. 'Thanks for dinner, and everything.'

Rivalaun added his thanks to mine and once the chorus of good evenings had been concluded we left the room and headed upstairs.

Out of the living room I could hear heavy metal music coming from Poppy's room, but I didn't feel comfortable with saying anything about it and led the way to the guest bedroom. As soon as we were inside the door Rivalaun crossed to stand in front of the painting. I went quickly to look at it with him.

'Did your father paint this?' he asked and I nodded.

'He left it to me in his will,' I said. 'But this isn't his usual style. I can show you an art book of his, if you'd like?'

'Yes, I'd like that,' he said instantly and I started rummaging in my bags.

It didn't take me long to find it. It had come out earlier this year, before my father's last illness, and I hadn't even finished reading it when he died. I'd brought it with me on an impulse but hadn't felt like looking at it again until now.

When I found the book, Rivalaun crossed to sit next

to me on the spare bed and we looked at the glossy cover together. *Felix Greenwood: Myth and Modernism* it read, and then in smaller type: *Produced for the National Gallery*. I traced the letters with my finger and Rivalaun looked curiously at the cover.

'The National Gallery,' he read out loud. 'That sounds important.'

'It is,' I assured him. 'My father was a great artist.'

Then, facing the inevitable, I opened the book.

I've never really known what to say about my father's work. I know things about art, of course. But most of what I know is from conversations my father's friends used to have. I know about techniques and schools of painting and even who the galleries hate and who doesn't get the notices they deserve. But at school, when teachers talked about my father, I was never sure what I was supposed to say. To talk about his reputation sounds like boasting to most people and I don't honestly think I've got the right to talk like an art critic. Besides, he's my father. I saw many of those paintings while they were still works in progress. In a weird way, it's a bit like seeing family photographs on display.

But Rivalaun didn't seem to expect me to say anything. He worked through the book methodically, reading the titles of each painting, studying them for a few moments and occasionally glancing at the main text before turning the page. I watched as compositions I've known all my life flashed past my eyes. The *Camera Obscura* painting that shot him to fame before I was even born. The *Broken Window* painting, showing the scenes of a lovers' quarrel in shards of splintered glass, its date a year before my parents' divorce. The famous *Still Life* which sold for millions, although I could never understand what it meant. People standing in a city street, each one engaged in some transaction and carefully detailed. But beneath them there are cracks on the pavement, which at the edges of the painting open up so that you can see through them to an ominous black void beneath.

The pages continued to turn and I saw more memories flashing past. The *Echo and Narcissus* which I keep seeing in poster shops. A girl with pale hair lies beside a small lake in a bank of small flowers. They cover her almost completely and she stares up at the sky with a small mad smile. I don't like that one and my mother didn't like it either. She always avoids looking at it at my father's exhibitions. Then *Morning Glory*, which is supposed to be one of his weaker works but I love it. Two figures stand on a balcony on a grimy skyscraper and look out across the city roofs towards the rising sun.

I lost myself in memories while Rivalaun turned the pages and I only came back when I realized he had paused. He was looking at a painting of Poppy. The one she still owns even though I know for a fact that people have tried to buy it several times. I've only really looked at it briefly before, but now that Rivalaun was studying it so intently I looked again, trying to see what he saw in my conceited cousin. She's about eleven in the painting and she's standing looking straight at the artist in a dark room that I appreciated for the first time must be the library here. Her red hair is thick and silky, but she's pushed it back from her face and looks straight out of the picture with a serious expression, the tiniest frown creasing her eyebrows.

'Look, Bethany,' Rivalaun said, pointing to the title.

'*Secrets*,' I said, reading it aloud. 'That's strange. I never noticed it was called that.'

Rivalaun said something like 'hmm' and turned the page. But five minutes later he paused again and said in a more excited voice, 'Look at this!'

I looked at the book and was instantly fascinated.

'I've never seen that one before,' I told him. 'It says it's loaned from the Staragi Collection.'

It was a painting of three people. My father stands in the centre, leaning forward with a paintbrush, which is flattened in the foreground as if he is pressing it against a transparent screen. A younger Sylvester is on his left, standing sideways on, looking up with a blank, distracted expression from a book he is holding. On the right is Daniel, standing further back from them both, and looking out through the painting to share a twisted smile with us.

❧❦❧

Changer of all things, yet immutable,
Before, and after all, the first, and last,
That moving all, is yet immovable,
Great without quantity in whose forecast,
Things past are present, things to come are past.
—Giles Fletcher

The Book of Secrets
Rivalaun's Book

When I saw the painting of Felix, Sylvester and Danaan I knew I couldn't put off the conversation I had to have with Bethany any longer. I'd been cautious about approaching the subject, remembering that Poppy had said her cousin despised her for her pretences to witch-craft. But Danaan's enigmatic hints had confirmed my belief that there was a power loose in this family which almost everyone was attempting to deny.

Looking down at the painting which placed each of the three brothers so firmly in a milieu I said, 'Does anything about your family ever strike you as strange?'

Bethany gave me a surprised look and then smiled a little.

'Well, you turning up . . .' she admitted. 'You and Daniel. Because I didn't even know I had a cousin until I saw you.' She blushed then and swung her hair forward in what I was coming to recognize as a customary defensive gesture.

'What about names?' I continued. 'Have you noticed that people use different names for one another?'

'Well, yes.' Now she looked really puzzled. 'But that's not strange.' She frowned at me as she added, 'A lot of families do that. My mother calls me Bethany now, but when I was little she called me Bethy. Emily calls Sylvester "Sylver" for a pet name. But she doesn't do it in public. And my father's friends . . .' She hesitated for a second before continuing. 'Well . . . some of them called him "Lucky", because that's what his name means. And sometimes they called him "Felix the Cat" because of this old cartoon . . .' Her voice trailed off and she looked at me expectantly.

'I didn't know that,' I said slowly. 'I think of names differently. What you're called is important.' I paused. 'What about other things,' I asked, 'like Poppy and her witchcraft?'

She gave me a disappointed look.

'That's not real,' she said. 'Poppy only does that to be interesting. She's into this whole goth thing and she and her friends pretend they have magical powers. But it's silly, really.'

'All right.' I left that topic for a minute and said instead, 'What about dreams?'

'What about them?' she said sharply and her voice was defensive.

I reached out and moved the curtain of hair away from her face so I could see her expression. She blushed again but didn't stop me. Then I gestured towards the painting hanging on the wall.

'I've dreamed about that place,' I told her. 'Before I saw that painting. And so has Poppy. And I've dreamed of seeing Poppy there, of a boy with grey eyes and a man with hair like white smoke.'

Bethany looked frightened for a second and made as if to hide behind her hair again but aborted the gesture. Instead, she turned away from me and looked at the painting.

'I dreamed about that too,' she said in a small voice.

I didn't speak, hoping she would say more, but when she didn't I added gently, 'Don't you think that means something? That we all dream about the same place?'

'Yes . . . it's strange,' she admitted. 'But it's not real. I dreamed I wrote something in my journal too.'

'That's a good idea,' I said, impressed. 'I didn't think of trying that. Is what you wrote still there?'

'Of course not!' she said quickly. And then a moment later, 'I mean, I haven't checked but . . .'

'Check now,' I told her.

She sat still for a while and she looked very uncomfortable.

'My journal's private,' she said eventually. 'I don't want you to see what I write in it.' She was blushing again and when she shook her hair back down I didn't stop her.

'I understand that,' I said. 'I keep one too. I don't want to see what you've written. I just want you to check if what you wrote is still there.'

'OK,' she said finally. 'But I know it won't be.'

She got up and crossed to the small cupboard by her bed and took out a book with a blue cover. She flipped quickly to the last page and then froze in place, still kneeling by the cupboard.

'It is there,' she whispered. 'Why is it there?'

It was hard for me to stay seated but to my relief she came back across the room, slowly. Then, still holding on to her journal, she showed me the words written neatly on the last page: *What happens to the dream when the dreamer wakes up?*

'I've wondered that as well,' I said softly. 'Especially recently.'

Bethany closed the book hurriedly and held it to her chest. Her expression was stubborn.

'I don't believe this,' she said firmly. 'I must have written this when I was waking up and just not remembered or something. Things like this can't happen. They just can't.'

'But they do,' I said. 'Look Bethany. You don't have to believe me. But tonight, when you sleep, look for me in your dreams, please?'

'I'll look,' she said finally. 'But I don't expect to see anything.'

❧❧

There she weaves by night and day
A magic web with colours gay.
She has heard a whisper say,
A curse is on her if she stay.
—Alfred Lord Tennyson

The Book of Lies
Poppy's Book

It was the irony that got to me in the end. I had woken up that morning desperate to regain control over myself. But after everything that had happened today I was back where I had started.

But when I thought that, I realized it wasn't true. I had progressed. I'd fought with Bethany and with my mother. Bethany had made it clear that she hated me, and my mother . . . my mother despised me. That was unpleasant to have to admit, even if I thought her reasoning was flawed. But at least it left me in no doubt of where I stood with either of them. It was Rivalaun I still didn't understand. When we'd talked he'd seemed so open, so honest. But he'd lied to me just the same. Of that I was certain. Rivalaun knew how to make that transition between different worlds. He knew how and he'd kept that information from me. It was that which finally made up my mind.

Everyone lies to me. Everyone. I'd given them

chance after chance to speak to me honestly. I'd been truthful with them all, even if they didn't believe me. But now I'd had enough of lies. I would go to the one person who'd promised they wouldn't lie. I'd take one last chance. And if it didn't work . . . if this doesn't work I don't know what I'll do. I won't think about that now.

I made my preparations carefully. Once the storm of tears had finally subsided I got up from my bed and looked at myself in the mirror for a long time. My skin was raw with tears and my eyes almost as red as my hair. I never cry in public. I would like to say I never cry at all. I looked at my reflection and told myself silently I was a mess. A witch shouldn't let herself be consumed by anger like this. A witch should walk lightly on the world, untouched and untouchable.

I couldn't stand feeling like this any more. I couldn't stand being like this. What reason did I have to stay here in the middle of hate and lies?

I had said, when I leave, I'll leave this journal behind me. I had meant to leave it so that my parents would know *why* I'd left. Now I just think, so what? It's not as if they'll care. I've given them every chance with me. Despite everything that's happened I still love them, even though I despise myself for that. OK, so I'm not an abused child in any conventional sense. My parents have given me the best of everything, every material advantage they could provide, every intellectual assistance, every advantage the world could afford. They've given me everything. But not the one thing I've always wanted. Have they once given me anything of themselves?

I'll leave this journal anyway, although I don't think

my parents will understand what it means to me. But I'll take the necklace that Uncle Felix gave me. I don't need anything else. Only myself. Even taking clothes seems foolish in the circumstances. I'll wear the black dress I wore to the will-reading. Of everything I own, it suits my mood the best right now . . .

I stared at my reflection long enough for my skin to cool down and to see the look of resolution in my eyes as I decided I wouldn't let myself by controlled like this again. Then I got seriously to work to try to cast a spell. The most serious and the most dangerous I'd attempted yet – a deliberate use of magic rather than the accidental outbursts of power I'd experienced up to now. Tonight there could be no room for failure.

I knew so little though. Too little to rely on one method alone. If I was going to break through the barrier that held me to this world I'd need power. As much raw power as I could find. If I had time for research I might have been able to manage a proper ritual, but as it was I'd have to work by intuition.

I wouldn't sleep tonight, although I had to dream. I needed to reach through to the land I had seen in my dreams while still conscious enough to do more than brush against it in sleep. I had to reach that trance-like state that magicians speak of, somewhere between sleeping and waking, where all possibilities are open to you.

As I write this, my materials are already assembled. This will be the last entry I write before attempting . . . no, before succeeding . . . in crossing over to the place I've only seen in dreams. I've chosen as carefully as I know how. What I intend to do may be dangerous but I tell myself that the blame for that rests on my parents' shoulders. If something goes wrong and they read this journal they should know that. I've worked with what I know. I've chosen things personal to me. I've chosen things with power. I've taken ideas from different disciplines and philosophies. This spell *is* me. I've infused it with every meaning in which I see potential truth. I've held it in my mind, testing its reality, and I like what I see.

I'm going. Tonight. No more of this. I feel breathless again with the sense of drama. I'm calm and excited at the same time. Somehow I *know* I'm doing this right. And nothing will ever be the same again.

CHAPTER TWENTY-SIX

~◦(●◦~

Let no lamenting cries, nor doleful tears,
Be heard all night within, nor yet without:
Ne let false whispers, breeding hidden fears,
Break gentle sleep with misconceivéd doubt.
Let no deluding dreams, nor dreadful sights
Make sudden sad affrights.

—Edmund Spenser

~ In Dreamland ~

Bethany stands in the middle of tangled greenery. At first she thinks she is in the forest but, turning, she sees corridors of hedges stretching out in different directions.

'I'm in the maze,' she says. 'But I don't know where to go. Where's Rivalaun?'

'He's here,' a voice says reassuringly. The boy with black hair is standing in an arch of twisted trees. 'But you have to find your own path.'

'What about Poppy?' Bethany asks.

'She's not here,' he says and she thinks he looks worried. 'I don't know why not.'

'She's sulking,' Bethany tells him, feeling pleased with herself. 'I hate her, you know,' she adds confidingly.

'Good,' another voice says and a figure coalesces out of nothingness. He seems realer than he has before. His white hair is less like smoke and she can see the individual strands lifting and coiling around each other with a prehensile life. 'That will help,' he tells Bethany in a satisfied voice.

'Who are you?' she demands angrily. 'And what business is it of yours?'

The figure only smiles enigmatically but, unexpectedly, the boy answers for him.

'He's Morpheus,' he says. 'Don't trust him.' Then he turns and walks around the next corner of the maze.

'NO! Wait!' Bethany calls and races after him, but when she reaches the turning there is no sign of him.

'Who are you?' she calls after him and hears laughter behind her.

'If you don't know that,' Morpheus says, 'you don't know anything.' And he disappears.

Rivalaun hurries down the paths of the maze, turning always to the left; he is looking for something but he can't remember what.

'Try to remember,' the boy tells him. 'It might be important.'

Rivalaun stops and looks at him while he thinks. The boy waits patiently but his long white fingers twist in and out of each other as if he is worried about something. Rivalaun would like to help him but there's something more important he has to do.

'Bethany!' he exclaims, remembering. 'I have to find Bethany.'

'Are you sure that's right?' the boy asks but Rivalaun is already hurrying on.

'I have to,' he calls back over his shoulder. 'She has to believe me.'

'It won't help,' someone says ominously and he sees a white, wraith-like figure walk out of the hedges.

'What do you know?' Rivalaun asks angrily. 'If you won't help me, don't hinder me either.' And he hastens on.

Poppy's eyes are closed. She sees only darkness. She sways where she is standing. A breeze brushes against her as lightly as a kiss but with a building force that she senses is strong enough to knock her over.

'I'm lost here,' she whispers. 'Help me.'

Rivalaun is lost in the maze. He knows Bethany is near but he can't find her. He comes out from a narrow corridor into a meeting place where different paths combine. The boy with black hair is sitting there on the rim of a small stone fountain.

'Is this the centre of the maze?' Rivalaun asks him.

'Don't ask me!' the boy says fiercely, grey eyes darkening. 'I can't tell you. I can't aid you. Stop asking me for help.'

'Stop asking me for help,' Poppy hears, and power crests in her like a wave.

'I'm not asking!' she says coldly and deliberately, her voice rising. 'I'm commanding. I claim this as my RIGHT!' Her last word is a shout and she opens her eyes. Mists swirl around her. Black, white and grey, they coil around her like vines and buffet her like a storm.

'I'm coming,' she tells them. 'I'm crossing over. Don't you dare try and stop me!'

'And why would I stop you?' a voice asks her and the mists retreat, contracting until they form a single figure and Poppy can see she is standing on the drawbridge of the castle, facing a pillar of smoke with violet eyes. 'This was meant to be,' he says. 'The land knows its own.'

There is a wrench and Bethany realizes she's not running down corridors of the maze any more. Instead she is racing

126

through narrow, dark city streets. Cobbles are underneath her feet, buildings loom on either side. She wants to get out from between the houses but every turning leads into another alleyway, darker and more twisted than the last.

'Stop it!' she screams. 'Let me go!'

She hears laughter from somewhere and she whirls but there is no one there.

The fountain stays the same but the maze has retreated. Rivalaun and the boy are standing in a market square. Old, crumbling buildings surround them and between the houses passages open into dark alleyways.

'This isn't the maze,' he says, testingly.

'What makes you think that?' the boy asks, puzzled.

Then Rivalaun hears a scream close by and he feels suddenly afraid.

'That's Bethany!' he says. He looks anxiously at the boy, forgetting he has been told not to ask questions. 'Nothing can hurt her here though, can it?'

The boy looks puzzled.

'What makes you think that?' he asks and Rivalaun turns and runs.

Poppy looks down the hill and sees first the city, then the maze, then the forests stretching out further and, beyond, the foothills of the purple mountains. A scream rings out from somewhere in the city and she laughs.

'That's Bethany,' she says. 'But she'll wake up.' She looks back at the figure with smoky hair and asks, not expecting an answer, 'Can I wake up?'

'You should know better,' the figure tells her and melts away.

★

127

Bethany is terrified. Shadows are closing in on all sides. Nothing is as important as escape. But on every side she is trapped. The maze has caught her and she doesn't know the way out.

'I want to wake up,' she says miserably, and then a voice answers her.

'But you can,' he says and Rivalaun comes quickly out of the shadows. Forgetting herself, she runs and clings to him.

'Is it really you?' she asks. 'Are you really here?'

'Yes,' he hugs her tightly. 'I said I'd find you, didn't I? I told you this was real.'

'Yes,' Bethany agrees. 'But please . . . I want to wake up.'

'I think I know how,' Rivalaun tells her. 'Hold on, close your eyes and jump.'

Something ripples across the landscape like a shock and Poppy turns to meet black eyes. They are standing together on the battlements once more.

'You're here,' the boy says softly. 'Now it begins.'

◦〜◦

A well of love — it may be deep —
I trust it is, — and never dry:
What matter? if the waters sleep
In silence and obscurity.
　　　　　—William Wordsworth

The Book of Dreams
Bethany's Book

I woke up suddenly, my heart pounding and my skin damp with sweat. Outside, grey light filtered through the curtain and I realized it was only just past dawn. There was no way I was going to go back to sleep tonight, I decided, and instead I got up and searched the bookshelves for something to read.

In the end I decided on a Jane Austen novel. Something as completely unlike my nightmares as I could imagine. I read all through the early morning, curled up on the window sill so I wouldn't accidentally fall asleep again. I saw the sun gradually get brighter as it burned up the damp haze of the morning. I saw Sylvester come round the side of the house and walk down the gravel path to the road. And I saw him come back again carrying a milk bottle and a rolled-up newspaper. His limp hardly seemed to trouble him at all and his cane crunched briskly on the gravel when he occasionally leaned upon it for support.

I saw Rivalaun come out of the stable block and stand in the back courtyard behind the kitchen garden. He was wearing only jeans and I blushed as I remembered how I had clung to him in my dream. But then I remembered I didn't want to think about that and closed the curtains so I wouldn't see him. I climbed back into bed with my book. It was a warm and cosy place to be, now that it was morning, and I found myself thinking cheerfully of breakfast. I hoped Poppy was still sulking so I wouldn't have to face her across the kitchen table. Food seemed like a good thing: a nice touch of normality with bacon and eggs.

I could hear the small noises of the household waking up as I continued to read, but it wasn't until about half an hour later that there was a sudden sharp knock on my door and my aunt Emily came in a fraction of a second later. I looked at her in surprise because she would never normally just walk in, but I hurried out of bed when I saw her face.

'What's wrong?' I asked.

'Sorry to disturb you, Beth,' she said quickly. 'You don't know where Poppy is, do you?'

'In her tree house?' I suggested. 'Doesn't she sleep there sometimes?'

'Sylver's already looked,' she said and then paused, her hand still on the doorknob. 'No one else has seen her either.'

I put on my dressing gown and came over to the door.

'You don't think she's left the house completely, do you?' I asked.

'Oh, Bethany, I just don't know.' Emily looked more distressed than I've ever seen her. 'Her bed hasn't been slept in. We had a terrible argument last night and Poppy . . . she's been so difficult recently. I really wouldn't put it past her to run away.'

As we stood there I heard a voice call 'Emily!' from somewhere else in the house and we both came out on to the landing to see Sylvester standing in the front hall.

'She's nowhere in the house and grounds,' he said conclusively and we came quickly down the stairs to join him.

As we arrived on the ground floor, Rivalaun and Daniel came through the kitchen door. I thought I'd never seen either of them looking so disreputable. Rivalaun was still shirtless but had acquired a pair of broken black combat boots from somewhere and Daniel was wearing a peculiar, long, green robe. Still wearing my own pale apricot dressing gown I felt like a small child compared to the rest of them. Everyone looked so shocked and worried that I felt guilty for hoping Poppy wouldn't be around this morning, almost as if I had ill-wished her.

'I wish we hadn't argued last night,' Emily said miserably. Sylvester reached out to put a comforting arm around her.

'You said yourself she was behaving abominably,' he reminded her gently. 'Don't worry, my love, we'll find her.'

'What can we do to help?' Rivalaun asked and Sylvester considered for a moment.

'I'll have to call the police,' he said. 'Although I doubt they'll find her nearby. If Poppy has run away, she won't still be in Cornwall now. But, darling, you'll need to check her drawers for any clothes she might have taken, they'll need to know that.'

'I'll do that now,' Emily said quickly and hurried back upstairs. Then Sylvester turned his attention to me.

'You don't know anything about this, Bethany, do you?' he asked.

'No! Nothing!' I said hastily. 'Poppy wouldn't have talked to me.' Then I felt embarrassed but Sylvester had already turned his attention to Rivalaun.

'Rivalaun?' he asked and my cousin frowned.

'I knew she was unhappy,' he admitted. 'But she didn't confide in me.'

At that point Emily came back down, looking confused.

'She's hardly taken anything, that I can see,' she said. 'At least, her room's a state but not much seems to be missing. And I'm not sure about clothes. I don't recognize half the things in her wardrobe, anyway.'

Rivalaun cleared his throat and then hesitated before saying, 'Did she leave a letter or any kind of diary?'

'No, nothing,' Emily said quickly and something about her tone of voice made me look up in time to see a glance pass between her and Sylvester. I was suddenly convinced that she wasn't telling the truth. 'Nothing of any use to us,' she went on and Sylvester nodded grimly.

'Very well, then,' he said. 'I'll go and telephone the police.'

He went off to his study and the rest of us hung about in the hall until Emily recollected herself.

'This is ridiculous,' she said to herself. 'Come into the kitchen, everyone, and have something to eat. Standing about here isn't going to help anyone.'

We all went into the kitchen but no one felt able to eat. Rivalaun gently took over making the coffee from Emily, and she sat down at the kitchen table instead. Daniel laid a hand lightly on her arm.

'You said yourself the child is intelligent and resourceful,' he said, obviously referring to some private conversation they had had. 'There's no reason to fear for her, just yet.'

'But . . . Poppy's so sure of herself,' Emily said in a shaky voice. 'She won't think twice about danger because she doesn't believe it applies to her. She could easily get into trouble just because she's so fearless.' She began to cry. 'She's so young and so lovely,' she managed to say through her tears. 'I wish I hadn't shouted at her.'

I looked on impotently as Daniel put his arm around her and Rivalaun crossed the kitchen to put a cup of coffee with a sprinkling of cinnamon on top in front of her. That made her smile and she looked up to touch his arm.

'Thank you, Rivalaun,' she said brokenly and he sat down beside her.

'I'm sure Poppy will be all right,' he said. 'She wouldn't run away without some idea of where she was going.'

'I agree,' Sylvester said from behind us and Rivalaun gracefully moved out of the way so he could sit beside his wife. She put her head against his shoulder and he held her easily. 'I don't think she'll be anywhere in Cornwall but she might go to one of her friends. Do you have any addresses for them, my love?'

'Yes, some of them.' Emily made as if to get up but Sylvester drew her back down.

'Drink your coffee first,' he told her. 'Beth, you know Poppy's friends. Who is she close to?'

'I don't know all of them,' I said awkwardly. 'But she rooms with Alys and Siona.'

'Siona's in America at the moment,' Emily said. 'We're looking after her horse. Oh, Sylver, she couldn't be at the stables, could she? She might just have wanted to go for a ride.'

'I'll call Angela next,' he said. 'It's possible. But we can discuss friends with the police when they get here.'

The police arrived in about half an hour; I was impressed by how quickly Sylvester had got them to come. It was he who showed them in, and we all sat in the living room while they took notes. Inevitably, they asked why Poppy might have run away and I was surprised when Emily cast a quick, anxious look at me.

'Poppy was unhappy last night,' Sylvester said smoothly, clasping Emily's hand. 'She did something her mother and I disapproved of and, when she was rebuked, she locked herself in her room for the evening.'

'Who was the last person to see her?' the male policeman asked.

Emily answered quickly. 'I was,' she said. 'At about

eight in the evening. It was me she had the argument with. I may have been too harsh with her.'

'Well, these things happen,' the policeman said comfortingly. 'I wouldn't worry about it too much, Mrs Greenwood. Teenagers often make too much of things.'

They asked to see Poppy's room and Emily took them upstairs. When they came back down she seemed a little bit more relaxed and the police didn't seem too worried.

'She doesn't seem to have taken much with her,' the policeman said to Sylvester. 'Quite an artistic kid, isn't she? Into all those black clothes, as well. My oldest is the same. Wanders about in rags and complains no one understands him. My feeling is she'll feel silly tomorrow and come back. But we'll search anyway.'

~⸎~

I wake and feel the fell of dark, not day.
What hours, O what black hours we have spent
This night! what sights you, heart, saw; ways you went!
And more must, in yet longer light's delay.
                    —Gerard Manley Hopkins

The Book of Secrets
Rivalaun's Book

As the morning dragged on I got steadily more worried. I suspected I knew where Poppy had gone, though I had no idea how she'd managed it. I had been a fool to let her know about different worlds; it had given her just the escape route she needed. But she could be anywhere now and, amidst all the fuss, I somehow didn't feel able to say what I thought had happened. I feared that my suspicions would be dismissed as impossible, even though I knew they were not.

Sylver and Emily closeted themselves in the study and talked quietly in voices too low for me to hear, but I could guess what they were discussing. I had caught the look that passed between them earlier when I asked about Poppy's journal. I was certain that they had found it and deliberately decided to hide it from the police. Maybe they were right to do so; knowing what I now did about this world, I could see that any talk of

136

magic would be seen as suspicious by the authorities. But it made no sense to keep the truth secret from the family.

I hoped Danaan might say something, but he held himself apart from the situation. Instead, he went into the kitchen to prepare lunch, finding things by instinct as he worked to prepare something Emily would eat. I hovered by the doorway for a while, reluctant to go in. I doubted that my father would tell me any more than he had yesterday. Then I went upstairs to look at Poppy's room and found Bethany on the landing. She was dressed now, in brown jeans and a white sleeveless shirt, and she started when she saw me.

'I was going to look at Poppy's room,' I told her and she nodded quickly.

'Me too,' she said and we went down the corridor together. Bethany paused before a door and tried the handle. 'It's locked,' she said.

I glanced at her and down the stairs. Then I sighed.

'I can fix that,' I admitted and put my fingers to the door. After a short pause there was an audible click and the lock snapped back.

'How did you do that?' Bethany asked in a frightened voice, and I gave her a level look.

'Magic,' I said briefly and opened the door.

I don't know what I had been expecting. Something unexpected, probably. But Poppy's room surprised me, nonetheless. It was like a stage set. Sunshine shone faintly through the open window but gave up just inside the room, sinking into the oceans of black velvet

137

that covered almost every surface. I found it hard to imagine that Poppy actually used this room, or that she slept in that huge, menacing iron bed. But then we came further in and we both stopped as we saw what Poppy had left behind.

'My painting!' Bethany exclaimed with shock and anger in her voice.

'This must be what she and Emily argued about,' I told her, stepping further forward to look at the mural on the wall. Something crunched underfoot and I looked down instead to see what the presence of the magnified painting had obscured.

Poppy had not lied when she called herself a witch. The litter of a spell-working lay strewn about the room. Danaan has often said, when telling his stories, that true power is in the mind and heart of the one who wields it. But there are symbols of power, like the crown of a king, which can hold their own magic. From what I could see, Poppy had not relied on the raw power of her own self-confidence but had hedged her spell with an alarming mixture of great symbols and the paltry trumpery of the hedge-witch.

Small bundles of dried flowers and twigs from different trees were woven together, and together with a scattering of candle ends traced out the shape of a five-pointed star in front of the mural. Other items lay here and there in the jumble: red and white flowers floating in a bowl of water; a plaited tress of long red hair; a little silver knife with a rust-red tarnish on the edge of the blade; and a cut crystal glass stained with dark dregs of wine. An open case held packets of dried leaves, stoppered bottles and a black flute-like pipe; and a heavy scent hung in the room, despite the cool, sweet air from the open windows.

Without a doubt Poppy had worked magic here, alone in this dark and sinister room, determined to pass through the boundaries between worlds. Drunk on power and drugged with her own spells, she had succeeded beyond what I had thought possible and stepped through the painting on the wall into the landscape of our dreams.

Bethany was standing in front of the mural and reached forward as if she couldn't help herself.

'Don't touch it,' I said sharply and she froze. 'It's been used as a spell focus,' I told her. 'It might not be safe to touch.'

To my surprise Bethany didn't argue with me. Instead, she turned with an appalled look.

'Is that where she's gone?' she asked. 'To the castle?'

'I think so,' I said, thinking fast. 'And that doesn't seem like such a good idea. I'm not sure the castle is a real place. I think . . . I think . . . she's gone to the place where dreams come from.'

'But how?' Bethany asked pleadingly and I could see her struggling for comprehension.

'I don't know,' I admitted. 'But it's been calling all of us, hasn't it? Poppy obviously decided to accept the invitation.'

'And she's there now . . .' Beth said wonderingly.

'Perhaps. If the spell worked. But I don't think she was meant to go alone.' I turned and looked at my cousin seriously.

'It wanted all of us, didn't it?' she murmured. 'I don't

know how she could go there. It was . . .' she paused and then shook her head. 'Terrifying.'

'I suspect it's what you make of it,' I said to myself. Then I added calmly out loud, 'I'm going after her.'

'You're not!' Bethany looked horrified. 'How can you?'

'How can I not?' I asked her. 'I think it's what I'm meant to do. Danaan told me I had to chose my own path. For the moment, this appears to be it. I think I can repeat what Poppy did, or something close enough. I'm going to follow her. If I don't I'll only end up there anyway when I fall asleep tonight.'

That seemed to strike a chord in Bethany and she looked scared.

'We will, won't we?' she said softly. 'And if you leave too, I'll be alone.'

'You could try asking Poppy's parents about it,' I said. 'But they seem determined to pretend everything is normal, even when all the evidence contradicts it. I'm not going to expect any help from them.'

Bethany didn't say anything for a long time and I waited, knowing she would have to make this decision on her own. Finally she turned to me with a determined expression.

'If you're going, I'm coming with you,' she said. 'I still don't like it but I like the idea that people have been hiding things from me even less. And this painting was a message to me. My father wanted me to do something about it. I'm involved in this, whether I like it or not.'

'All right then,' I agreed. 'We'll go through tonight.'

'What about my uncle and aunt, though?' Bethany

said. 'Even if they do know more than they're telling, I can't just leave. Look how distressed they are about Poppy.'

'Leave a letter?' I suggested. But I didn't share her concerns. I was grateful to Sylver and Emily for bringing me into their family, but I didn't consider that I was their responsibility. If Danaan had given me the freedom to make my own decisions no one else had any claim to stop me.

~❦~

Into the nothingness of scorn and noise,
Into the living sea of waking dreams,
Where there is neither sense of life nor joys,
But the vast shipwreck of my life's esteems;
And e'en the dearest — that I loved the best —
Are strange — nay, rather stranger than the rest.
—John Clare

The Book of Dreams
Bethany's Book

The day dragged on nightmarishly. No one seemed to be able to do anything. Sylvester shut himself in his study and Emily played the cello in the drawing room. They both came out briefly for lunch but didn't speak much. Instead, Daniel told us stories. Fairy tales, really, but, still coming to terms with what Rivalaun had told me this morning, I wondered if they were also true.

I felt guilty all day knowing I would leave tonight. I sat up here in my bedroom for most of the afternoon, wondering if I really dared go. But I can't see how I can dare not go. I keep thinking that my father's waiting for me. That he's somewhere in that castle or in that maze. And, although it shames me to admit it, if Poppy and Rivalaun both leave I don't want to be the one left behind. I don't want them to go off on an adventure together while I stay at home because I wasn't brave enough.

In fairy tales, when three princes or princesses set off to seek their fortune, only one has a chance to succeed. I don't see why Poppy should have all the chances there as well as here. So I suppose I'm going because of what the boy in my dream said. I'm going to see if there's a place for me at the centre of the story. I'm going to give the story a chance to prove that Poppy isn't the heroine. Because I don't see what she's ever done that even my dreams should love her that much.

I wanted to write a letter to Emily and Sylvester but I don't know what to say. I won't have any use for this journal where I'm going, however, so I'll leave it behind and hope that maybe they'll understand why I left. I'm not ungrateful. Rivalaun says that anything is possible when you walk the different worlds.

His plan is simple. Tonight we'll go to Poppy's room and stand in front of the mural she painted, while Rivalaun attempts to work whatever spell or conjuration it takes to travel between worlds. He says he doesn't think that the dream kingdom is exactly a place, but he believes the attempt will be enough. There's something in our dreams that's been calling to us. It's been trying to draw us in night after night, and if Rivalaun can open the way it will do the rest of the work for us.

So I'll go tonight although I don't know where I'm going and maybe, when I'm there, I'll be able to understand what's happening.

~⟨~

There are three books lying on the polished wooden desk. Each of them tells a story. Professor Greenwood, whose desk this is, has reason to believe it is the same story. But the titles of the books would appear to contradict him.

The first book has a blue cover and the pages are slightly rough to the touch. Inside the front cover, blockish capitals read: THE DREAM JOURNAL OF BETHANY GREENWOOD. The second book is bound in black leather and the pages are smooth and creamy. The book's title is stencilled in silver on the cover above a delicate red flower: *A Book of Lies*. The third book is handmade. Although the title has been burned on to the cover, the same words are written again inside with a plain black biro in a careless scrawl: *Rivalaun's Secrets*.

Outside in the library, five adults are sitting. It has been a while since anyone has spoken. For hours there has been no sound other than the soft rustle of turning pages. But now the journals have given up all they have to offer and the occupants of the library must seek elsewhere for an answer to their questions.

Cecily Markham sits on one side of a long russet sofa. The clothes she is wearing are borrowed and her short hair is untidy. Her posture is defensive, her legs curled up underneath her, and she is frowning to herself. Her husband, David, sits beside her. He looks tired and thoughtful and has allowed himself to relax against the back of the sofa. Danaan, the storyteller, sits in the armchair by the fireplace. His eyes are hooded as he looks dreamily into the empty grate. On the other side of the fireplace, Sylvester occupies the opposite chair. One of his hands fiddles with the silver knob of his walking stick. The other hand rests gently on his wife's hair. Emily Greenwood is half-asleep. Sitting on the floor at Sylvester's feet, she has finally been able to rest and is leaning against her husband as she stares into the distance with unseeing eyes.

In the study three books lie on the polished wooden desk. Three incomplete stories abandoned when their authors disappeared. In the library the adults have nothing to do but wait for the end of the tale.

David shifts suddenly and leans forward to meet Sylvester's eyes. He is frowning.

'All right, then,' he says into the silence of the library. 'What's next?'

'Next?' Cecily asks nervously, and her husband glances across at her before turning back to Sylvester.

'We agreed not to show the journals to the police until we'd read them ourselves,' David says. 'Now that we've seen them I'd like to know what you plan to do next.' His eyes are still on Sylvester. The older man frowns.

'There is little we can do,' he says. 'I asked you to read the journals so that you'd understand what had happened. The children have crossed into the land of dreams. In the circumstances, there is nothing the police can do.'

David's expression is incredulous, shifting rapidly toward anger in the face of Sylvester's steady regard.

'You can't be serious,' he exclaims and Cecily turns towards him with a beseeching expression.

'I know it sounds insane,' she says. 'But believe me, it's true.' Her face twists as she adds, 'It was because of things like this that Felix and I didn't stay together. Things that can't be explained by normal terms.' She looks around the room for help before adding: 'Magic.'

At the sound of the word they have been avoiding Emily looks up with a jerk and then looks away again quickly. Sylvester reaches to touch her hair lightly. Danaan turns away from the fire to watch David with speculative interest and Cecily holds her breath.

'I don't think you've quite understood me,' David says grimly. 'It's not this story, strange though it is to believe, that I doubt. For the sake of argument I will accept that my stepdaughter and her cousins are trapped in a landscape of dreams. What I find hard to believe is that you refuse to do anything about it.' He stands up suddenly, the gesture of a man who cannot sit still any longer, and paces back behind the line of the sofa.

'I'm appalled,' he says angrily, shaking his head. 'If I'm to believe any of this, I'm forced to conclude that your behaviour has been entirely irresponsible. Not only do the three of you . . .' his eyes rake Danaan, Sylvester and Emily in turn, and Cecily turns round on the sofa to stare at him in surprise, '. . . not only do you claim that our children are subject to magical influences, which up until now you have kept woefully secret, but that now that they have apparently run away to a fictional place and there is nothing you can do about it!'

'What do you expect us to do?' Sylvester asks, the strain in his voice evident as he endeavours to keep his words calm.

'For a start, you can explain how this all began,' David snaps. 'What is this dreamland in Bethany's painting, what are those children caught up in and where exactly are they now?'

Sylvester bows his head under David's criticism and Emily bites her lips, unable to speak. From the empty fireplace Danaan watches them with an unusual expression on his face before clearing his throat and drawing all eyes towards him effortlessly.

'Our story is ambiguous,' he begins. 'As dreams often are.' His voice is relaxed and his quiet figure has become the focus of the room, his listeners caught in the spell he casts out with the web of his story. Although he has told a thousand thousand stories on half a hundred worlds, this is one he will tell for the first time tonight – the one in which the storyteller becomes part of the tale – and for the first time he feels uncertain of where to begin, although his words roll smoothly through the library, sinking into the book-lined shelves.

'Just as stories exist somewhere between truth and lies,' he says, 'the land of dreams is on a boundary between real and unreal. In this world, and in an infinite number of other stranger worlds, there are things which hold constant. People are born, they live, they die. They accept the reality of the world in which they live. But some things remain a mystery, even to the wise. Mysteries that have existed since the beginning of time. Mysteries like death. And dreams.

'To dream is to journey into another world. A world where the rules are inconstant and changeable. It is a landscape of endlessly twisting paths and possibilities, creating stories with an infinite number of endings and subject to a multiplicity of interpretations. The land of dreams is the landscape of the mind: everything that can be conceived of is possible there; anything imaginable can be true. Since the beginning of time people have filled it with their beliefs, fears and desires, and it has used that belief as fuel for its existence. It is a world of story, built out of myth and magic, inhabited by half-real creatures whose ways are as capricious and unpredictable as the landscape itself. It is a magical and mysterious place. It is also the place that we came from.

'Felix, Sylver and I were creations of the dream landscape. Symbols sprung fully formed from the landscape to play a role in its reality. Three princes in a castle, figures from legend and story, part of the panoply of possibilities the visitor may encounter in their journey to the land of dreams. A mythological aristocracy in an invented landscape.

'But being real in the land of dreams we were also real to ourselves and, accepting the reality of our own existence, we came to wonder about other forms of reality. It is always night in the landscape of dreams, and night after night the dreamers would arrive and wander through a shifting landscape of story before waking into their own worlds. As time passed we became curious about those worlds and wanted to explore them ourselves and leave the landscape of dreams as the dreamers did. I have said that anything is possible in the dream kingdom but this, even to us, seemed beyond our powers, and so we went to the only creature in the dreamland who we thought capable of helping us.

'As all who dwell there know, the land of dreams has but one ruler. He is Somnus, the Sleeping God, and is the greatest of all the creations of the dream landscape in all things, including the mystery that surrounds him. Somewhere at the heart of the landscape is the silent citadel in which he has his palace. But where that is I do not know. The god's sleep is guarded in secrecy by Morpheus, Councillor of Dreams, second only to Somnus and deviser of the intrigues and intricacies which beset all visitors to this land. He is the architect of nightmares, and even those of us who lived in the dreamland feared him and called him lord, although there were many among us who were mighty ourselves.

'But it seemed to the three of us that Morpheus alone could help us, for we had no way to plead with the Sleeping God or with the landscape itself to release us. So we went to Morpheus and asked him if he knew of a way that we might leave the dream kingdom and pass into the worlds that the dreamers inhabited in their waking lives. He was loath to let us go; warning that, even if such a thing might be accomplished, outside the dream landscape we would be mortal, subject to disease or death. But we were seeking our fortune, no matter what foreign lands it took us to, and so Morpheus interceded with us and wrought from Somnus a passage through to this world and also for each of us a gift.

'The eldest, Sylver, whose symbols had been the

forest and the hunt, wished for wisdom and came into a world where he could study in seclusion, untroubled by the strange magics of the dreamland. The second brother, Felix, who had lived as a prince in a castle of dreams, wished for art and followed the eldest so that he could share with that world his visions even if they would not be seen as truth. And I, the youngest brother, decided to travel. I wished to follow the stories I had glimpsed fragments of in dreams to the end of the universe, throughout every possible world that existed.

'And so the dream became reality and the three of us came like sleepers waking into new lives in which the memory of our beginnings began to fade. More real were the constant worlds into which we were newly born, to live and love, and in which we would eventually die.

'But in our liberation we forgot that Morpheus was not known for benevolence and that gifts from him can prove double-edged. We escaped him and in this world have passed beyond his power, for we no longer dream. But our children, with dream creatures and dreamers as parents, come under his dominion. Now they have found the way into the land of dreams where, save for the Sleeping God, everything is under his sway.'

Danaan stopped speaking and, although he had not finished the story, no one challenged him. Only Emily stared into the space in front of her as if he was telling it still, her hand reaching up to cling tightly to Sylvester's. Cecily also shifted and turned to look at David. Noticing, Sylvester said, 'Don't blame yourself for what's happened, Cecily. The responsibility for this is mine. I should have been more wary. I wasn't prepared.'

'No, you weren't,' David said sharply. 'And I'd like to know why you think you have the right to claim responsibility when you've behaved so irresponsibly!'

'David.' Cecily's voice was pleading. 'I'm sorry. I thought when Felix and I divorced I wouldn't have to deal with this any more. I didn't want to understand it.'

'I don't blame *you*, Cecy,' he said hastily and came to stand directly behind her, reaching over the back of the sofa to touch her shoulders reassuringly. 'I can see how little you've been told about this. It's you I blame.' He looked straight across the room at Sylvester and Emily. 'I don't care what your reasoning was. No matter how strange or difficult this story was to tell, you should have tried – even if you thought we might not believe you. How responsible is it to keep knowledge of a child's danger from its parents? If Cecily had known earlier what you've told us today perhaps we could have protected Bethany. It seems to me those children have been playing with fire and it was inevitable that sooner or later they'd be burned by it. And you both kept silent right up until the last moment. What other knowledge have you kept from those children that they need right now?'

'He has a point,' Danaan agreed. 'Bethany and Poppy may be woefully ill-prepared for what Morpheus has in store for them.'

'And Rivalaun is prepared?' Cecily rounded on him, her eyes blazing. 'We've all read his journal. He's obviously grown up completely in your shadow. How responsible is it to do that to a child and then, when he really needs you, tell him to find his own path?'

Danaan looked about to reply but he was cut off before he could begin.

'Stop it!' Emily said, her voice strained and full of unshed tears. 'This isn't helping.'

'No, it isn't,' Sylvester agreed. 'But is there anything that can help now? The children are already beyond where we can reach them.'

'We can't just wait!' Cecily's voice was alarmed. 'Not when we have no idea what's happening to them there.'

David came back to sit beside her. His expression was dark but when he caught Sylvester's eye he looked pleading.

'Is there anything that can be done?' he asked in a quieter tone. 'Some way to reach the children or speak to them?'

Sylvester frowned and looked at Danaan and then Emily. 'Maybe,' he said slowly. 'We have the journals.'

'There's an established link between the children and the stories they have written,' Emily said suddenly, looking up from the empty fireplace with a new hope in her eyes. 'It might be possible to use the journals to find out more.'

'And the story has already begun,' Danaan agreed. 'Even if Morpheus won't let us be involved in it, he might permit us to follow it.'

'What do you mean?' Cecily asked, glancing quickly at David.

'A way to find out what's happening,' Emily told her. 'A chance at least.'

'I'll need your help, my love,' Sylvester told her. 'And yours, Danaan.' He looked at David and Cecily. 'Will you permit us to attempt this?'

'I don't see that we have much choice,' Cecily replied and David nodded.

'At least for now,' he agreed. 'We'll wait and see.'

CHAPTER THIRTY

~*~

Shall I meet other wayfarers at night?
Those who have gone before.
Then must I knock, or call when just in sight?
They will not leave you standing at that door.
—Christina Rossetti

The Book of Secrets
Rivalaun's Book

Rivalaun and Bethany stood on the drawbridge of the castle. The painted landscape on the wall of Poppy's room had seemed more unreal than ever as Rivalaun had called on the power needed to make the shift between worlds. But the misty greys and purples of the landscape had drawn them closer to the mural until the colours blended into a blurred fog and all other sensations retreated as the world spun and shifted and they stepped forward, hand in hand, into the nothingness.

The whirling mists had only just retreated and, disorientated by the change between worlds, it took a while for Rivalaun to realize that all the activity around them wasn't part of his imagination alone. Down the hill, in the city, dark crowds were gathering among the buildings. He could only glimpse shadowy figures until a firework erupted suddenly and lit up the night sky.

'Look,' Bethany said, touching his arm, and he turned.

The castle ahead of them was illuminated. Lights glowed from every window and opening. Even high above on the battlements he could see the glow of torches. There were sounds of a celebration in progress. But the castle doors were shut.

'Come on,' said Rivalaun.

Bethany turned uncertainly to follow him as he walked up to the heavy double doors of the castle entrance. He lifted the heavy door knocker and knocked three times. They could hear the booming sound echoing back into the stone interior of the castle. There was a pause and Bethany tapped nervously on Rivalaun's shoulder.

'The city's gone silent,' she whispered.

Rivalaun glanced back to see that she was right. He couldn't see any further than the other side of the drawbridge, everything else was black. Before he could say anything else the castle doors swung open and he saw a wide stone corridor opening into the castle courtyard. Shadowy figures were hurrying down the passageway and milling in the courtyard. Since the corridor was only lit by flickering lights he couldn't make out how many there were but had the impression of a large crowd, bustling around and past him.

'Hurry up please, it's time,' a voice said and eager hands grabbed at him. Then suddenly he was being hustled and bustled along with the crowd. He looked back to see Bethany's small, pale face somewhere in the confusion of shadows before it disappeared and he found himself being hurried along a long, curved gallery and then into a large chamber.

The room was some kind of armoury. Weapons hung

155

on hooks and in stacks. Other unidentifiable items sat on shelves or on racks glowing enticingly with mystery. In the centre of the room was a mirror. Rivalaun stepped up to look at it to find it covered with a black cloth.

'Rivalaun,' a voice said behind him and he turned to see Marten, his friend from the village, stepping through the doorway with a smile. 'We thought you'd never get here,' Marten said. 'It's almost time for the quest.'

'The quest?' Rivalaun asked, frowning.

'Here, try this on,' Marten said and started handing him objects. Still frowning, trying to remember what had happened, Rivalaun struggled into a long, black cloak and allowed Marten to strap a sword to his belt and place a silver circlet on his head. Then the cloth was swept away from the mirror and Rivalaun saw himself.

In black and silver he looked alien to himself and menacing. He touched the mirror uncertainly to feel his fingers slip through it.

'The picture of a young prince,' a voice said and Rivalaun turned, expecting to see Marten, and saw a shadow instead. It formed itself into a figure with smoky hair and purple eyes. 'And now the players are assembled,' it said.

CHAPTER THIRTY-ONE

Not where the wheeling systems darken,
And our benumbed conceiving soars! —
The drift of pinions, would we hearken,
Beats at our own clay-shuttered doors.
　　　　　　　—Francis Thompson

The Book of Dreams
Bethany's Book

Bethany was feeling lost. She had been swept away from Rivalaun by a tide of shadows and deposited in a bedroom fit for a princess. Maidservants attended her deferentially, dressing her in an elaborate silk ball gown. Through the windows of the castle room she could see the celebrations in the city down the hill but felt distant from them, in her unreal fairy-tale surroundings.

But the bedroom and the maidservants seemed real and somehow comforting. As Bethany submitted to them dressing her and winding her long hair into ringlets, they spoke together softly about the quest she would attempt.

'Quest?' Bethany asked in confusion, as they put strings of jewels about her neck and arranged her elaborate cascade of curling hair around a silver circlet.

'To find the end of the world,' one of them said enviously.

'To reach the heart of dreams,' another added.

Bethany had thought about this as they smoothed the long skirts of the embroidered silver dress. She was having difficulty thinking clearly.

'Are you sure?' she asked. 'That it's me going on the quest?'

The maid attending to her hair had smiled then and Bethany had almost remembered her name. Louise, wasn't it? Weren't they friends? But the moment had passed when the girl said, 'It could be Poppy.'

'Or Rivalaun,' someone else suggested.

'But one of you will save the kingdom and come back with the treasure at the end of the world,' Louise said reassuringly. 'We know you will.'

They had stopped dressing her then and looked expectant instead. Bethany had stood awkwardly, not knowing what silent signal had caused them to stop.

'Is that it?' she asked. 'How do I look?'

'Like a princess,' someone said.

There was a blur and Bethany realized with a sudden jolt that the surroundings had changed and she was surrounded by a laughing throng of people, dressed in silks and velvets and forming a whirling mass in a massive hall, flickering with light and shadow. She moved slowly through the crowd, feeling dazed.

'I'm really here,' she told herself. I'm through the mural, inside the painting, in the land of dreams'. But nothing seemed real and the shifting changes of perspective left her feeling so dazed it was hard to believe she wasn't in a dream. She moved uncertainly through the room, past dancing couples and laughing crowds, unsure of what she was seeing or low long it might last. It was the sight of Poppy that jolted her out of her daze.

The end of the hall was dominated by a raised dais on which stood a massive carved throne of black stone and a little to one side a smaller silver chair in which Poppy was sitting. A small group clustered around the dais and Poppy was leaning forward to speak with them, her hands flying as she gestured swiftly to illustrate something she was saying. Her red hair was pushed back from her face by a slender silver circlet and Bethany reached up a hand instinctively to touch its twin in her own hair.

Poppy laughed suddenly and Bethany frowned as she realized she was now only a few steps away from the dais where her cousin was sitting. A space was opening up in the crowds in front of the dais. Into that space someone suddenly walked out and Bethany recognized Rivalaun, dressed like a prince with a sword at his side and a silver circlet glinting in his silvery hair.

'On him it looks right,' she thought to herself and then blushed and looked down at the silvery skirts of her silk dress. 'But I probably look like an idiot.' Automatically she looked back at Poppy and saw her cousin staring at Rivalaun with a strange, distant look as if she had never seen him before. Her expression was puzzled, drawn into a small frown, as if trying to remember something.

'Bethany!' someone said and Bethany turned to see Rivalaun moving quickly to her side. He reached out to take her hand and Bethany blushed as she felt his long fingers clasping hers. 'I lost track of you,' Rivalaun said hurriedly. 'Stay close by, everything seems to keep changing somehow.'

'What else should it do, in the land of dreams?' a voice said quietly behind them and Bethany and Rivalaun turned to see a slim figure in the shadows at the side of the hall. In the whole hall he was the only thing with no colour to him. Night-black hair and marble skin, his expression was as inhuman as a statue and, as they stared at him, reality seemed to leach out of the bright crowds surrounding them to leave them standing with him in a pool of darkness.

'You again,' Bethany said and saw Rivalaun look at the boy with recognition.

'You refused to help me before,' Rivalaun said coldly. 'Is there any use talking to you now, whoever you are?'

'I am Dream,' the boy said, still in his swathe of shadows. 'If I have answers to give you must find them yourselves.'

Rivalaun frowned but Bethany's expression was thoughtful.

'If you can't give us answers can you ask questions?' she wondered aloud. 'Perhaps there's something we can tell you . . .'

'Why did you come here?' he asked softly, grey eyes considering them and silently weighing up the balance. 'What is it you are seeking?'

Bethany hesitated, unsure of what to say, and then glanced at Rivalaun. Her cousin was silent but the boy nodded as if they had both answered his question.

'Your quest awaits,' he said and stepped back, the shadows swallowing him into nothingness as the light returned, leaving Bethany and Rivalaun staring at each other.

'What . . . what should we do now?' Bethany asked unsteadily and he answered quickly.

'We should talk to Poppy,' he replied at once, and Bethany turned away to look with him at the stone dais and saw that Poppy had vanished.

As they turned there was a lurch as if they had turned too far. Simultaneously, the torches flared up in a blaze of firelight, throwing shadows out across the great hall. Bethany clutched Rivalaun's hand in a sudden panic and felt him squeeze her hand back reassuringly. The torchlight danced and flickered and a thick grey smoke poured from the edges of the hall to envelop the shining throng, deadening all sound as it coiled up to the black stone chair and built up into a pillar in front of the dark throne.

'Morpheus,' Bethany whispered and the smoke fluttered like tatters of a cloak, falling back like a hood about a deathly pale face.

'You brought us here,' Rivalaun said, keeping hold of Bethany's hand as he stared up at the wraithlike figure. 'Why?'

'You know less than nothing,' Morpheus informed them coldly. 'This is your heritage.' An arm swept out suddenly and he gestured sweepingly, the smoke vapours hastening to keep his shape as he did so. 'All this might be yours.'

Rivalaun and Bethany turned their heads to look where he gestured. At the other end of the hall the darkness melted away like a curtain lifting, revealing to them the vista from the painting.

Down the hill they could see the muddled shapes of the city merging with the maze of gardens that extended beyond it. Flowing slowly through the landscape and into the far distance they saw the grey snake of the river. Mists moved gently over the surface of the flat grey water, as floating and fluid as the water was lifeless and still; clouding the rest of the landscape so that they could only make out a few scattered images of trees and hills and, beyond that, the purple peaks of the cut-out mountains at the end of the world.

'What do you mean, it might be ours?' Bethany asked, swallowing nervously, as she looked back at Morpheus. 'It's not real, it's a dream.'

'To those who stand outside it, it might not be real, but for we who dwell within this land it's real enough. All you hope and all you fear, fantasies and nightmares, memories and desires, every possibility awaits you as you begin your quest.'

'Our quest?' Rivalaun asked quickly and the smoke sketched a smile underneath the dark hood.

'The landscape has called you,' Morpheus said. 'To take the place of the three lost princes.' He gestured to where three delicate silver chairs now stood on the dais. 'The royal line returns once more to the castle of dreams and the land rejoices.'

In the darkness of the hall the layers of mist thinned for a moment to reveal the glittering crowds. The hall rang with an echo of their merriment before the mists returned.

'Here is where your story really begins,' Morpheus told them. 'Here only can you find what you seek. To begin the quest that I shall devise for you.'

Bethany stared at the phantasmal figure. Her mind seemed as cloudy as the hall. Something was eluding her as she looked at that smoky figure and the three silver chairs. She shook her head to clear it.

'What quest?' she demanded. 'What are we supposed to be looking for?'

Morpheus stared down at her, his lambent purple eyes gleaming through the misty swirl of his hooded robe.

'Haven't you learned yet that no one here is bound to answer your questions?' he said coldly. 'In the land of dreams you must find your answers for yourself.'

'Why should we play your games?' Rivalaun asked, his voice politely enquiring, causing Morpheus to smile.

'Because here is where your heart's desire lies,' he said softly. 'In the land of dreams what else should you seek but your fortune?' Then the mists swirled suddenly and Bethany and Rivalaun blinked as fog rose about them. Out of the coils of darkness Morpheus added, 'Besides, now you have crossed over you have no choice. You belong to the dreamland now and there's no escape in waking.'

Bethany's heart lurched as she felt the room spin around her. A dream that you couldn't wake up from was a nightmare. Her suddenly sweaty hand began to slip out of Rivalaun's as the darkness coiled around them. A thousand fairy-tale images poured into her head like the flowing mists that made the shape of Morpheus; not Arcadian Disneyland fairy tales but the shadowy menacing images of Brothers Grimm stories.

163

'No escape,' she whispered, and as the last shapes of the great hall swam into darkness her hand slipped from Rivalaun's grip and she stumbled forward into nothingness.

∽⊂∾

Will he give a champion
Answer to my question
Or will his words be dark
And his ways evasion?
　　　　—Louis MacNeice

The Book of Lies
Poppy's Book

Poppy's thoughts were overshadowed by darkness as she passed through a stone archway and into the formal gardens. Overlapping memories formed blurs of colour and light as she wandered through the castle of dreams. She couldn't remember when she had arrived in the castle any more; in the whirl of the ongoing celebrations, as the sky shaded grey and black in endless night, the passage of time became meaningless. Companions and entertainments came and went, stirring a fleeting recollection in Poppy of other people and places somewhere else.

The air seemed to hum with magic, and space in the castle was fluid, spilling Poppy from one scene into another in a fantastic pageant of majesty. Now, finding herself unexpectedly alone, Poppy breathed in the silence and the cool night wind. She could see figures, lit up by thousands of tiny coloured lanterns, walking across the cultivated lawns, and shadows chasing each other around the topiary trees. Further down the hill near the river there were more lights. Small riverside pavilions and pagodas attracted people out of the gardens and down towards a flotilla of little boats moving silently along the dark surface of the water.

Poppy had the sensation of someone following her and, not wanting to rejoin the crowd, she ducked into the concealment of a colonnade of statues. Each statue she passed shifted under her gaze, evolving from one alien image to another. Ignoring the distracting transitions, Poppy moved up to the balcony on one side of the colonnade and looked down at the river below snaking its way into misty distances with a smooth, placid motion. The water was black, reflecting the starless sky above, and the boats bobbing gently on the surface could have been flying through the black void of night.

She looked back suddenly at the sound of running footsteps and saw a flying figure racing down the colonnade. He didn't see her until the last moment and almost fell as he skidded to a halt and exclaimed:

'Poppy! What happened to you?'

His hair was silver blond and his raiment black and silver like her own; the same silver circlet glinting in his hair. His face looked serious as she tried to place him in her memory, until a memory twinged like a sore tooth somewhere in the back of her head.

'Rivalaun,' she said and his expression lightened with something that looked like relief.

'I've been looking for you,' he said. 'You or Bethany.'

A sensation of annoyance turned over a pile of

memories like a drift of leaves and Poppy shrugged them off irritably.

'Don't let me hinder you,' she said, politely drawing aside a little and Rivalaun frowned.

'You're different, somehow,' he said, coming closer to look at her with narrowed green eyes. 'What are you doing?'

'Looking at the boats,' she replied, gesturing down at the spots of light on the river. 'Have you been enjoying the celebrations?'

'Not exactly,' he said slowly. 'But I can see that you have. How long have you been here?'

She shrugged, annoyed at the irrelevance, and summoned a half-answer from the clouds in the back of her mind.

'A while,' she said. 'Does it matter?'

'It might.' He looked at her seriously. 'You seem very relaxed here. You do remember that it's not a real place, don't you?'

'It's a different kind of reality, true enough,' Poppy replied. 'But yes, it's relaxing. Makes a pleasant change from lies.' She frowned, as something unpleasant roiled up in the mists of her memory, then her expression cleared again and she smiled. 'Let's go down to the river,' she said.

Rivalaun fell into step with her as she began to walk along the colonnade of statues to where a wide sweep of stone steps led gradually down to the river. He watched her in silence for a while before saying:

'Your parents miss you, you know.'

Poppy's pace faltered for a half-beat and then she continued on.

'Let's not talk about the past,' she said smoothly. 'It's all so far away now, anyway.' She paused for a moment before adding: 'Like a dream.'

'All right then, what about the future?' Rivalaun asked her. 'What do you plan to do next?'

'Whatever I feel like,' Poppy said vaguely but her eyes were distant with displeasure. 'I can do what I want here.'

Rivalaun looked grim. He grabbed her shoulders, forcing her to turn away from the snake of the river and look directly at him.

'Poppy!' he said loudly and clearly. 'Snap out of it! You realize we're trapped here until he releases us? Do you really want to spend all your time in a dream?'

Almond-shaped eyes narrowed as Poppy looked straight at him. For the first time since she'd come here she was beginning to feel angry and it added clarity to her memories.

'It beats reality,' she told him coldly.

'And what makes you think you *can* stay here for ever?' Rivalaun asked her. 'We're all dancing to Morpheus's tune. He's set us a quest and you're already failing, Poppy!'

Poppy looked down the long slope of the gardens towards the river. She was struggling to think clearly.

'What happens to those who don't finish the quest?' she asked slowly.

'I don't know,' Rivalaun said, shrugging his shoulders helplessly. 'I didn't think this through when I followed you here. I shouldn't have brought Bethany either, not without being sure I knew my way back. But back at your home she showed me something she wrote. She asked, "What happens to the dream when the dreamer wakes up?" ' His voice was pleading as he tried to force Poppy to understand what he was saying. 'I think now that we're here we're the dreams, and Morpheus said that we can't wake up. Who knows what'll happen if we don't attempt to complete this quest – maybe we'll just fade away?'

'I certainly didn't come here to fade away,' Poppy said, with an edge in her voice for the first time. Uncomfortable memories had surfaced about exactly why she had come here and suddenly the bright festivity of the castle seemed shallow and meaningless in comparison to the surge of fury that had originally propelled her into the dreamland.

'Neither did I,' Rivalaun told her. 'I'd like to be part of the story for a change instead of just watching it . . .' He hesitated and then looked at the river. 'Instead of just watching it flow past.'

Poppy smiled at him radiantly.

'All right,' she said, still grinning. 'Let's go find the story's end.' She turned away from the river. 'Where shall we look for it?'

Rivalaun sighed with relief at her decision but he was already shaking his head. 'I don't know,' he confessed. The landscape keeps shifting. I don't understand how this world works. Nothing here is real.'

Poppy struggled to think logically.

'It follows its own rules,' she said slowly. 'But there's a pattern to it.' Her thoughts raced as she looked about the graceful curves of the formal gardens and the long, slow snake of the river. 'Bethany's painting made it look like a real place you could travel in.'

'Morpheus showed it to us that way as well,' Rivalaun agreed. 'He showed us the landscape laid out like a map, with the castle at the beginning.'

'Then we must be allowed to explore,' Poppy said thoughtfully, her eyes still roving about the twilight-shrouded gardens. Then, abruptly, she narrowed her eyes as something caught her notice. 'Look!' she said out loud.

Rivalaun looked in the direction of her pointing arm and saw the walls and pathways of the formal gardens extending into the distance. At the end of the colonnade of statues they could see that the next turning would take them in between tangled hedges.

'We're already in the maze,' Poppy said.

'No wonder,' Rivalaun said dryly and Poppy nodded at him.

'So it seems,' she agreed. 'The world shapes itself around our thoughts.'

'Whether we like it or not,' Rivalaun added and together they stepped forward into the maze.

~◖~

She wander'd in the land of clouds thro' valleys dark, list'ning
Dolours & lamentations; waiting oft beside a dewy grave
She stood in silence, list'ning to the voices of the ground,
Till to her own grave plot she came, & there she sat down,
And heard this voice of sorrow breathed from the hollow pit.
—William Blake

The Book of Dreams
Bethany's Book

When the darkness had swallowed Bethany up she had panicked and lurched forward trying to find anything visible in the choking blackness. Her hands had scraped on rock and she'd clung to the cold stone, feeling her way along. She'd taken only a few more steps when the dark had gradually lightened and shown her the huddled shapes of stone buildings surrounding her. Somehow she had moved from the castle to the city.

Her first intention had been to go back, but the twisted streets had quickly swallowed her up. Now she wandered along narrow passageways and across the crossroads formed by several baffling paths. Sometimes the passageways were roofed over and she had the impression of wandering aimlessly underground. At other times they opened up into gardens and she walked between tangled hedges for a while. Determined not to repeat her previous panic in the

171

maze, Bethany attempted to accept the changes in her environment with equanimity. Ever since she had spoken to Morpheus she was determined not to fail his test. And so she drifted through the maze with a thoughtful curiosity, still assimilating everything that had happened so far.

So much had changed so quickly. Everything she knew about this strange place just led to more questions. She still didn't understand how the dream landscape could exist outside of dreams, or why her father had painted it. More than anything else she was puzzled by what her fortune could possibly be and how she could seek for it if she didn't know what it was. She was reeling from the discovery that Poppy's claims to magic were not as spurious as she'd always believed and that Rivalaun, too, had similar abilities. She would have liked to test whether or not she had them as well but wasn't sure how to begin. Instead she wandered ever deeper into the tangled maze, her thoughts revolving around and around as she wondered.

Although she travelled the maze of passages on her own, she would occasionally hear footsteps not far away, as if there were someone just around the next turning or on a nearby path. Sometimes she would hear snatches of conversation or catch a brief glimpse of another figure in the distance of a long pathway. But apart from that she was alone in the maze. The sky above had shifted from black to grey and, as she walked along, it was easy to imagine that it was late evening instead of the starless blackness which had alarmed her before.

She was beginning to wonder if all of the land of

dreams was like this, twisting turning pathways which led nowhere, when she came upon a section of the maze where the walls were beginning to crumble. Stone blocks had tumbled from the ruined walls and twining strands of ivy were growing over them. The next few turnings presented the same scene and Bethany paused in her explorations.

'Is this the centre of the maze?' she wondered aloud but there was no reply. The grey sky above was tinged with the red of sunset and Bethany climbed up on top of the nearest wall to try and see a clear path through the ruins.

From the top of the wall she saw that the ground where she stood was higher than she had expected. The maze stretched out in all directions. She could still see the pointed roofs of the city behind her and, up on the hill, the battlements of the castle. Still some way ahead she could see the endless depths of the forest like a green ocean. To her left and right the maze rambled onwards, although far in the distance she could see it opening out on the edge of the forest into low hills. The river was still the most noticeable presence in the landscape and she could see its broad, flat greyness sliding back into the distance behind her and winding on as far as the mountains in the distance ahead. The river thinned down to a narrow stream, however, as it met the crumbling walls of the ruined section of maze. A little way ahead the walls seemed to have collapsed entirely and other structures replaced them. In the increasingly dim light Bethany couldn't make out the shapes well but tentatively identified them as a cluster of small stone houses.

She climbed down from the wall and made in their general direction. She had doubts whether the maze would allow her to reach them, but the ruins continued to advance in their state of decay as she trekked onwards. Eventually she turned a corner and saw the structures almost directly ahead of her, barred by a rusty iron fence with bars shaped like spears. At once she realized her mistake as the last trace of light left the sky. It was a graveyard.

Bethany walked uneasily up to the iron bars of the fence. Like the walls, they were in an advanced state of disrepair and several bars had pulled away from the fence to present an opening.

'This isn't a real place,' she whispered, looking at the tombs ahead. 'It's just a dream.' But it was a dream she had had many times before and her words didn't reassure her. She remembered the branching pathways of the graveyard where they'd buried her father. Between the glittering and eloquent church service and the media event of the wake, the funeral procession had made its way to Highgate Cemetery. Graves had proliferated in all directions, hidden among the gnarled stumps of trees and thickets of unwelcoming plants. Crosses and stone angels appeared at intervals out of the wilderness, testifying to the accomplishments of the illustrious dead. Amongst the litter of mortality the procession had made its way down muddy paths. Only family members had followed the coffin to the graveside. Bethany had stood at the edge of the gathering, watching damp clumps of soil fall on the shining wood of the coffin until the procession had reversed and started to wander back out of the cemetery. Since then she had walked in that cemetery in dreams and night-mares. The graves now ahead of her seemed more familiar than the real thing.

She ducked through the gaping cavity in the fence and into the resting place of the dead. Like the walls of the maze, the tombs were old and crumbling. The stone angels were missing limbs or heads and the crosses were thick pillars of twined ivy. Where the greenery was most tangled she could make out the single thread of the river making its own route through the graveyard. Bethany searched the tombs methodically. It was inevitable that what she was searching for would be here, though when she finally saw it, it was with dread.

The white marble stone was simple but expensive: intended to display a discreet celebrity. Bethany saw it from some distance away, the newly cut stone bright among the older graves. She had to leave the earth path to reach it, and struggled for a while in a proliferation of foliage before finding a route across the stream. She lost sight of it for a while but, coming out from between two larger tombs, saw it again only metres away. She crossed to stand in front of it and read the words carved into the stone.

Felix Greenwood. B. 1959 D. 1999. Between dark and dark a shining space.

Before she had finished reading the words Bethany was crying. She crouched down at the foot of the grave and let the tears fall, only wiping them away whenever the salt stung her eyes too much for her to see the gravestone. Whatever she'd been hoping for, it wasn't this.

The wet leaves and the damp earth seeped into

her bones. When she tried to adjust her position she stumbled and almost fell. She clutched at the gravestone for support and then, suddenly and violently, slammed her fist into it.

'Is this all there is?' she said in a low, harsh voice. 'I've come all this way and this is it?'

'What were you expecting to find?' a voice asked and she looked around angrily.

The speaker was the boy from the castle. Dream, he had called himself. Now he stood among the graves like another marble angel and looked at Bethany with a level gaze devoid of any expression.

'I thought maybe here, he wouldn't be dead,' Bethany said bitterly. 'I was hoping to find him.'

'Be careful what you wish for,' Dream said seriously. 'Sometimes it's possible to find the dead here but the experience isn't always pleasant.'

Bethany looked at him distrustfully. 'Are you going to explain that?' she asked. 'Because I can do without you turning up just to be mysterious. It's not you I wanted to find here.'

'I'm not so sure,' he said quietly and then walked forward to seat himself on the gravestone. His pale skin looked more like marble than ever when set against the grey-veined stone and Bethany, who had been about to object, didn't say anything. 'What is it you wanted?' the boy asked levelly. 'Consolation or punishment? It's one or the other with ghosts.'

'What do you mean?' Bethany asked suspiciously, dragging the sleeve of her jumper across her wet eyes.

'This is as close as the waking world can come to Death's kingdom,' said Dream. 'But the boundary is still there. If you come seeking the spirits of the dead you will find them, but only as much of them as exists within the borders of your own mind. Seek them in peace and you'll find consolation. Seek them in anger and you will be punished. But when you wake they will still be dead.'

'Then where are they?' Bethany asked, kneeling at the foot of the gravestone and looking up at the still figure above it.

'In memory,' he said. 'Or other realms where you cannot follow them.' He stepped down off the stone and reached to help Bethany to her feet. 'What would you have said,' he asked, 'if you had found the one you seek?'

'That I miss him,' Bethany said, looking at the gravestone. 'And that sometimes I hate him for leaving.' She paused for a moment. 'But you're right,' she said eventually. 'There isn't anything he could say that would change that. He'd still be dead.'

Dream nodded once solemnly and stepped back from her.

'What will you do now?' he asked.

'Go on, I suppose,' Bethany replied. 'But the maze seems to last for ever.' She sighed. 'You can't tell me the way out, can you?'

'Not really,' he said and she thought he sounded apologetic. 'But perhaps you're closer to it than you think.'

'All right then,' Bethany said. She looked one last time at the gravestone and then turned away. 'I think I've spent enough time here.'

~✺~

Do I dare
Disturb the universe?
In a minute there is time
For decisions and revisions which a minute will reverse.
——T. S. Eliot

The Book of Secrets
Rivalaun's Book

They had been walking for some time before either of them spoke. Rivalaun was thinking about what had happened back at the river of dreams. He felt that he should say something to Poppy of what had happened after she'd disappeared but he doubted that now would be a good time to bring up the subject. Poppy had already run away from her past once and he didn't want to lose her in the maze.

At each turning he paused and looked at Poppy and each time she turned left with him. But the maze showed no signs of ending and each turning took them through more hedges. Like the gardens, this part of the maze had the same atmosphere of cultivation but every now and again they would stray into a more tangled section and had to tread carefully between the spiked hedges.

'I don't think this is working,' Poppy said after a while. 'I'm not sure the usual rules for mazes will be the same in this place. Do you feel we're making any kind of progress?'

'Not really,' Rivalaun said thoughtfully and stopped walking. It was quiet in the maze and the sky above was a pale pearl–grey he could almost imagine was the early light of the morning. He looked down the long gravelled path in both directions. 'We know it leads into the forest at some point though. And back to the castle.'

Poppy shrugged.

'We may as well go on as back,' she said. 'Perhaps we should look for the parts of the maze that are more tangled.'

'All right,' Rivalaun agreed. 'At the next turning then.'

They walked on for a while and then Poppy spoke again. There was a touch of amusement in her voice when she said:

'You said Bethany was here, too.'

'Yes,' Rivalaun frowned to himself. 'We both came here together. But I lost her in the castle.'

'I can't believe you got Bethany to go with you,' Poppy said with a touch of scorn. 'She's *sooo* mundane about this kind of thing.' She drawled the words with an idle contempt that Rivalaun didn't like.

'You never give her a chance,' he said. 'You only see her in your shadow.'

Poppy shot him a sharp look and her eyes narrowed like a cat's. Rivalaun wondered if she was going to say something unpleasant but her words surprised him.

'You're really worried about her, aren't you?' she said. 'It's OK.' She laughed suddenly. 'Look,' she said.

179

'I'm not worried about her, am I? And I know her better than you do. For all that you're championing her you still don't think she's going to cope with this, do you?'

Rivalaun had to think about that for a while before admitting to himself that Poppy was right. He *had* been worrying about Bethany and he wondered now if his concern was misplaced. When they'd lost Bethany while out riding Poppy had been close to frantic. Now her mood was different. But he, having got closer to his other cousin since then, was more worried. He decid–ed that Poppy's casual contempt for Bethany was less genuine than Bethany's more sullen hatred of Poppy.

'I am worried,' he said. 'But maybe I shouldn't be. You're right that I don't know her as well as you do.'

'You don't know either of us very well,' Poppy told him. There was an edge in her voice. 'I think you making me remember myself makes us even now. I mean, kudos for the help, but you owed me something for lying to me before.'

'What do you mean?' Rivalaun asked, stalling for time.

Poppy hissed under her breath and he realized she was becoming angrier.

'What do I mean?' she echoed, slashing violently at a trailing spray of ivy. 'I mean you lied to me, Rivalaun. You broke our agreement. Your secrets for mine, remember?' They were coming up to another turning. She gestured quickly towards the route that seemed more overgrown and he speeded his pace to meet hers. 'You said you couldn't make the shift between worlds,' she continued. 'But you're just as much here as I am.'

'And that's why I didn't tell you,' Rivalaun said defensively. 'Because I thought if I did, you'd leave. And I was right.'

'And?' Poppy glared at him. 'That somehow gives you the right to lie? You don't have the right to control my actions.'

'And you don't have the right to control mine,' he replied sharply. 'I broke our agreement because I saw what I thought was a good reason to lie. Did you ever consider that there are times when dishonesty isn't a betrayal?'

'No,' she replied coldly. 'I'm sick of being lied to for my own protection. You could have just told me you wouldn't answer that question. That would have been fair. But no, just like everyone else you lied to me and thought I was too dumb to figure out the truth.'

Poppy slashed at another trailing strand of greenery, cursing fluidly under her breath. Rivalaun looked down at her and saw red beads of blood lining up along her hand. The hedges were now wound with thorns. Underneath, the gravel had given way to ankle-deep grasses and he thought he saw brambles underfoot as well.

'I think we might be getting close to the forest,' he said.

'No kidding,' Poppy said sharply, licking the blood from her wrist. 'You know, I bet we'll find Bethany there. I wonder if you can fall asleep in the land of dreams.'

A protruding spray tangled in Rivalaun's hair and he stopped to remove it. Poppy headed on. When he looked up she had disappeared around the next turning. Cursing, he ripped the strand of hair away from the branch and ran after her. To his relief she was there when he turned the corner and he hurried to catch her up.

'Poppy!' he said, when he reached her. 'I'm sorry.'

She darted a look at him and pushed the increasingly dense bushes out of her way.

'Expand and enhance,' she said.

'I'm sorry for lying to you,' he replied, helping her clear the path ahead. 'It wasn't fair. And you were right. I was thinking of you as a child and humouring you. I apologize. It won't happen again.'

Poppy looked up with a twisted smile.

'When you apologize you really do it in full, don't you?' she said. 'OK then. We're quits. But don't do it again.'

'I won't,' Rivalaun said, relieved.

They pushed onwards and then Poppy added:

'Out of interest then, why?' She was frowning to herself. 'What made you think of me as a child?'

'Because you're so impulsive,' he said with a sigh. 'I did have an idea of how my father's magic works but I thought if I told you how you'd use the power to leave home. I didn't want to be responsible for that.'

'Responsible?' she sounded incredulous. 'You hardly know me, Rivalaun, or my family. Why should you care what I do or what they think?'

'Because they're my family too,' Rivalaun told her. 'At least, I wanted to think of them that way.'

She laughed.

'A real family will love you whatever you do,' she

said. 'They can't help it.' She stamped casually on a bramble.

'Then do you still love your parents, despite the fact they lie to you?' Rivalaun asked.

'Of course,' Poppy said with an edge in her voice. 'Now drop it, Rivalaun. My relationship with my parents is really none of your business.'

'All right,' he replied, satisfied for the time being that she did at least remember the past. 'Look, I think this *is* the forest now, don't you?'

Poppy looked around at the surrounding foliage and the taller trees beyond it.

'I suppose so,' she said. 'But I'm not sure what difference it makes.'

'I think paths in the forest are more likely to go somewhere,' Rivalaun replied. 'Let's look for one.'

~❁~

So now it is vain for the singer to burst into clamour
With the great black piano appassionato. The glamour
Of childish days is upon me, my manhood is cast
Down in the flood of remembrance, I weep like a child for the
past.

—D. H. Lawrence

~ *In Camomile House* ~

'It stops there,' Danaan said, putting down Rivalaun's journal. His son's careless scrawl had reproduced itself on the empty pages, just as Bethany's neat script and Poppy's black swirling handwriting had appeared in their journals, describing the children's progress through the dream landscape in response to the spell Sylvester had worked. As the story moved onwards Danaan had taken on his familiar role as the storyteller; reading from each journal in turn to the rapt group of adults. Now that he had stopped reading his voice was hoarse, although moments before no signs of strain had shown in his even cadence.

'Stops?' Cecily was alarmed. 'What about Bethany?'

'Nothing more since the graveyard,' Emily said, checking quickly.

David touched his wife's hand gently.

'I'm sure she's all right,' he said quietly. 'She's done well so far.'

'But she shouldn't have had to do it all alone,' Cecily said

184

bitterly. Across the table Emily made a small choking noise and then ran out of the room. Sylvester and David both stood, the first nearly falling in his haste. 'Oh, damn,' Cecily cursed. 'No, it's my fault. I'll go.' She quickly left the room.

Sylvester and David looked at each other and then both men reseated themselves.

'She's not the only one taking this hard, my brother,' Danaan said quietly from his own seat by the fireplace. 'Felix's death shadows us all and Bethany's not alone in not knowing how to mourn him. But, Sylver, there's no shame in grief.'

'It's not grief that shames me,' Sylvester replied. He looked at David. 'You were right,' he said. 'And I owe Poppy an apology. I did lie to her, as she well knows, and the fact that I did it to protect her is no excuse.'

'I'm not so sure I was right now,' David replied. 'This isn't the kind of thing it's easy to warn against. And the children have acquitted themselves well so far.'

'Bethany has,' Sylvester said. 'Although I wish she didn't feel so much in the shadows. And Rivalaun is finding his way. But Poppy . . .' he paused. 'With all my care I've taught her exactly the wrong lessons. I wanted to protect her from the vagaries of magic, and now she craves its unreality.'

'We can't predict the end of our stories,' Danaan said. 'Perhaps that's not such a curse.'

David shifted awkwardly and the other two men looked at him.

'What happens now?' he asked. 'It's getting late.'

'Perhaps we should rest,' Sylvester agreed. 'I don't think Emily can take much more right now.'

David frowned. 'What happens when we sleep?' he asked. 'I mean, if the children are in the land of dreams . . .'

185

'I doubt you'll see them there,' Sylvester told him. 'It takes experience to find someone in the dream kingdom and as for us, Danaan and I, we don't dream any more.'

'Morpheus kept his word to that extent,' Danaan confirmed. 'When we sleep, it's without dreaming. That was the price we paid for leaving.' They were silent for a while and in that pause Cecily and Emily came back into the room.

'I'm sorry,' Emily said when she entered. 'Please don't let me make this harder on anyone than it is already. I'm just finding this difficult.'

'It is difficult,' Cecily agreed, sighing. 'I feel as if my skills at parenting are on trial. And right now I'm not giving the best account of myself.'

'They say eavesdroppers never hear good of themselves,' David said lightly. 'And I think we're proving that now.'

Emily shook her head. 'But I don't feel as if I'm eaves-dropping,' she said. 'I feel as if I'm there with them. Wandering about in the same maze.'

'The dream landscape is heavily symbolized,' Sylvester told her. 'As much metaphor as myth. They wander confused and misled by meaning and find themselves in a maze. When they come to a decision, they escape from it. It's the patterning of dreams. What I think should be our main concern is how far does Morpheus intend to keep testing them and what the object is of this quest he has devised?'

The others looked at him but no one said anything for a while. Finally Danaan voiced the thought in the minds of the others.

'There's nothing we can do about that now,' he said. 'We can't know the end of our stories. Or even of other people's until they've finished. Perhaps we should sleep and come back to this tomorrow.'

186

'We know more than we did before,' David agreed. 'And our first aim was to find out what's happening. Let's discuss the next step tomorrow.'

'If any of us can sleep,' Emily said ruefully.

'You can and you will, my love,' Sylvester said. 'You need rest, and if you have difficulty finding it I have power enough to give you sleep at least. Even if that's all.'

Emily leaned her head against his shoulder and sighed.

'All right then,' she said. 'Let's leave this for now. The children will have to find their way out of the maze without us.'

~c~

(They fear not men in the woods,
  Because they see so few.)
You will hear the beat of a horse's feet,
  And the swish of a skirt in the dew,
  Steadily cantering through
The misty solitudes,
  As though they perfectly knew
The old lost road through the woods . . .
But there is no road through the woods.
— Rudyard Kipling

The Book of Lies
Poppy's Book

It was dark in the forest, much darker than it had been in the maze. The tall trees were densely packed and through brief gaps in the green canopy the sky was black.

'I wonder why it's always night here,' Poppy mused to herself, leaning back against a tree trunk.

Rivalaun was sitting across from her in the small clearing. By mutual consent they had agreed to rest for a while when they reached it. Poppy had taken the silver circlet out of her hair and was absent-mindedly flipping it between her fingers. Rivalaun had unsheathed his sword with a view to hacking the brambles away, but the slender rapier wasn't really suitable for the task and he tilted it into the dim light to study it instead.

'I don't know,' Rivalaun replied after a moment. 'I've had dreams where it was daylight.' He met Poppy's eyes steadily. 'But people dream mostly at night, don't they? It makes an odd kind of sense that it would be night here.'

'Perhaps,' Poppy agreed. 'I still don't really understand how this place works. Is it a real place . . . ?' She glanced across at Rivalaun. 'You know more about that than me,' she reminded him. 'You've known more than one world.'

'I think I might have known too many,' Rivalaun said thoughtfully. 'In some ways our travels were a lot like this place. All of a sudden everything's different and you find yourself grasping at fragments of meanings.' He sighed. 'Like Danaan's stories there are common elements though.'

'Hmmm.' Poppy studied the slender silver circlet glinting through her fingers. 'Tell me more about your father's stories. Is that really all he does? Travels from world to world telling stories?'

'More or less,' Rivalaun sighed and resheathed the silver sword, turning to face Poppy properly. 'I don't know who my mother was,' he said. 'As long as I can remember, back to when I was very small, it's been me and Danaan travelling together.'

'How come you call him Danaan?'

'You mean rather than Daniel?' Rivalaun asked. 'I think your mother changes his name to make it sound more normal. Like Sylver and Sylvester.'

'Obviously.' Poppy rolled her eyes scornfully. 'I'm not

189

talking about that. I mean why don't you call him Dad or Father or something?'

'Oh.' Rivalaun was silent for a moment. 'I imagine it's because he doesn't seem very much like a father,' he said. 'He's always just . . . the Storyteller. That's the important thing about him; the thing that's the most real.'

'But it's not real.' Poppy frowned blackly. 'That's just like my parents. How can the things that seem most real about them be such a lie?' She shook her head in irritation.

'Is it all a lie though?' Rivalaun asked and then went on quickly when Poppy glared. 'I'm not arguing with you . . . It's just that in lots of ways your parents are just what they pretend to be: normal people living a normal life in your world. I think that's what they want to be so they pretend it's true. Maybe pretending makes it true . . .'

'And your father, Danaan?'

'Whether his stories are all true or all invented they're still real, aren't they?' Rivalaun pointed out. 'They're still real stories. And the people who listen to them, in palaces and villages, on ships and on caravans, they find some kind of meaning in them. Danaan says that his stories are universal, although the meaning shifts and changes for different people; that telling the story is the same as living it.'

Poppy laughed. 'He likes to be cryptic, your father, doesn't he?' she said, grinning. 'He's about as helpful as Morpheus.'

Both children were silent for a while, thinking about the Councillor of Dreams, and Poppy spun her circlet more rapidly through her fingers as her mind raced.

'You know,' she said eventually. 'I think we might be on to something here. There's a connection between all of this, we know that, right?'

'Go on,' Rivalaun urged and Poppy held up a hand and began to tick off points on her fingers.

'OK,' she began. 'Firstly, we know that there's a connection between this place and our family. Uncle Felix painted that picture of it, we all dreamed about it, and Morpheus called us here rather than anyone else.'

'Danaan said we were bound together by blood and by dreams,' Rivalaun told her and couldn't help laughing when Poppy rolled her eyes again.

'*Okaaay*,' she drawled and then ticked off her next point on her middle finger. 'We also know that there's a magical connection. No matter what my parents pretend, we know that both of us, and maybe Bethany too, have abilities that can be described as "magical", right?'

'Agreed,' Rivalaun nodded, impressed by the methodical way Poppy was considering the situation.

'Now comes the tricky bit,' Poppy went on. 'Morpheus said that there's something we're expected to do here.'

'To seek our fortune,' Rivalaun agreed.

'To reach the end of the story,' Poppy added.

'To finish a quest.'

'And we have to decide our own path,' Poppy finished. 'find our own way through this dream landscape.'

'You said before that the world shapes itself around our thoughts,' Rivalaun reminded her.

'Yes, but not our wishes,' Poppy said thoughtfully. 'In

the castle it was all eat, drink and be merry. But things were different by the river and it wasn't until we agreed to start the quest that we ended up in the maze.'

'And now we're in this forest,' Rivalaun added, looking up and around them.

As they'd been talking the light seemed to have got even dimmer and he wondered if the clearing was as large as it had seemed at first. They had found their way into it by hacking through what had appeared to be one of the hedges of the maze. But once they were through, it had become clear that they were in the forest. When they had first arrived the trees had not been quite as densely packed as they were now and Rivalaun remembered that they hadn't appeared much taller than the hedges of the maze. They were tall now though, over three or four times his height, and looking around he couldn't see where they had entered this clearing.

'The places are like the different stages in a story,' he pointed out. 'But we move through them like people in a dream.'

' "Stage" is a good word for it,' Poppy agreed. 'We're placed here like puppets and Morpheus watches us to see what we do.'

'And what are we going to do?'

'If I knew that . . .' Poppy shrugged expressively. 'I still haven't worked this place out yet. But I'm guessing that until we pass this test of Morpheus's we're basically screwed. What were those options again? Complete the story or fade away?' She shook her head. 'I don't much like the sound of that.'

'And it seems to be a competition, doesn't it?'

192

Rivalaun said slowly. 'We're supposed to be competing against each other. You and me and Bethany. One of us is intended to succeed and the other two fail.'

'Fight it out like gladiators?' Poppy said. 'Yeah, I'll bet you're right. But I don't see that working, really. How are we supposed to compete if we don't know what we're competing for?'

'I'm not certain,' Rivalaun said, considering Poppy warily. 'But I don't like the idea much.'

Poppy smiled. 'Well you're the one with the sword, Prince Rivalaun,' she said lightly. 'I've just got this thing.' She flipped the silver circlet again before settling it back in her thick glossy hair and jumping to her feet. 'Look, until we get set against one another *mano a mano* let's cooperate, OK?'

'OK,' Rivalaun repeated. 'In that case we ought to agree on a direction, in case we get separated.'

'In Bethany's painting the very last thing, in the distance, is the mountains,' Poppy reminded him. 'I think they're still ahead of us at the moment and I'm guessing we'll end up there sooner or later.'

'So if we get separated the plan is to head for the mountains,' Rivalaun said.

'Seems reasonable,' Poppy agreed. 'Though Bethany may object, of course.'

'Let's cross that bridge when we come to it,' Rivalaun said neutrally and Poppy grinned.

'Be careful what you wish for,' she said. 'You might get it.'

CHAPTER THIRTY-SEVEN

Meanwhile the mind, from pleasure less,
Withdraws into its happiness:
The mind, that ocean where each kind
Does straight its own resemblance find;
Yet it creates, transcending these,
Far other worlds, and other seas;
Annihilating all that's made
To a green thought in a green shade.
                              —Andrew Marvell

The Book of Dreams
Bethany's Book

Bethany wasn't sure at exactly what point the maze had melted away into the forest but it had been a long time since the path she was on had twisted or turned. Tall trees grew on either side of her and the undergrowth made straying off the path a less than desirable choice. The sky above was dark and the expanse of the forest a deep verdant green. Occasionally she thought she could see shadowy figures in the distance and once or twice she glimpsed what might have been lights far away. But she kept walking down the path she had originally found herself on thinking there wasn't much point in leaving it until she had some idea of where to go.

Loose twigs crunched under her feet as she walked.

She could smell woodsmoke somewhere in the air. Occasionally, she saw wild flowers growing in the undergrowth on either side of the road, but she didn't recognize any poppies. The thought reminded her of her cousins and she wondered if they were also somewhere in the wood. But when she found herself considering whether or not they were making the journey together she shook her head and tried to concentrate on something else. It wasn't that hard to let her mind wander. Although it was night the forest was peaceful. The grassy path meandered through the trees and past thick banks of flowers. Any distant noises were too soft and far away to trouble her. She was reminded of the little wood she'd explored on the horse ride, and she winced at the memory of Poppy's scathing contempt.

'And she's here too,' she thought to herself. 'After stealing my painting to use in her miserable magic spell.' She ignored the fact that Poppy's magic had proved to be real after all and wondered instead if Poppy had got through the maze and if Rivalaun was with her.

The path was opening out, and Bethany felt a kind of recognition at the scene ahead of her. Green light filtered down through the trees into a small shady clearing strewn with flowers. Still remembering her ride in the woods near Camomile House, Bethany took a few steps into the space and sat down on the thick, lush grass with a sigh. Ever since she'd left the graveyard she'd been alone. She remembered how alone she'd felt on that ride as well, with Poppy and Rivalaun off having fun somewhere else. Ever since her father's death she'd felt separated from everything else. Now she thought of the letters he had written to her during his last illness and how he'd made her promise not to spend too much time grieving.

'I came here to look for him,' she admitted out loud. 'But he's not here.' She bent her head to her knees and stared through her hair at the ground as her eyesight went blurry with tears. Then suddenly she was scrambling to her feet as a mound near the centre of the clearing humped itself upright and she saw that what she had assumed was grass was the green robe of a resting man.

He was old. A crackling cloud of snow-white hair straggled to below his shoulders. As he stood up Bethany saw that he moved carefully, resting his weight on a bleached wooden staff. The robe that had misled her into not seeing him was a dark mossy green for the most part, but shaded imperceptibly into darker and lighter greens as subtly as the natural colours of the ground. Despite his apparent age his face was not deeply lined, and she took in a hawklike nose and a thin, cruel-looking mouth before her frightened gaze was trapped by the dark caves of his eyes.

'You are afraid,' he said quietly. 'There is no need. I am no threat to you here, child. Nor would I harm you were I capable.'

Bethany's heart was still beating wildly as the man continued to stare unblinking into her eyes and he went on in the same measured tones.

'Others will judge if I brought good or ill to the world but I do not believe it was ever said of me that I gave children reason to fear me.' The thin mouth tightened with something that might have been amusement. 'Indeed, I once had a student of your age and for a long time my company pleased him greatly. It was not until he became a man that he saw that I might be feared. But I assure you, child, here I am powerless.'

Bethany's heart was calming down due to the steady pace of the old man's words, which were beginning to convince her. Standing still in the middle of the clearing and leaning heavily on his staff, he didn't look like much of a threat. She wet her lips before speaking.

'You startled me,' she explained. 'I didn't know there was anyone else here.'

'And why should you have done?' the old man agreed. 'You have troubles enough of your own, it appears.'

Bethany flushed and wiped at the drying tears on her face, embarrassed that he had seen them. His dark gaze was dispassionate as he considered her and an uncomfortable thought occurred to her.

'Are you . . . are you something to do with Morpheus?' she asked.

An expression she couldn't recognize passed across the man's face and she had the feeling that she had managed to surprise him but all he said was, 'I am not under his command as the creatures of dream are, but I have been prisoner in this land for long enough that I know him and his.'

'You're trapped here?' Bethany said in surprise. 'Did you cross over too?'

'Cross over?'

'Come here really, I mean,' she explained. 'In the flesh.'

'Ah.' He nodded his understanding. 'No, child, the manner of my captivity is other than that. In sleep I am imprisoned. A magic spell binds me that I do not wake, and so now all else has left me, my last freedom is here, in a cage of dreams.'

Bethany stared at him from across the clearing and tried to convince herself that he was telling the truth about not being able to harm her.

'How were you trapped then?' she asked, playing for time. 'And how long have you been asleep?'

'Long indeed if you do not recognize my tale,' he said thoughtfully. Bethany shivered at the thought that he was assessing her in return as she studied him. 'And the instrument of my capture was a child's trick, one I might have evaded with ease had I not been blinded by pride and selfish love.' For a moment the dark eyes flashed with anger before the old man shook his head, dismissing the thought. 'But, tell me truly, child,' he said and for the first time a wistful note entered his voice. 'Are there none left who remember me? Has the name of Merlin in truth passed from the waking world?'

Bethany's eyes widened as she stared at the old man, taking in for the second time the moss-green robe, the smooth wooden staff and the straggling, long white hair.

'I see I am not completely forgotten,' Merlin said, with an air of satisfaction, and Bethany blinked.

'Yes,' she said. 'I mean no.' She blushed. 'I mean, you're . . . he's not real. It's a made-up story.'

'Ah.' Merlin nodded as if her stumbling words had

conveyed something of interest to him. But all he said was: 'Whether or not I am who I believe myself to be, I am here, as you are. So tell me, fellow prisoner, who you are and how you come here.' His eyes gleamed out from thatched white eyebrows with a mild curiosity which made Bethany feel nervous even from the other side of the clearing.

Bethany sighed. In the quiet forest she had almost convinced herself that she was back in England. Now, confronted by this sinister old magician, the impossible reality of her situation was returning and she quailed at the thought of it.

'I'm Bethany,' she said. 'And I came here by mistake.'

~◁~

Like as the waves make towards the pebbled shore,
So do our minutes hasten to their end;
Each changing place with that which goes before,
In sequent toil all forwards do contend.
                              —William Shakespeare

The Book of Secrets
Rivalaun's Book

It seemed to happen in an instant. One moment Poppy was walking beside him and just a little behind. The next she was gone. Rivalaun looked around, alarmed, but there was no indication of what had happened to her. The path behind and ahead was clear and the undergrowth on either side was undisturbed. He shouted her name a few times but heard nothing except his own voice echoing back from the trees. Eventually he gave up and started walking on. At least they had made plans about their destination, he thought. But he wondered why the forest had separated them.

Not much later the path began to narrow. For a while Rivalaun wondered if he had circled around and was coming back to the maze but the track didn't twist or turn, it just got fainter and smaller. The undergrowth straggled on to the earthen track and the tree branches menaced his face and arms. The going became slower and more difficult and after a few more minutes Rivalaun was brought to a complete stop. The path had run out and the way ahead seemed impassable. He turned to go back in the direction he had come and was not unduly surprised to see that the path had disappeared in that direction as well.

Sighing, he took out his sword and began to make his way through the greenery, slashing at trailing sprays of thorns whenever they got in his way. Once he'd got used to the slower going it didn't seem so hard, but he wondered why the path had disappeared so abruptly and whether it was connected to Poppy's almost simultaneous disappearance. Eventually he gave up wondering and just concentrated on going in a straight line.

Although Rivalaun didn't believe that the forest obeyed normal rules of direction he hoped it would understand that he was trying to go straight ahead and towards the mountains. He was beginning to remember his tracking skills from the village and hoped that, unless the dream landscape was deliberately thwarting him, he could make his way with a degree of certainty. Whenever it seemed suitable he used the rapier to make a marker on a convenient tree and he scoured the earth for signs of any other inhabitants. Although he didn't see any footprints there were some animal signs which he tentatively identified as having been left by deer. He stopped using his sword to cut through the brambles and moved more slowly, concentrating on being quiet. If there were animals here he'd like to see them, and hacking through the forest was beginning to seem a bit inelegant, besides the fact the sword wasn't ideal for the purpose.

Rivalaun stopped when he heard soft rustling ahead and began to creep forward to see what had caused it. A little distance away the forest opened out into a small clearing and, to his surprise, he saw a human figure standing near the tree on the other side. At first glance he seemed to be wearing a spiked crown on his head. But, as Rivalaun moved slowly closer, he saw that the spikes were the prongs of antlers growing from the man's skull like the horns of a stag.

A stick broke underneath him and the great head turned quickly. Huge liquid-brown eyes met his and then the stranger raised a hand in greeting. His expression was sorrowful and Rivalaun felt embarrassed for sneaking up on him. He came out into the clearing slowly, careful not to make any threatening movements.

'Greetings,' he said, when he was only a few paces away from the mysterious figure. 'I'm sorry to disturb you.'

The horned man looked surprised and he frowned very slightly.

'Are you not a hunter?' he asked, and his voice was touched with a lilting accent Rivalaun didn't recognize.

'No,' he said hastily. 'Not at all. Just a traveller. Currently lost in this forest.'

'You wear a sword,' the man said.

'It was given to me,' Rivalaun explained. 'If it makes you uncomfortable, I'll remove it.'

'I do not fear it,' the stranger told him. 'You may keep your weapon if it pleases you. Or leave it if you will. It makes no matter to me.'

'I'll keep it then,' Rivalaun said slowly.

'Perhaps wisely,' the stranger told him. 'There are others here who may challenge you.'

'Others?' Rivalaun stepped another pace forward. 'Can you tell me about them?'

'If you will walk with me,' the man said. 'The Hunt is near to beginning and I must be far away by then.'

Rivalaun moved closer and followed the man as he headed back into the forest on the other side of the clearing. The stranger was an expert at moving unheard or unseen. Each step was placed precisely and he bent his great antlered head carefully to avoid the lower branches. Rivalaun followed in his footsteps, trying to tread where he trod, and was reminded of hunting expeditions in the past. That in turn reminded him of something else and he asked:

'What is the Hunt?'

'It is a celebration,' the horned man told him. 'Of life and death. It is as inevitable as the tide and it sweeps through the forest like the strongest wind. I would warn you to be well away once it begins.'

'Who are the hunters?' Rivalaun asked, trying to feel his way towards some understanding.

'They are many,' the man replied. 'But the elves lead the Hunt.'

'Then the elves are some of those you mentioned who live here?' Rivalaun clarified.

'That is so,' the man agreed. 'And others who are harder to find.'

'And you,' Rivalaun added, trying hard not to offend the stranger. 'Do you have a name I might use?'

'A name?' the man turned his head and looked at Rivalaun.

'Yes, something I may call you,' the boy replied. 'My name is Rivalaun. Please use it if you wish.'

'It is a good naming,' the man said thoughtfully. 'It speaks of natural things, of the meeting of water and earth.'

'Then do you have a name I could use?' Rivalaun pressed.

The stranger considered for a while and then finally answered.

'You may call me Quarry,' he said.

CHAPTER THIRTY-NINE

~❈~

In sweet music is such art,
Killing care and grief of heart
Fall asleep or, hearing, die.
—William Shakespeare

The Book of Lies
Poppy's Book

She had noticed a group of lights somewhere in the distance and stopped to try and make them out more clearly. 'Look, Rivalaun!' she had said and then, when there was no answer, turned to see that her cousin was no longer there. Frowning, she looked about for a while, but he was completely gone. After a few moments she abandoned the search. Turning back to the lights she could see that they were brighter now and, without any misgivings, left the path and headed in their direction.

Immediately, the forest closed in about her. The undergrowth didn't present too much of a problem but the trees seemed taller and darker and obscured almost all the light there was. The only thing she could see was the dancing circle of light ahead of her like a cloud of fireflies. It retreated as she headed towards it and, when she speeded her pace, winked out. Poppy blinked for a moment and then caught a glimpse of something from the corner of her eye.

Turning, she saw that the lights had reappeared in a new direction.

'*Okaaay,*' she drawled slowly. 'Very clever. How about we wait each other out, then?' She stopped walking and leaned against the nearest tree, keeping her eyes trained on the lights. A few moments later they winked out as well but she still didn't move. She doubted she would be able to find the path again now and she wanted to see what the lights did next.

Five minutes later they appeared again, much further away this time, and back in the direction she thought she had come from. Poppy considered them for a while and then grinned as a new thought occurred to her. Bending to the forest floor she picked up a few short twigs and then carefully extracted a thread from the embroidery at the hem of her dress. She bound the twigs together and then looked at them.

'Burn,' she said and smoke began to drift up from the little bundle. Smiling, she tossed it away and then repeated the process several times more. While she was working, the lights in the distance disappeared again, but she didn't stop what she was doing. By the time they appeared again she was enclosed in her own circle of tiny flickers and she sat down in the centre.

'Now I know you can see me, whoever you are,' she said in a normal tone of voice. 'Come and get me, if you dare.'

With the lights surrounding her, her night vision disappeared and she could barely make out the shapes of the nearby trees. She sat, cross-legged, in the centre of her circle and waited. She didn't have to wait long.

With a sudden rush the surrounding brightness

increased to a painful intensity and the space around her seemed to swell in size at the same time. Poppy found herself in the middle of a crowd of people. Lights twinkled from the branches around the clearing and glowed from torches staked into the ground. She was in the middle of a shining throng of people. They were dressed in hunting clothes but each of them also wore a king's ransom in elaborate and ornamented jewellery. When Poppy rose to her feet they ignored her studiously, but before she could become annoyed there was a movement in the mass and then the crowd parted like a wave.

Two people stalked slowly towards her. Poppy didn't need to be told that they were the leaders of the group. From the silver spurs on their boots to the tips of their delicately pointed ears they reeked of nobility and it hardly needed the bows of the rest of the crowd to confirm it. The man was as handsome as any film star and smiled at Poppy with the confidence of justified vanity. The woman, whose long golden hair formed a cloak over her clothing, had a cool, remote beauty, which seemed suddenly and overwhelmingly magnified when her ice-blue eyes met Poppy's.

'Greetings, child,' she said, with a smooth smile. 'I notice you do no homage to us.'

'And why should she, my Queen?' the man asked, laughing the comment off. 'We are all royalty here. Come, Princess Poppy. You need not curtsy if you wish but come join our Hunt.'

Poppy hesitated for a moment and the Queen's smile grew brilliantly.

'Come, child,' she said softly. 'Dreams and magic flow

in your blood, come take your rightful place in the elven court.' She reached out to take Poppy's hand and the redhead didn't resist as the Queen drew her gently into the throng. As the group closed in around her, her eyes began to shine and she began to look about her with fascination. Above her head the Elf Queen met her husband's gaze across the clearing and a small smile of triumph curved her pale lips.

CHAPTER FORTY

~❦~

Thou blind man's mark, thou fool's self-chosen snare,
Fond fancy's scum, and dregs of scattered thought,
Band of all evils, cradle of causeless care,
Thou web of will, whose end is never wrought.
—Sir Philip Sidney

~ In Camomile House ~

Danaan put down the black-and-silver book and turned to look at the rest of the gathering. The group of adults sat silently in the summer house and watched the drizzle of Cornish rain splatter the windows.

'Ill met by moonlight,' Sylvester said softly and Emily looked quickly at him.

'I don't like the sound of that at all,' she said in a tight voice, although it wasn't clear if it was the passage Danaan had finished reading or her husband's comment that she objected to. 'Who is that woman?'

'Exactly who she claims to be,' Sylvester said with a sigh, looking out at the puddles of rain turning the lawn to mud. 'She is the Elf Queen and her followers are indeed the elven court. They're creatures of dream.'

'And the others?' David asked. 'Merlin and the horned man?'

'Other mythological mimes,' Sylvester said with a shrug.

'Not good enough, Sylver. I don't want technical terms,'

Emily said tersely. 'Who are these people and how dangerous are they?'

'They're part of the story,' Danaan explained. 'That's what the forest tries to do. It likes to populate stories. Unlike the repetitions and confusions of the maze, the forest is a scene of paths and meetings.'

'And characters,' Sylvester added. 'It provides the appropriate ones for your story. Which, unfortunately, means that if Poppy found the elven court it was because she wanted to.'

'Why "unfortunately"?' Cecily asked carefully.

'Because they're dangerous,' Sylvester said candidly. 'Elves are callous and vain creatures who care only for their own amusement and take pleasure in the discomfort of others.'

Cecily and David exchanged glances but neither of them said anything. They didn't need to. Emily's face was white and she twisted her fingers fretfully.

'Then we've protected Poppy from witchcraft all her life, only to have her run straight into the arms of everything we most distrust,' she said bleakly. 'I could never have imagined a daughter of mine would be so foolish.'

'We've given her bad advice, my love,' Sylvester said. 'She doesn't see power as something to be feared. We concealed it from her and now she doesn't believe us or trust us.'

David took a deep breath, even as he spoke unsure whether or not he had a place in this discussion. Then, when Sylvester glanced at him, he asked cautiously, 'But I don't understand why you did conceal it. Especially when she seems to have found her way to it, anyway.'

Sylvester answered slowly. 'We did plan to tell her eventually,' he said. 'When we thought she was old enough to deal with the issues involved. But magic isn't what Poppy thinks it is. There is no system that we know of that encompasses all the rules of what can and cannot be done. Any use of power can have unpredictable results, and with Poppy's intelligence an undisciplined use of her natural abilities could create havoc. I tried to encourage her into areas which would make use of her other talents and leave this kind of power for a time when she had the wisdom to approach it with caution.'

Emily took her husband's hand and looked seriously at David.

'Sylver is sparing my feelings as well,' she said quietly. 'Poppy inherits her abilities from both of her parents.' She glanced at Cecily for support. 'I had . . . gifts when I was a child but they scared me. I grew up thinking I was cursed. It wasn't until I met Sylver that I could learn not to be frightened of what I was. I didn't want Poppy to go through that.'

'I understand,' David said sympathetically.

'But you still think we were wrong,' Emily replied. 'And I agree with you.'

'We've all made mistakes as parents,' Cecily said. 'All of us.' She turned to look at Danaan.

The storyteller raised his eyebrows at Cecily. He looked almost amused as he answered her unspoken accusation.

'Is that comment directed at me?' he said. 'I don't see that Rivalaun is experiencing any particular difficulties so far.'

'You wouldn't,' Cecily replied scornfully and David looked anxious.

'Darling . . .' he began, but Cecily stopped him.

'No, let me say this,' she said. 'He's watched us for two days now, worrying about the lessons we've taught our children, but have you seen him once question his own?' She looked directly at Danaan. 'How can you be so confident that you haven't harmed Rivalaun? What gives you the right to lord it over the rest of us?'

Danaan spread his hands placatingly.

'I wasn't aware that I was,' he said. 'But if you choose to challenge me I'll admit I'm content with Rivalaun's behaviour so far. I think he stands the best chance of completing this task Morpheus has set them.'

'You do, don't you?' Sylvester said suddenly, looking at him thoughtfully. 'You were the most reluctant to leave, Danaan. Did you intend that Rivalaun should return to take the place we abandoned?'

The storyteller shrugged.

'I rarely intend anything,' he said. 'But Rivalaun has grown up with magic and story as his heritage. If he wishes to stay and take the place the landscape is constructing for him, I would have no objection.'

'No, you wouldn't, would you?' Cecily said contemptuously. 'That's what you like to do . . . stay back and let events take care of themselves. It's a parent's role to provide some kind of guidance and at least we've all attempted that. But you . . . you've ignored that aspect of raising a child. Rivalaun doesn't have a value system of his own, he doesn't even have an identity of his own. Maybe he's the most adept at solving problems but he doesn't have any real emotional connection to them. It's obvious that the first human reaction that child has ever had came when he encountered a real family.'

She stopped speaking and David stared at her in shock. Danaan looked unmoved but Sylvester frowned and said quietly:

'She's right, brother. A child isn't an apprentice or an experiment.'

'Oh, for God's sake, let's not argue any more,' Emily said

212

with some distress. 'Bickering among ourselves isn't going to help things.'

'A valid point,' Sylvester admitted and the group subsided into an uncomfortable silence.

∼❀∼

Turn away no more;
Why wilt thou turn away?
The starry floor,
The wat'ry shore,
Is giv'n thee till the break of day.
　　　　　　—William Blake

The Book of Dreams
Bethany's Book

Bethany sat on a cool, wet rock, staring down into the dark-green depths of the forest pool. Dripping greenery surrounded them. In one direction the pool thinned down to a small brook which wound back through the forest. In the other direction water splashed down over a scree of rocks and Bethany could see that, beyond the rock face, the forest had developed an increasing gradient, steepening in the low foothills of the mountains.

She wasn't sure how long she and Merlin had spoken for or how they had come from the small grassy glade to this wider clearing. Her story had bubbled out of her before she knew what she was saying and she had told the magician everything, from her father's death and her unwilling visit to Camomile House to Poppy's inexplicable disappearance and Rivalaun's insistence that she travel to the dream landscape of the painting. Improbable as the story was, her audience had accepted it all only murmuring with encouragement when she faltered in her recitation. Now, as she finally came to an end, he continued to listen from where he sat a short distance away, as still as moss on a rock.

'Morpheus said we should look for our heart's desire,' she concluded bitterly. 'But all I wanted was to see my father again. And I never will. Not in this world, or the real world, not unless I die. I know that now. But I'm still trapped here.' She raised her head to look at Merlin as she added: 'Just like you.'

'But no,' the old magician said immediately, surprising her. 'Our situation is not the same. I am here because in my long imprisonment I dream. You are imprisoned in dream, which is something else again. The rules are different for you.'

'What rules?' Bethany asked, brushing a scattering of small pebbles from the rock beside her so that they skittered down to splash in the pool. 'Nothing here stays the same for more than five minutes.'

'You must not pay attention to that,' Merlin told her. 'That is simply a feature of this land, like trees in a forest or sand in the desert or the flow of water in a river. In the world which I came from, which remembers me now only as a children's tale, there were some places similar to this; places where the land itself was magic. It may be in your time they are gone but surely you have legends of them?'

Bethany shrugged angrily.

'We do,' she admitted, tossing another small stone into the pool and watching the ripples spread slowly across the emerald water. 'But I don't . . . didn't believe in magic. It's Poppy, my cousin, who goes in for that stuff. She's probably casting spells right now.'

Merlin nodded but Bethany had the feeling that her objections meant little to him, and she wondered if he was capable of giving her any useful advice. She still wasn't entirely convinced that he really existed, instead of just being a more complicated part of the dream-land. But, she reflected, at least he was giving her advice, which was more than anyone else in this world was willing to do.

'So if you think I should ignore the landscape,' she asked reluctantly, 'what should I concentrate on? This quest I'm supposed to complete?'

'Perhaps,' said Merlin in a tone that she was fairly certain meant 'no'. 'There is something to be said for seeking your heart's desire, even if you do not yet know what it might be. I have known men who set out on such a search and returned believing they had triumphed, and still others who did not return at all, whether because they perished in the endeavour or in faraway lands found a fortune they had but dreamed of.' He picked up a smooth, flat stone and turned it over in his fingers before sending it flying with a quick flick of his wrist so that it skimmed the surface of the pool, bouncing three times before it sank.

'But . . .' Bethany prompted and the old man turned to meet her eyes.

'But,' he said gently. 'The knights I knew set out on such quests for love of the King who commanded them. It is not for love of Morpheus that you do his bidding but out of fear.'

Bethany shivered. Although the little pool was shielded by the surrounding trees, she was suddenly conscious of the black night above. The forest might have provided an illusion of safety but it was just that: an illusion. Now, remembering Morpheus, she felt chilled and huddled tight on the wet rock.

'What else can I do?' she asked in a small voice and Merlin did not answer. Again the words 'no escape' echoed in her head and a cold fear clenched in the pit of her stomach. She sat in silence by the lush greenery of the pool, her head numb with indecision, and it wasn't until an eerie call cleft the silence that she started upright and stared wildly across at Merlin.

'What was that?' she asked and the magician looked back at her, his expression incomprehensible.

'A hunting horn,' he said.

Bethany craned her neck but heard nothing and, still straining for a repetition of the call, she asked, puzzled:

'Is there someone else in this forest?'

'Many others, I believe,' Merlin told her. 'But it is the elves who hunt.'

'Will they come this way?' Bethany asked, her eyes scanning the thick vegetation, but she could see no sign of any movement in the trees.

'They go where the quarry leads them,' the magician told her, not moving a muscle so that he might have been a stone shaped like a hunched old man. Bethany opened her mouth to ask another question, but before she could speak the horn call rang out again from the depths of the forest. This time it was joined by others, fainter but nearing, as the hunters gathered in the chase.

CHAPTER FORTY-TWO

Enough for me: with joy I see
The different doom our fates assign.
Be thine despair and sceptred care;
To triumph, and to die, are mine.'
He spoke, and headlong from the mountain's height
Deep in the roaring tide he plunged to endless night.
—Thomas Gray

The Book of Secrets
Rivalaun's Book

The clarion call of a hunting horn rang out from the woods and Quarry stilled suddenly. Rivalaun almost ran into him and had to struggle for balance when he abruptly stopped. He looked anxiously at his companion. The man was as still as a statue, his horned head cocked a little to one side as he listened. For a second time the horn called and was answered by more of its fellows. It sounded as if the forest was full of people, although Rivalaun couldn't be sure of where all the calls were coming from.

Quarry lowered his head and then nodded to himself. His large eyes were wider than before and he was trembling slightly.

'What's wrong?' Rivalaun asked with a sinking feeling.

'The Hunt is beginning,' his companion said quietly. 'The elves are already on the move.'

'It's you they're hunting, isn't it?' Rivalaun asked. 'How can they?' He shook his head in incomprehension. 'What have you done?'

'I am the quarry,' the horned man told him. 'Without a Quarry there would be no Hunt.' he looked at Rivalaun seriously. 'It is their nature to hunt and mine to flee them.' He looked about himself. 'I cannot stay here long,' he said. 'I wish you well.'

'Wait!' Rivalaun said. 'I wish you well.'

'I'm coming with you.' Quarry looked back at him, his brown eyes were wide with animal fear and he seemed on the brink of flight.

'You are not hunted,' he said. 'Why should you want to come with me?'

'Because . . . because it's not fair!' Rivalaun said. 'I can't just stand by while they hunt you. Please, let me come.'

'I must go with speed,' Quarry told him. 'Keep up if you can.' And then, with a bounding leap, he began to run. When he touched the ground his form shifted and, when he turned his head to look back at Rivalaun, it was the head of a stag, although the velvet brown eyes were the same as before. Its look was sorrowful and Rivalaun felt his heart clench in fear. As the stag began to run, he pelted after it.

They raced through the forest, the stag finding almost invisible paths through the trees and Rivalaun chasing after it as best he could. The forest seemed menacing now he was running, and the horn calls of the Hunt ringing out behind him inspired him with terror. Every branch that whipped at him, the tree roots that threatened to trip him up, the thorns that tore at his clothes, they all seemed as if the forest itself was the enemy.

He ran as he had never run before, striving to keep the stag in sight. His heart thundered in his ears and his breath whistled in his throat as he tried to keep his breathing even. His muscles strained. The trees were little more than a green blur as he ran; the stag was the only fixed point in his universe. But behind him was the Hunt and he could feel it getting closer, even if he couldn't see it yet. Howls went up behind him, though they were the cries of wolves, not of dogs.

He ran until he thought he couldn't run any more and then he kept going. The animal fear of the stag had infected him and the idea of stopping for the huntsmen to find him was more terrifying than anything he had ever contemplated. It was impossible to stop running, although his muscles already ached with the unaccustomed strain. He felt caught in a fugue state, dislocated from the movements of his own body. He wondered if he would ever be able to stop or whether he would keep running forever. Then the horns called again and he remembered that the Hunt would not go on for ever. He and Quarry were only two. It sounded as if there were thousands in pursuit of them. Thousands of hunters, armed and thirsty for blood. Escape was impossible and yet he couldn't stop running.

Then an uneven patch of ground caused him to stumble and he lost the rhythm of his pace. He lost his balance and staggered onwards, no longer sure of his direction, until he realized he was falling, not running, and fell full length with a jolt that shook the breath from his body. He staggered to his feet, still dazed and shaken, and tried to start running again. But now it was as if his muscles were made of glue. The world slowed down around him. Each step seemed to take an eternity. He tried to cry out to Quarry to wait but he couldn't make a sound; his throat was too tight with terror. He fell again and this time he couldn't get up. He cringed into a ball waiting for the wolves to leap upon him.

Something touched him and he shuddered.

'We must hurry,' a voice said in terror and he looked up to see the stag staring down at him, its whole body quivering with fear.

'I can't!' Rivalaun gasped, trying to get to his feet. 'I can't run any more.'

'Then ride!' the stag said and he found himself swinging up on to its slender back. With a leap the animal gathered itself and then bounded away. Still shaking with terror Rivalaun rode the stag. He tried to shift his weight with its weight, to move his muscles at the same time as it made its springs, trying to aid instead of hampering its flight. Then, as they tore through the forest, even that sensation passed and he rode as if he and the animal were one. They were Quarry together and behind them was the Hunt. Nothing else mattered in their headlong flight. There wasn't room for another thought when the horns sounded behind them.

222

CHAPTER FORTY-THREE

~❦~

The long light shakes across the lakes.
And the wild cataract leaps in glory.
Blow, bugle, blow, set the wild echoes flying.
Blow, bugle; answer, echoes, dying, dying, dying.

—Alfred Lord Tennyson

The Book of Lies
Poppy's Book

The wind of her progress whipped Poppy's red hair into a vivid flag of colour and she couldn't help shouting with glee. She could feel Claret's body beneath her and knew that the horse was as excited as she was. They held their place at the front of the crowd easily as the Hunt jockeyed for position. The air around her hummed with magic as the elves' exuberance conjured a mayhem of fantasies into being. Colours too bright to see, sounds and smells she could taste and touch, a riot of sensation engulfed her and she heard herself laughing.

She looked back to see the rest of the Hunt spread out behind her like a ribbon of light through the forest and thought she had never seen anything so wonderful. The elves themselves were like gods: beautiful and terrible. The forest itself quailed before them. Nothing could stand up to such power and force. And Poppy, at the head of the Hunt, felt like the spear point of all that power. She turned to look at the Elf King riding to her right and saw his face fixed with savage concentration. The Elf Queen called to the rest of the Hunt in a strange, high, inhuman voice like the call of the horns. She saw Poppy looking and her smile intensified. With a flick of her long, thin fingers she summoned a hunting horn out of the air and tossed it towards the girl.

Poppy caught it as it tumbled. The Elf Queen smiled and indicated she should sound it. Raising the horn to her lips, Poppy felt the presence of the Hunt behind her, all of them churning onwards like a tsunami. Then she blew the horn and felt the magic build behind her, lifting her into the air. As she raised her arms she heard the Elf Queen give a cry and then the Hunt thundered down and she could hear her own blood singing.

'It's all so beautiful,' she gasped and she saw the Elf King turn and smile.

'You are one of us, Princess,' he said. 'You hear the call of the Hunt in your blood.'

'I do,' Poppy whispered. Amongst the bedlam of the stream of hunters she felt a still point of calm control within her that delighted not only at the exotic madness but in her separation from it.

'Those others follow where we lead,' the Elf Queen told her. 'The court will always fall in line behind nobility. In us, in whom power is centred, the court is defined.'

'You were born to lead,' the King said in her other ear. 'Embrace the power, Princess, and delight in it. We lead the Hunt.'

'We lead the Hunt,' Poppy repeated. Skeins of power

rippled about her, ribbons of magic caressed her skin as they whipped back and forth through the company. The elves were lords upon the earth and there was none among them who did not know it and none before them who would dare deny it.

A howl went up before them and one of the great wolves, who had been running like a bitter wind over the earth, lifted its frosted muzzle and turn to howl back at them.

'They scent the quarry,' the Queen said with a pleasant malice. 'Now we'll see some sport, my darling daughter.'

Poppy blinked for a second before she smiled back, but the Queen was looking at her intently and the blue eyes were glowing with pride.

'Sound the horn, my child,' the Queen said. 'Call the Hunt down upon the quarry, daughter of my heart.'

Poppy's blood sang beneath her skin. Her eyes were blurred with tears and the magical wind stung with sharp delight. She breathed in deeply, savouring the building euphoria.

'Yes, Mother,' she said and sounded the horn.

The Hunt cried as one and their shout was pure power. The wolves bayed and the elves shouted back. Their voices rang like bells from the forest. The long train of the elven court condensed into the sharp point of the spear and Poppy felt the presence of the court behind her impelling her on. They were a thunderstorm, a tidal wave, an earthquake. They were power and magic and inevitability. She could feel the quarry ahead of them now. She could taste its fear in her mouth and it was sweet. She had never felt so free, and the trapped thing running before her seemed as remote from the terrible power of the elves as an insect in a whirlwind.

The wolves pounded on and the horses followed them. Poppy was almost shaking with excitement as she guided Claret after the quarry. She could just about see it now – a horned, brown creature carrying something on its back. The wolves could see it too and they pelted after it with a greater speed than before.

'Time to call the wolves back,' the Elf King said. The Queen called out something in a language Poppy didn't recognize and the wolves whimpered and slackened their pace.

'Why?' Poppy asked.

'They would tear the quarry to pieces, Daughter,' the Elf Queen explained. 'We choose to deal death with more . . . elegance.'

Poppy nodded, the words seemed to make sense, but she felt a pang of sympathy for the wolves. A minute ago they had spearheaded the Hunt, power and hunger in motion; now like whipped dogs they clustered almost under the feet of the leading horses, yipping small cries of protest.

'The Hunt is not an animal thing, Princess,' the Elf King said, seemingly reading her thoughts. 'It is not seemly that it should end in animal rending of flesh. The killing blow must be struck by one in full knowledge of what he does.'

'I understand,' Poppy said. But she still pitied the wolves: called back before the Hunt had ended.

The ground was rougher going now, even though Poppy felt more as if she were flying than riding.

'The quarry makes for the mountains,' the Queen said. 'But he won't reach them.'

Poppy looked up and saw that they were nearing the edge of the forest; ahead the trees began to climb the low foothills of the purple mountains. In only a few more miles they thinned out entirely and only the mountain remained. The sight surprised her. She had been forgetting there was anything beyond the forest. For a few moments she forgot her horse as she tried to remember. Something beyond the forest and a castle behind it. And also something else behind that.

'Ware the wolves, daughter,' the Elf Queen called out. Poppy blinked, realizing she had almost overrun the grey bodies of the creatures in her abstraction. She reined Claret back quickly and turned to see the Elf King pointing.

'We have him now,' he said. 'There's no way out.'

~c~

The sense that every struggle brings defeat
　　Because Fate holds no prize to crown success;
That all the oracles are dumb or cheat
　　Because they have no secret to express;
That none can pierce the vast black veil uncertain
Because there is no light beyond the curtain;
　　That all is vanity and nothingness.
　　　　　　　　　　—James Thompson

The Book of Dreams
Bethany's Book

A hunting horn startled Bethany. This one was much closer than before. She could hear a sound as well; a rushing noise like a great wind. Automatically she stood, trying to see from the vantage point of the scree of rocks.

The whole forest was rippling as if a giant snake was making its way through the trees towards them. The movement was heading uphill and the trees bent and swayed as whatever it was came closer.

'The Hunt,' Merlin said, not raising his bent head from contemplation of the green water, and Bethany felt suddenly afraid. She could hear more horn calls and the howls of wolves mixed in with the rushing noise. She wondered for the first time what it was the elves were hunting and wondered if they were able to distinguish between animals and people when caught up in that mêlée of activity. Suddenly something shot out of the trees at the side of the clearing and leaped into the pool, sending up a great spray of water as it did so. Bethany shook with fear for a second before she recognized what she was seeing.

The creature was a huge stag, branching antlers growing from its great head. On its back lay a human figure. Silver blond hair spilled into the antlers as the person clung to the stag's neck.

'Rivalaun!' she shouted and the figure stirred.

Slipping down from the stag's back he stood in the centre of the pool, looking dazed. A horn called out and both boy and stag jumped and looked wildly about them. With a pang of terror Bethany realized they were trapped. The only way out of the pool was back the way they had come or up the slippery wet rocks at the back of the pool. The stag tensed its muscles and sprang for the small waterfall but lost its footing on the wet rocks and fell back down into the water. Rivalaun rushed to its side and helped it to rise.

Then the Hunt was upon them. They came out of the trees, a crowd of hunters and animals, eyes bright with blood lust, halting at the edge of the clearing as they saw the scene ahead of them. Rivalaun put his arms around the stag and faced them. The wolves howled at the sight.

Bethany watched the confrontation with wide eyes, afraid even to blink lest she miss anything. She seemed to see everything with vivid clarity. The stag and the boy waist-deep in the green water, the trees enclosing the clearing like a cage, the leaders of the

Hunt standing at the brink of the water, looking down at the trapped figures. Then her eyes widened further as she realized what she was seeing. Three figures had dismounted at the front of the Hunt. The man and woman were both richly dressed. The man was hand-some but somehow blank-looking. The woman had the brilliant eyes of a snake in a small pale face. The girl between them wore a black dress and a silver circlet held back her lustrous red hair.

'Poppy!' Bethany gasped, only realizing that she had spoken when her cousin glanced in her direction. But there didn't seem to be any recognition in Poppy's shining eyes.

'What's this?' asked the Elf Queen, looking at the trapped figures in the centre of the water, and her voice was faintly amused. 'Two where there should be one?'

'The stag is mine, my lady,' the Elf King said in a harsh voice. 'You promised me it should be so.'

'Speak not to me of promises,' the Elf Queen said, her voice as brittle as ice. Then she smiled and her voice was warm and honeyed, and Bethany wondered how she could have thought the woman plain when her beauty was now almost too painful to look at. 'But, yes, my love. The stag shall be yours. Dispatch it as you will.'

The Elf King produced a spear and hefted it easily in his hand but paused when a voice shouted:

'No!'

It was Rivalaun. His clothes were torn and there was blood on his arms and on his face. His eyes were wild and staring and he shook where he stood in the water.

But he stepped in front of the stag and faced the elves as he said in a hoarse voice:

'No, I won't let you kill him.' With fumbling hands he unsheathed his rapier and faced the Elf Queen. 'No,' he said again as he looked at her.

'Foolish child,' the Elf Queen said, her voice still soft. 'You understand little, although you feel much. The stag must die. It was intended from the first. Let him tell you himself if you will not hear me.'

She gestured and Bethany bit her lip as she saw the shaking figure of the stag shift into the shape of a man. He still bore the antlers on his head and his large brown eyes were those of the stag but he stood in human form taller than Rivalaun and, with a sinking heart, she saw him turn to speak to her cousin.

'She speaks truth,' the horned man said. 'All things must end and this is my time.' And then he stepped away from Rivalaun and into the path of the spear the Elf King had already thrown.

His body shifted as he fell and once more it was a stag that lay at the edge of the water, heaving his last breaths as blood bubbled from his chest. Rivalaun fell to his knees beside the animal and Bethany saw that he was sobbing. Then the Elf Queen smiled and Bethany clenched her fists, her nails digging into her palms.

'We still have a quarry left,' she said, and Bethany jumped down into the pool, sliding painfully down the rocks and scraping her hands and knees in her hurry to reach Rivalaun.

'No, you don't!' she said. 'You've got what you came for. Just go away!' She stumbled up to her cousin and helped him stand up. Rivalaun's eyes were full of tears.

She wasn't sure if he recognized her any more than Poppy had as he whispered:

'I couldn't save him.'

'At least you tried,' Bethany told him and tried to hold him up. She was uncomfortably aware that she was now playing the role Rivalaun had for the stag as she faced down the Elf Queen. 'Leave us alone!' she said fiercely.

The Queen smiled down at her, causing Bethany to shiver at the tender malice in her face. The woman put her hand on Poppy's shoulder and the red-headed girl looked up at her.

'Come now, my daughter,' the Queen said. 'You have a quest to finish, do you not? You may end part of it here and now.' She put a second spear into Poppy's hand and gestured at Rivalaun. 'He ran from us,' she said. 'By our laws he is fit prey for the Hunt.'

Poppy's hand closed round the shaft of the spear and she turned to look at Bethany and Rivalaun. Her expression was strange and inhuman like that of the elves and her eyes were still dazed.

There was a noise from the edge of the pool. Bethany turned to see that Merlin had stood up and was skirting the edge of the pool as he came towards the elves. She had almost forgotten he was there and now felt a sudden flood of relief that intensified when she saw the look on the Elf Queen's face.

'You!' the Queen said and her voice was displeased. 'You have no part to play here. Go back to sleep, old man. Your day was done long since.'

Merlin leaned on his staff as if weary but his face was stern as he spoke:

232

'It is done,' he agreed. 'And you had some part in its ending. But grass grows over the bones of the past and I speak now to remind you only of your own laws. You may not harm those who are not your subjects.' His head turned towards Poppy as he added, 'You, however, are free to act as you will.'

Poppy weighed the spear in her hand. The elves clustering behind her cheered at the sight and the Elf Queen smiled tenderly.

'You only may strike, my daughter,' she said. 'But see how we have delivered your enemies to your hand. Already you could be one of us. Your magic, your intelligence and your beauty fit you well for the court of the elves. Make the kill and you will be one of us in truth. I swear it.'

Poppy raised the spear and levelled it at Rivalaun and Bethany. Bethany felt a thrill of fear. Even though there was only one spear she didn't doubt that in this place it could kill them both and she trembled as she waiting for the killing blow.

It didn't come. The spear dropped from Poppy's hand to fall in the water and the redhead stepped away from the Elf Queen.

'Who would trust your promises, elf?' she said and her small, cold smile was the mirror of the Queen's. 'Everything about you is a lie. I'm not your subject or even your daughter. And I won't be your dog.' She walked forward to stand on the other side of Rivalaun. When she looked back at the Queen, Bethany saw that there were tears in her eyes. 'You may leave us,' she said and the air began to blur.

~⁂~

CHAPTER FORTY-FIVE

Though truth and falsehood be
Near twins, yet truth a little elder is;
Be busy to seek her, believe me this,
He's not of none, nor worst, that seeks the best.
To adore, or scorn an image, or protest,
May all be bad. Doubt wisely; in strange way
To stand inquiring right, is not to stray;
To sleep, or run wrong is. On a huge hill,
Craggéd and steep, Truth stands, and he that will
Reach her, about must, and about must go;
And what the hill's suddenness resists, wins so.
Yet strive so, that before age, death's twilight,
Thy soul rest, for none can work in that night.

—John Donne

The Book of Secrets
Rivalaun's Book

They stood in a small ring on an empty hillside. The forest had receded although Rivalaun could still see its green shadows behind them. The snags and tears had gone from his clothes and he blinked in the pale-grey light as he looked at his two cousins.

'They're gone,' Bethany said with relief and Poppy nodded.

'Yes,' she said. 'And so has the forest.'

234

They both turned simultaneously to look at Rivalaun and Bethany took his arm anxiously.

'Are you all right?' she asked.

It took Rivalaun a while to regain his composure. When he did he stared at both of them trying to find the words to speak. Bethany had appeared beside him so suddenly that it had taken him a while to register her presence, although he thought it was her who had come to him while he stood by Quarry's bleeding body. He looked at Poppy and saw again in his mind the spear she had levelled at his heart. They had both appeared out of nowhere, like dream creatures, and after Quarry's death he still felt unreal himself.

Bethany's expression was distressed and she held Rivalaun upright supportively, reminding him of how their positions had been reversed the first time they'd found each other in the dream world. Poppy stood facing them, as she had in the clearing, her expression unreadable.

'This is your fault,' Bethany said bitterly to Poppy. 'You and your elves. You were hunting him!'

'No,' Poppy shook her head, still staring back at the forest. 'It wasn't about him. There had to be a quarry but that wasn't all there was to the Hunt.'

Bethany glared at her.

'Oh, right,' she said scornfully. 'I've heard it all on the nine o'clock news. Maybe you *don't* care what you're chasing, all dressed up in your finest clothes and your stupid riding jacket, but it makes a hell of a lot of difference to the thing you're hunting.'

'You think I don't know that?' Poppy looked straight

at Bethany for the first time. 'I'm trying to say things seem different from the point of view of the hunter.' She paused and then shrugged dismissively. 'But I can see I'm on to a losing streak here. It's not as if you have any experience with seeing things from someone else's perspective.'

'And you *do*?' Bethany demanded with outraged disgust.

Rivalaun shook himself, realizing that an argument was building at an alarming rate.

'Bethany,' he said gently. 'Poppy wasn't the one who killed Quarry and she didn't throw the spear at us.'

Bethany stepped back, releasing Rivalaun's arm. There were tears in her eyes and her expression was furious as she stared at her two cousins.

'Don't fool yourself into thinking that had anything to do with us,' she said angrily. 'Poppy was only doing what she does best . . . being selfish as usual!'

'And why should I be anything else?' Poppy demanded coldly. 'Haven't you worked it out yet, Bethany? In this place we *can* do what we want. Everything we look for we find. Everything we want, we get — except the landscape twists it and changes it. So what if I'm selfish, anyway?' She shook her red hair out defiantly, stepping back from Rivalaun and Bethany to look down at them from the hillside. 'Dreams *are* selfish.'

'Like the elves,' Rivalaun said quietly and Poppy looked away for a moment.

'Well, maybe not that selfish,' she said thoughtfully. Then she looked directly at Bethany, her eyes narrowing. 'And where do you get off claiming the moral high

ground?' she sneered. 'This has nothing to do with the anti-hunt lobby or the nine o'clock news. The only reason you're acting so saintly is because you're jealous, and I know why even if he doesn't.' She jerked her head in Rivalaun's direction and Bethany flushed red, although Rivalaun couldn't tell if it was with anger or embarrassment.

'You're a snake, Poppy,' she burst out, her breath catching in an angry sob. 'I hate you!'

'Oh, give it a rest,' Poppy told her in an exaggeratedly bored voice. 'I'm tired of suffering the results of your inferiority complex.'

Bethany stared at her, speechless, then swung away to turn her back on them both, hiding her face behind her hair. Quickly Rivalaun stepped between them.

'Stop it both of you,' he said and his voice was tense. 'I don't need the two of you ripping at each other right now.'

They both turned to look at him with almost identical expressions of hurt and betrayal. Then Poppy shrugged dismissively, feigning uninterest in the quarrel, but Bethany answered him shakily:

'Then you can chose who you want to be with,' she said. 'Because I'm not staying with her for another moment.' She looked deliberately away from Poppy.

'Like I give a damn,' the other girl said contemptuously. 'Go ahead and pretend we're not in competition with each other if you want. I don't need either of you.' She turned and started walking down the hillside towards the nearest valley.

Rivalaun sighed with frustration, still feeling emotionally battered by the events of the forest. Now he'd finally managed to find both of his cousins at the same time they seemed determined to break up the group and he didn't feel fit to deal with the situation.

'Now you've antagonized her,' he said, turning to Bethany with some measure of annoyance.

'Then go with her if you care about her so much,' she said in a choking voice and then turned and ran. He called after her but she didn't stop, stumbling away along the ridge of the hillside.

Rivalaun stopped where he was and looked after them. Like waves of an ocean, the land dipped and rose in a sequence of hills and valleys leading onward towards the mountains. Poppy's small figure was still marching down toward the valley. Bethany's was already dipping out of sight on the other side of the hill. He groaned in frustration and sat down on the hillside, burying his head in his hands.

'I can't deal with this right now,' he said to himself and wasn't surprised when a voice chose to answer him.

'Then when will you deal with it?' Morpheus asked, and Rivalaun looked up to see that mist had descended on the hilltop and that the Dream Councillor's figure was resolving out of the white haze.

'Since when do you care?' Rivalaun asked savagely and then dropped his head back down on his knees. 'I don't know,' he said. 'I need to think.'

'Think then,' Morpheus told him, his figure fading back into the mist. 'But don't imagine the quest will wait for you.'

CHAPTER FORTY-SIX

~❦~

Courage was mine, and I had mystery,
Wisdom was mine, and I had mastery:
To miss the march of this retreating world
Into vain citadels that are not walled.
                              —Wilfred Owen

The Book of Lies
Poppy's Book

Poppy walked down into the valley, deliberately not thinking of anything except her next footstep. There was a blank, white misery in the back of her mind and she didn't feel equipped to deal with her own thoughts, let alone anyone else's. She didn't look back, not wanting to see Bethany or Rivalaun behind her.

The curves of the hillside were gradual, flattening out when they reached the valley. She walked at a regular pace, concentrating on the next hill ahead.

'This had better not go on for ever,' she said out loud and then laughed to herself as the words keyed off a train of associations in her mind. 'And what doesn't?' she asked in a softer voice.

That thought kept her occupied as she climbed the next hill. At the top she turned and looked back. There was no sign of either of her cousins. A white mist had settled over the tops of the hills and lay like a blanket in the dips of the valleys. She sighed to herself and kept walking, taking each step with measured care.

She couldn't keep herself from thinking for long. Too much had happened and Bethany's words still haunted her. For the first time in her life Poppy felt an obscure sense of shame. She'd allowed the Elf Queen to use her, she thought. Enchanted by the glory of the Hunt, she hadn't properly registered that it was Rivalaun they had been hunting. It was only the triumph in the Elf Queen's words that had brought her back to herself. Even now she wasn't entirely sure what had stayed her hand from throwing the spear. When Bethany had challenged her she'd been furious and, in the middle of her anger, had felt an unpleasant delight in realizing that Beth cared more for Rivalaun than she was prepared to admit. But her words had also held bitter anger that Bethany so obviously loathed her.

Poppy thought back to Camomile House and Bethany's behaviour there. It seemed that her cousin had always been awkward and jealous in her company, but Poppy hadn't appreciated until recently how deep those feelings went. She didn't hate Bethany. She'd never had any reason to. But now she felt that her cousin's constant antagonism had worn her down to the point where she would have done almost anything to make it stop.

'How many other people hate me?' she wondered aloud, thinking back to the real world. She couldn't remember a time when she hadn't been popular, when she hadn't been surrounded by friends and well-wishers. But now she began to wonder about the people, like Bethany, who were beyond that enchanted circle of popularity.

She frowned to herself, looking ahead through the mist and thinking hard. Success had come so naturally to her she'd never really taken it seriously. While her parents had so obviously kept the real truths hidden from her nothing else had seemed important. She wondered now how much that alone had caused Bethany to resent her. Her cousin had never found it as easy to win friends and influence people. Poppy sighed to herself.

'It's just a game,' she said to herself. 'Why should it matter so much?'

She had half expected Morpheus to appear and answer her, but instead there was only a dry, rasping noise from somewhere ahead. Poppy peered through the mists warily. She had crossed several small hills as she walked but now she was on level ground and it had been a while since the land had curved or dipped. Although the mist lay everywhere, she could still make out a few shapes in the whiteness ahead of her. She moved cautiously towards them.

Something shifted under her feet, causing her to look down and freeze. She had trodden on one of the femurs of a human skeleton. Perfectly preserved, stripped clean of flesh but still wearing rags of clothing. With extreme caution she bent to examine it more closely. A broad sword lay beside it along with some strips of broken leather that could have been a scab-bard. Nothing else gave any clue to its origins. Poppy studied it for a few more minutes and then walked on. Only a minute later she came across another one.

Instead of a sword, this one had carried a rifle and she frowned at the tangle of bones and weaponry as she passed it.

The mist was clearing slightly. As Poppy walked on she could see that there were more ancient skeletons lying about the valley. Nothing else grew here except for a few stunted trees. The earth was strangely reddish in colour and in some places had been dug up to form huge earthworks and trenches. All of the bodies had been armed, and weapons of all kinds lay scattered about. Poppy paused to examine some of the more esoteric ones but she didn't feel the urge to pick them up. Instead she trudged on across the battlefield, trying to make out the landscape through the trailing curls of mist.

The rasping noise came again and Poppy stiffened, her eyes roving quickly across the bone-strewn earth. Grey light glinted on harnesses and weapons. A sudden shift in the landscape dazzled her momentarily. Screwing up her eyes she could see something moving among the ancient bones, rising up with a sinuous sway to address her.

'Where are you going, little witch?' it enquired in a dry, dead voice like the crackling of autumn leaves.

Poppy blinked quickly, her eyes watering, and saw the dazzle resolve itself into a coiled shape crouched by a nearby tree. About twenty foot long, snout to tail, and covered with silver-grey scales except for its leathery taloned wings; it was a dragon. Poppy approached cautiously and answered:

'I'm seeking my fortune.'

'Ahhh,' the dragon sighed and the air was briefly

thick with a burnt meat smell. 'I had a fortune once,' it said wistfully, blinking lambent moonstone eyes. 'A glittery hoard of swords and crowns.'

'What happened to it?' Poppy asked, interested but still hanging a few paces back from the creature.

'All gone now,' the dragon said sadly. It raised its wedge-shaped head a little higher and studied Poppy with interest, opalescent eyes fixing appreciatively on her silver circlet. 'Are you a princess, little witch?' it asked.

'Why do you ask?' Poppy said cautiously, rapidly trying to remember everything she'd ever read about dragons. 'This had better not be a culinary interest.'

The dragon flattened its ears back in displeasure and hissed like a cat.

'Curiosity,' it insisted. 'A witch princess is food for thought merely.' It blinked slowly and then began to unwind itself from its sleeping place.

Poppy hesitated, watching it. She wasn't sure if she entirely believed its claim that it didn't consider her a candidate for lunch, but on the other hand she didn't really want to run off and leave it either. While she vacillated the dragon made up her mind for her, finished unwinding itself and stalked slowly towards her. On all four legs it was almost as tall as she was and its long snake-like neck lifted its head above her.

'You smell of magic,' it told her, the scaled head bending to sniff at her hair. 'Magic and majesty and metal.' Poppy jumped as a forked tongue escaped the dragon's mouth and licked the silver circlet. 'Ahhh,' it sighed. 'I had a hundred such once. Trappings of royalty and riches.'

'Look.' Poppy stepped back so she could look it in the face again. 'Do you want this? I'll trade it to you if you like.'

'Hmmm.' The dragon's eyes glowed with interest as it considered the offer. 'What for?' it asked.

'Information,' Poppy replied, removing the circlet and spinning it through her fingers invitingly. 'What can you tell me about this place?'

'It is a battleground,' the dragon said plainly, extending its neck towards her again.

'I can see that.' Poppy held the circlet out of reach. 'That's not my real question.'

'Some answers are secret,' the dragon said, almost plaintively. 'Even from me. I can't answer those.'

'All right.' Poppy thought for a second. 'Tell you what. I'll ask you three questions and you answer them as well as you can, OK?'

'And in exchange the jewel is mine?' the dragon reminded her, sniffing at the circlet hopefully.

'Yes.'

The dragon sighed and again a gust of burnt air warmed Poppy's face. It flapped its wings a couple of times and then sat back on its haunches, fixing her with an expectant look.

'Your first question?' it asked.

Poppy thought carefully, reluctant to ask too hastily. Ever since coming to this world she'd been given cryptic answers to the most simple of questions. Now she wanted to actually learn something from this bargain. Remembering the points she had made to Rivalaun what seemed like an eternity ago she asked her first question.

'What does this place have to do with my family?' she demanded.

The dragon's tongue snaked out suddenly to flicker at the circlet, tasting the silver metal and rasping across Poppy's fingers. When she snatched the circlet back it hissed crossly and ruffled its wings as it settled back again.

'You came from here,' it told her. 'I can taste it on you. Half mortal. Half myth. You're one of us. Perhaps one of Morpheus's creatures strayed into your world to birth you.' The wings rose and fell as the dragon shrugged. 'That is all I know.'

'OK.' Poppy nodded. 'That's fair enough.' She paused for thought. 'Second question then. What powers do I have here?'

'Dream and dreamer . . . you change and are changed,' the dragon breathed in a whisper like burning leaves. 'All creatures of dream are under Morpheus's law. In the mists we drift. Patterns repeating over and again, as night follows night, set in our courses like the stars. But you, I saw you come down from the hills to cross the battleground, you move through the landscape like the breath of a god.' There was a deep longing in its desiccated voice as it hissed: 'You are free.'

Poppy frowned as she thought about that for a while, flipping the circlet as the dragon watched greedily.

'I'm not arguing with you,' she said. 'But I don't feel all that free. So far I've ended up half amnesiac by the river, wandered for ages in a maze, been hypnotized by a bunch of homicidal elves and spent the last ten minutes walking through skeleton soup. I don't exactly feel very powerful.'

The dragon's tail lashed back and forth.

'Did you use to have a hoard as well?' it asked with unexpected sympathy. 'Shiny and sparkling?'

'Yeah,' Poppy grinned at it. 'I did, actually. Full of swords and crowns and everything.'

'Gone now, though.' The dragon blinked its moon–stone eyes mournfully, reflections of Poppy's circlet dancing in the round orbs. 'Better get another one.'

'Yeah,' Poppy smiled. 'OK then, third and last question . . .'

'Ask and be answered.'

'How do I win this competition?' Poppy asked, meeting its limpid eyes. 'How do I pass the test? Where do I look for my heart's desire?'

The dragon sighed heavily and Poppy had to step back from the wave of sulphurous air.

'How am I to know that?' it asked her and then, before she could object, went on quickly, 'The way to win is for your enemy to lose. To pass a test you must know all the answers. Your heart's desire is the one true thing you long for and you should seek it where the land of dreams is most real.'

Poppy stared at it.

'And where is that?'

The dragon shifted and scales rippled along its flanks.

'You have had three questions,' it reminded her and this time Poppy sighed.

'All right then,' she agreed and extended the glinting circlet of silver toward the creature.

The dragon blinked rapidly and hissed with pleasure, lifting one of its front claws to grasp the circlet in a surprisingly careful grip.

'Ahh,' it sighed, licking the metal affectionately.

'Something to begin a new hoard with,' Poppy said smiling and the dragon crooned softly in agreement. 'I guess I'll be going then,' she added.

The dragon, engrossed in its new treasure, barely spared her a glance as she began to walk away. Ahead of the small red-headed figure the landscape suffered another abrupt change. The bones of the battlefield gave way to a glassy plain of black earth; a single tower outlined against the dark and lowering sky.

As Poppy came to the border the dragon looked up with a fleeting interest to watch her.

'They never ask the right questions,' it mused to itself, nuzzling its snout affectionately against the slender circle of metal. Its eyes were bright with interest as Poppy took a step across the boundary and was instantly swallowed up by the black land. 'Ahhh,' it sighed one last time and, caressing the bright metal, sank back to sleep.

~ ‹ ~

CHAPTER FORTY-SEVEN

They step into their voluntary graves,
Sleep binds them fast; only their breath
Makes them not dead:
Successive nights, like rolling waves,
Convey them quickly, who are bound for death.
—George Herbert

The Book of Secrets
Rivalaun's Book

Eventually, Rivalaun started walking again. The hills and
dales rose and dipped before him and the mist made it
difficult to see in any direction. He walked on regardless, wondering to himself why he was even continuing
in this endeavour and how it was supposed to end.

'Is it all just about fighting?' he asked out loud,
wondering if Morpheus was still pacing him. 'Are we
just going to go on and on like this until one of us wins
through to the end or kills the others in the process? Is
that what this is about?'

There was no answer and he continued to walk,
thinking miserably about the argument he had had
with his two cousins. It seemed as if he hadn't helped
either of them and they were determined to continue
their own conflict regardless of anything he said and
did. He'd entered the dream landscape because he'd felt
himself part of the family he had met for the first time
in Camomile House. Now, with Danaan and the rest of

the adults far behind, he thought how useless he had proved. He hadn't really affected anything here and it didn't seem to matter to anyone what he did. He hadn't saved Quarry. The stag had just let itself be killed and its last words had convinced him that nothing he could have done would have saved it. The Hunt had simply continued to its inevitable ending, just as Quarry had said it would, and Rivalaun didn't have any experience with endings.

'We always leave before then,' he said out loud. 'Just move on to the next story.'

He looked around at the dream landscape and wondered where this quest was taking him, what he was supposed to be looking for in this untrustworthy place. The low hills had given way to a flatter prospect of smaller dips and mounds and the earth had a raw look to it, as if below the pale-green grass it was churned up by some force of nature. The mist still lay heavily all about him and he sat down on one of the low hillocks to rest his legs for a while. Looking down at himself he realized with a sudden disgust he was still wearing the silver sword. Unbuckling it quickly, he tossed it to the ground. He looked down on it for a while and suddenly felt lonely for Bethany. He thought now he had been too harsh with her earlier. Although he didn't like her antagonism towards Poppy, he didn't have any real right to discount the strength of her feeling. The cousins had known each other for a lot longer than he had – a fact Poppy had pointed out in the maze. In his eagerness to become a part of their family and trying to be fair to all sides he had ending up hurting Bethany by equally distributing his frustration between them. She had, after all, been standing up for him.

He remembered Poppy's enigmatic comment that there had been something behind that support and he wondered what she had meant. He would have liked to have asked her about that. He felt ashamed of his part in the quarrel. The emotions his cousins felt for each other were real and they had been simply displaying how much strength of feeling existed there. He, the outsider, had stood by and judged them without any genuine experience of what being in a family was all about.

'I should just stop now,' he said out loud. 'I deserve to fail.'

'It's not meant to be a punishment,' a voice remarked behind him and he turned to see, with a kind of inevitability, the boy he had last seen when Bethany was lost in the maze.

'You're here,' Rivalaun said, frowning to himself. 'Where've you been?'

Dream came to sit beside him and stretched out his legs. He was slighter than Rivalaun and his black hair was tied back neatly from his pale face with a small silver clip. His clothes were the same dull black as his hair: a complete absence of colour that made him seem more like a hole cut in space than a physical presence.

Rivalaun studied him and the boy smiled under his scrutiny, apparently not self-conscious at Rivalaun's steady regard. His skin was almost translucently pale. Rivalaun imagined that he could almost see straight through it to the grass and the red earth behind him.

'Are you real?' he asked, remembering another part

of the conversation he and Poppy had had in the maze. 'And was Quarry real?' Then he stopped, remembering, and said, 'Or won't you answer my questions?'

'I don't think that's an answerable question on any terms,' Dream said, his own face equally serious. 'And that's by anyone's standards, not just mine. What is the reality of any experience save in how real it appears to the one who experiences it?'

'That sounds like something Danaan would say about storytelling,' Rivalaun said and then asked, testingly: 'Do you know my father?'

'Yes,' Dream answered. 'I did.'

Rivalaun was conscience of a tension in him and realized he might be in danger of driving his companion away.

'You said being here wasn't supposed to be a punishment,' he said. 'What did you mean by that?'

The boy sighed and looked straight ahead at the landscape before them. He bent suddenly and picked up Rivalaun's sword.

'Why did you throw this away?' he asked.

'It sickened me,' Rivalaun answered honestly. 'I don't know why I was given it to begin with. Is it supposed to make me a soldier? No one gave Bethany or Poppy a sword.'

'It's part of the landscape,' Dream said simply. 'It's only really there when you think about it. If you leave it behind it can still turn up again, either that or you may suddenly become aware of its absence. Or it may just lie there if you abandon it in your mind.'

Rivalaun blinked at the flood of explanation. It wasn't telling him anything he hadn't guessed already.

He wondered with a brief annoyance if the only things Dream intended to tell him were things he already knew for himself. He was suddenly annoyed by the memory of how cryptic Danaan had been as well. Nothing he knew about this place seemed really satisfactory.

Dream touched his shoulder lightly and gestured at the mound they were sitting on.

'Look where we are,' he said.

Rivalaun looked around him and remembered an image from one of the worlds he'd visited: an overgrown field outside an empty castle, where once a great battle had been fought. Danaan had told that story to a group of nomads camping on the battleground as if he knew all the details, but Rivalaun had heard many similar stories and wondered if his father really knew what had happened or whether he had simply invented it.

'It reminds me of a battleground I saw,' he said. 'Thousands of people died there, but when my father told their story he only talked about two of them. Brothers who ended up on opposite sides.'

Dream nodded.

'It is a battlefield,' he said. 'These are burial mounds.' He gestured over to their right. 'Some way away the earth hasn't covered the bodies and you can see them lying with their weapons beside them. Here they're more hidden. But I still know they're here.'

'Are they real?' Rivalaun asked.

'Everything is real to me,' Dream answered with sorrow in his voice. 'I remember the ones who have left just as if they were still here now. There is no visitor who doesn't leave his mark on me.' He stood up suddenly and said, looking down at Rivalaun, 'It really isn't supposed to be a punishment. Whether or not an experience is beneficial is a matter of personal choice.' He looked about him, adding, 'The landscape is ultimately honest; at least as much so as you are to yourself.' With which he put the sword down carefully at Rivalaun's feet and began to walk away.

'Dream!' Rivalaun called after him and he turned and looked back without expression.

'I hope I didn't offend you,' Rivalaun said and the boy smiled.

'No,' he said, 'you didn't,' and disappeared into the mists.

~c~

Here death may deal not again for ever;
    Here change may come not till all change end.
From the graves they have made they shall rise up never,
    Who have left nought living to ravage and rend.
                              —A. C. Swinburne

The Book of Dreams
Bethany's Book

When Bethany left Rivalaun she ran without thinking, embarrassed by the fact he had seen her cry and by the fact she had tried to make him choose between her and Poppy. Her headlong flight took her down the side of the hill and into a misty valley and she didn't stop running until she came to the side of another hill. At that point she wondered if she was going in the same direction as Poppy and looked around hastily for any sign of her red-headed cousin.

There was no one in sight and she began to walk slowly up the hill, rubbing the tears away from her face. Poppy's comments about competition were still ringing in her ears. It was clear the other girl had decided that she would try to win the quest the landscape had set them. Bethany felt a deep-seated resentment mingled with a certainty that Poppy would win this battle as she had every other one. Her thoughts were interrupted when the ground suddenly twisted under her feet and she fell forward on to something sharp.

With a yelp of pain she stumbled to her feet and then stared at the ground in horror. It was littered with bones. A low mist hung in the air and the landscape was eerily still as Bethany looked out across what at first appeared to be a mass grave. She shuddered as she looked at it. Skeletons lay this way and that across muddy red earth. Weapons of all shapes and sizes were discarded beside them and the earth was torn as if a great battle had once been fought there. Streamers of mist wreathed the broken bones as if the smoke of cannon still hung in the air an eternity after the battle had ended.

'How horrible,' Bethany said. 'Why is this world so full of dead things?'

It was with inevitability that she saw the mist roil upwards at her words to form a hooded shape before her.

'Sleep is the younger brother of Death,' Morpheus said. The mists swirled as he moved to stand by her side, gesturing smokily at the scene before him. 'But Death alone of the gods receives no offerings.'

'You think I don't know that?' Bethany demanded, forgetting her fear of Morpheus in her anger. 'I'd have given anything to have my father back. If Death's a god he's a cruel one.'

'Your father believed differently,' the figure told her and Bethany's heart skipped a beat.

'What . . . how do you know that?' she asked, past a lump in her throat.

'It's what he wished for,' Morpheus breathed in a

whisper of air, stirring the edges of his hood. 'The three lost princes: Felix, Sylver, Danaan . . . Death has no power here but when they left this world they put themselves under his sway.'

'They came from here,' Bethany said softly and it felt as if it was something she had always known. 'Who am I, then?'

She hadn't expected him to answer, talking to herself more than to the Councillor of Dreams. But his figure swirled with a sudden motion and drifted apart so that there was only the barest suggestion of a floating figure.

'The landscape called you,' he said and she remembered him saying the same thing in the castle when he had shown them the map of the land.

'To take the place of the three lost princes,' Bethany said, remembering. In this dead wasteland Morpheus didn't inspire in her the same fear that he had in the castle, but her voice was cold and suspicious as she asked: 'Did you do this to my father as well then? And . . . Sylvester and Daniel? Did they have to seek their fortunes on an endless quest through this impossible world?'

Twin purple lights regarded her from the robe of mists.

'The royal line left the land of dreams. The castle stood empty. I have given you this quest to determine whether you are fit to take their place.' The mists stirred with a violent swirling, disturbing the coiling patterns that made up the phantasmal figure. Then Morpheus said, 'I gave you this quest. Now it is your own.' His voice held complete certainty and a confidence that Bethany was at a loss to interpret and, as she stared at him, the threads of mist thinned down and he vanished as if he had never been there.

Bethany said his name but there was no answer. Even the low-lying haze on the battlefield was fading; leaving the red earth bare and allowing her to see the next features of the landscape awaiting her. Ahead, the shapes of the cut-out purple mountains were nearer now, but separated from her by a featureless black plain.

≈⟨≈

'O where are you going?' said reader to rider,
'That valley is fatal where furnaces burn,
Yonder's the midden whose odours will madden,
That gap is the grave where the tall return.'
—W. H. Auden

The Book of Lies
Poppy's Book

Poppy stepped on to the blackened plain and a shadow fell across her, a cold presence shivering her skin. In all directions the black ground stretched with an oily smoothness, its surface fused into a flat sheet like molten glass. The air was still and muffled with the same oppressive heaviness as before a thunderstorm, and the black sky seemed to be not only above her but all around her: as if the air was transparent blackness.

Poppy shook her head to dispel some of the tension and tried to focus. Jutting out of the smooth obsidian ground a single tower stood some distance away. As she concentrated on the jagged shape it seemed to be moving across the land and then Poppy's perspective shifted and she saw that the land itself was moving with a slow relentless drag so that she was being pulled inwards and around towards the tower, which was like a black hole at the centre of the plain. As the sliding motion dragged at her silently Poppy felt ill with it, her stomach tight with tension, and she closed her eyes.

Nothing changed. The same scene stood before her and, as a silent scream caught in her suddenly dry throat, Morpheus's grey figure appeared. The streaming trails of his hazy robes shaded from grey into black as if he was part of the darkness or tied to it with coiling tendrils reaching into his misty form.

'Welcome to the Sea of Nightmares,' he said.

Poppy's eyes flew open and Morpheus was gone. Unwilling to close them again she spoke into nothingness.

'Another of your games,' she said. 'I'm not afraid of you.' Remembering the dragon's words she added: 'I'm not one of your creatures. I'm not under your laws.'

The darkness laughed.

'You think that's the answer?' Morpheus's voice asked inside her head as the black tower spun closer out of the distance. 'No one commands dreams. I don't make the laws, I administer them. It's not my power you're under. This is the Sea of Nightmares and this is what it feels like to be helpless and alone.'

The black plain swirled under the black sky, bleeding inwards to the centre of the landscape where the tower nailed the darkness to the ground. The air tasted tannic with the smell of metal as Poppy was brought up sharply and suddenly at the gaping maw of the entrance. Inside, the first few steps of a staircase twisted steeply up the side of the wall in a tight spiral around a central column to an immeasurable and impenetrable darkness above. The surface was a montage of elaborately shaped figures, entwined in agonizing shapes as they wound their tortured way upward. Steeling herself against horrors, Poppy put her foot on the first step.

By the time she reached the third step she was shaking. Although she was determined to face whatever was in the tower her muscles were twitching with fear as she began the climb. Something against all reason or rationality was commanding her body and her legs were numb with a purely physical terror that was beyond conscious control. She forced herself up another step, still shaking, drawing away from the hideous drop increasing behind her. The darkness intensified and she continued to shake, her mind deadened with the strength of her body's fear, as she climbed upwards. With a frozen detachment she wondered why she was still climbing and then realized, as her legs stiffened, that she was now equally terrified to turn and go down. To stop climbing was to fall, and if she fell in a dream and she couldn't wake up, what would happen? Where would she fall to in the darkness below?

CHAPTER FIFTY

~⚬~

> The splendid silence clings
> Around me: and around
> The saddest of all kings
> Crowned and again discrowned.
> —Lionel Johnson

~ In Camomile House ~

'They're nearly at the end,' Sylvester said quietly and Cecily looked up with hope in her eyes.

'The end of the dream?' she asked and Sylvester nodded.

'They're getting closer to the mountains at the edge of the world,' he said. 'I think when they reach them it means the end is in sight.'

'Don't you mean "if" they reach them?' Danaan said, raising his bent head and looking directly at the others with a discomforting expression. 'Poppy's in the Sea of Nightmares now and Bethany is almost certainly on her way there.'

Cecily looked shocked at the sudden violence unspoken in his words and David glared at Danaan. But Emily broke the tension by saying in a surprisingly level voice:

'I trust Poppy to deal with her nightmares,' she said. 'I'm proud of what she's done so far.' Her eyes were bright, as they had been with tears when Poppy had held the spear at the end of the Hunt, but now there was an expression on her face that reminded Danaan of how the Elf Queen had been described.

Emily turned that look of calm pride on Cecily and relieved it with a smile.

'I think Bethany will be all right as well,' she said and then she looked at Danaan. 'And Rivalaun,' she said. 'We have to trust our children to have learned something positive from what we've taught them, even if they have suffered for our mistakes.'

Sylvester took his wife's hand and smiled more genuinely than he had in days.

'I hope you're right, my love,' he said.

'I apologize,' Danaan said suddenly and unexpectedly. He looked at Cecily and met her eyes directly. 'Bethany's behaviour has done her credit.' He paused. 'And you,' he continued. 'In the graveyard and in the forest. She's shown maturity about her situation that speaks highly of the values you've taught her. I think Felix would be proud of her as well.'

There was a long silence and then Cecily said, 'Thank you,' and the group relaxed into a more companionable mood. In that spirit Cecily turned to Emily and said with a wry laugh:

'And I'm sorry I haven't done more about this resentment Bethany feels for Poppy. I think I've been ignoring it for too long in the hope it would blow over.'

'I don't think I was even aware of it,' Emily admitted, 'I've made a lot of assumptions about Bethany that I shouldn't have. And I think Poppy's attitude hasn't helped the situation, even if she feels the antagonism less.'

'Poppy can be quite thoughtlessly cruel,' Sylvester said from the side of the room and Emily nodded.

'But it does come from thoughtlessness,' she said. 'She's self-involved but not, I think, malicious.'

'No, I don't think she's malicious,' Danaan said. 'But she's certainly tenacious.' He looked again at David and Cecily. 'As is Bethany,' he added. 'I would hope Rivalaun has the wisdom to appreciate her regard.'

Cecily blushed at the comment, much as Bethany might have, but then the flush faded and she said in a level tone of voice, 'I think in part he reminds her of Felix. Rivalaun's upbringing makes him seem different in much the same way Felix and you two . . .' she paused to look at Sylvester as well as Danaan, 'were when I first knew you.' She thought for a while and then added. 'He's been well educated in how to think and express himself.'

'But he's uncertain of what feelings to express,' Danaan admitted. 'I think his social education has been lacking.' He looked at Emily and said, 'And since he can't ask himself, would you in theory have any objection to overseeing the next phase of his education? If and when he returns I'd be grateful if you could give him that sense of family he seems to desire.' He looked at the others as well. 'All of you,' he added.

'It would be my pleasure,' Emily said gently and the others added their agreement to hers.

Danaan looked down at the books he was holding and said, 'The story begins again in Bethany's book. Are you ready to continue?'

Cecily and David nodded quickly and Emily said, 'Yes, if you're willing to go on.'

'I find myself missing Dream,' Sylvester said unexpectedly. 'I've forgotten too much.' He looked sorrowful and Emily touched his arm sympathetically.

'What exactly is *Dream?*' David asked and Danaan smiled at him.

'If we knew that,' he said, 'we'd be at the end of the story.'

CHAPTER FIFTY-ONE

∽•∾

'O do you imagine,' said fearer to farer,
'That dusk will delay on your path to the pass,
Your diligent looking discover the lacking
Your footsteps feel from granite to grass?'
                                    —W. H. Auden

The Book of Dreams
Bethany's Book

Bethany stood on the brink of the black wasteland. After the unpleasant scenery of the battlefield she hadn't thought things could become much worse but, staring out across that virtually featureless expanse, she realized she'd been wrong. Even the air over the black plain seemed different: rippling as if with a heat haze, so that Bethany couldn't focus on the single stump of a tower which rippled somewhere on the horizon.

At this point in the landscape there was no gradual shading of one territory into another. At her feet Bethany could see the reddish earth of the battlefield come to an abrupt end as it met the smooth border of the black plain. Then, as she watched, the edge of the darkness trembled and slid slickly over a few inches of the dead earth so that it was almost lapping at the toes of her shoes. There was a suggestion of colour in the depths of the glassy blackness like the rainbow film on a pool of petrol, a polluted quality to the obsidian sheet

265

of ground. Bethany couldn't think of anything she'd liked the look of less.

'Come on,' she told herself. 'I bet Poppy didn't hesitate.' And she stepped out on to the plain.

She sank instantaneously, throwing her arms out to break her fall, her mouth opening in a gasp of surprise as the blackness closed over her head. She choked as an acrid, smoky taste invaded her mouth, and struggled in the viscous darkness, forcing herself upwards towards air and light. She didn't find air, but her feet stumbled against an unexpected footing which was marshy and yielding as she pushed herself upright against it. Waist-deep in the darkness, she coughed compulsively, her eyes watering and throat stinging with the taste of the black liquid. Rivulets of darkness poured out of her clothes, back down into the dully gleaming flood plain. As she coughed she took an involuntarily step forward and lost her footing so that the process was repeated and she was drowning again in darkness until she floundered on hands and knees on to another slimy footing. No change in the surface of the water gave away these treacherous stepping places and, slipping and sliding across the black plain her heart was in her mouth as the ground continually gave way to plunge her again into the murky liquid. Only the jagged shape ahead, now revealed to be a tower, remained constant, growing gradually nearer with painstaking slowness.

Her final lurching fall took her so deep that she was convinced this time she would not reach the surface. The pain hit her with a dull slap as her body was thrown against a hard surface. Her body ached with the same uncomfortable tightness as a sudden flu and she got to her feet in a shocked daze to find she was standing in the doorway of the tower. She viewed the steeply increasing spiral of the stairs with dismay, too exhausted by the liquid plain to face a single step, let alone what might be hundreds.

'Or thousands, or millions, or an infinity,' she thought hopelessly. It seemed like the final injustice to crown all the unfairness of her life that she should be faced with this impossible challenge with no idea of what it was for or how she had come to this place. 'It's all Poppy's fault,' she thought automatically and unreasonably, wanting to believe her own words.

Her footsteps were muffled as she took the first steps, her thigh muscles protesting at the steepness of the ascent, and rounded the first curve of the staircase. Above there was only darkness, the next steps virtually invisible, and the sense of the crushing force of the tower.

'It could go on for ever,' she thought again, hearing her own voice but uncertain whether she had spoken aloud. Another step, and another again, and she wondered if she was moving at all, or if her feet were just shuffling endlessly in the same place. Her stumbling footsteps echoed up and down the tower with a sibilant echo that made her feel dizzy. She sobbed suddenly and hopelessly out loud:

'I *hate* this. I hate it!' Her voice rang out sharply, sending the word 'hate' echoing up and down the tower, and she heard the echo continue with words she hadn't said.

'Please, just make it *stop*!'

Bethany shuddered. The desperate voice, high with fear, sounded just like her own.

'Did I say that?' she asked, testingly, wondering if she was finally going mad.

'I don't know. I don't care,' a voice answered her from breaths away and she started and flailed out with her arms, only to feel the rough stone walls scraping her hands with agonizing reality.

'Who's there?' she shouted and heard a quick slipping scuffle and a suddenly caught breath before a voice said shakily:

'I am.'

There was something about the tone of the voice that made Bethany suddenly concentrate harder. It wasn't an echo and it seemed much more familiar than anything she'd encountered in the world so far. Not like Morpheus's cryptic pronouncements or Dream's distant compassion. More like someone she knew.

'Poppy!' she said suddenly and after a few moments the voice returned in a slow cautious agreement:

'Yes . . . Bethany?'

Bethany's head swam and she put out her hand to the central column only to feel carved figures slippery under her fingers. She recoiled abruptly to fumble for her footing on the black stairs.

'How did you get here?' she asked carefully and heard Poppy's voice speak softly out of the walls.

'I walked right into it. The Sea of Nightmares. Morpheus stood by and laughed. He said that . . .' her voice faltered and broke off fiercely: 'Never mind.'

Two sets of footsteps shuffled onwards and upwards, overlapping in a series of echoes descending a muted scale. Wondering what to say, a thought suddenly occurred to Bethany and, unable to help herself, she asked:

'What about Rivalaun?'

'*What* about Rivalaun?' Poppy's voice rang with mockery. 'He doesn't seem to be here.'

Bethany didn't say anything for a while. She wished it had been Rivalaun whose voice she could hear. She would have liked to talk to him about their fight earlier and she thought it might be easier if they weren't face to face. Having Poppy laughing at her from somewhere in the distance was no substitute. The thought made her want to cry and she set her lips tightly, determined Poppy shouldn't hear her sobbing.

There was a soft sound from the other side of the wall that sounded like a sigh and then Poppy spoke quietly:

'I won't tell him, Bethany.'

'Won't tell who what?' Bethany demanded, defensively.

'I won't tell Rivalaun you fancy him,' Poppy said in the same quiet voice and then fell silent.

Bethany would have liked to insist that she didn't, but there was a question she wanted to ask more and, steeling herself, she asked:

'Why not?'

There was a hiss from the other side of the wall and then Poppy said:

'Why would I, for God's sake?' Her voice was hoarse and strained with anger. 'Damn it, Bethany, I'm not actually out to thwart you at every turn. My life doesn't revolve about you. I couldn't care less if you fancy him, except when it makes you take his side without thinking about mine.' Bethany blinked at this and then Poppy added, as if she was talking to herself, 'I don't know why I even try to talk to you. You're just going to keep hating me whatever I say.'

Bethany wondered what to say. It was hard to believe she was actually having this conversation with Poppy.

'Do you actually *care* that I hate you?' she asked sarcastically.

'I don't give a damn,' Poppy rejoined. 'Why the hell should I care about someone who hates me?' There was silence for a second. 'But I don't think I've done anything to deserve it.'

"You've done everything to deserve it!' Bethany said angrily. 'I don't see why I should pretend that I like you just because you're my cousin. You're a horrible, cliquey social climber and devious user of people to get your own way *all* the time!'

There was only a second's pause before Poppy returned, 'And you, Bethany, are a complete nonentity who's terrified to demonstrate one tiny particle of individuality just in case it makes you look like me.' Bethany blinked back tears and Poppy continued remorselessly: 'And if you could forget your incredible envy of me for just one second you'd realize that I don't get my own way all the time and there isn't anything I've got I actually want.'

'Even your own parents,' Bethany said, no longer trying to conceal the fact that there were tears in her voice. 'You just ran away and left them without a thought and you didn't give enough of a damn to tell them why!'

'Don't you dare try and guilt–trip me about my parents!' Poppy said furiously and her voice was unsteady. '*Everything* you hate about me is because of them. Everything! They've made me what I am, the same way yours have with you . . . except that your father loved you enough to tell you the truth. He left you that painting so you'd find out that dreams are real.'

Her voice broke off and now Bethany could hear her breathing unsteadily in what sounded like sobs. She stopped walking, her own tears blinding her, and began to lean against the wall. Then she caught herself and shuddered and began to cry in earnest, unable to speak any more.

~c~

Not to have fire is to be a skin that shrills.
The complete fire is death. From partial fires
The waste remains, the waste remains and kills.

It is the poems you have lost, the ills
From missing dates, at which the heart expires.
Slowly the poison the whole blood stream fills.
The waste remains, the waste remains and kills.
—William Empson

The Book of Lies
Poppy's Book

Poppy walked faster up the stairs as she spoke, still trying not to touch the walls. She was blindingly angry at Bethany's self-centred justifications for her hatred and she wished that, for just one second, her cousin would stop hating her and actually see her as a person.

'Don't you dare try and guilt-trip me about my parents!' she said furiously. '*Everything* you hate about me is because of them. Everything! They've made me what I am, the same way yours have with you . . . except that your father loved you enough to tell you the truth. He left you that painting so you'd find out that dreams are real.'

She was crying as she stumbled up the next few steps and then suddenly her footing slipped and she felt herself falling and screamed. She fell sideways down one whole curve of the spiral, grabbing frantically for something to stop her slide, and came to a rest, bruised and bleeding, ten steps from where she'd fallen. Her vision was blurred and her head throbbed where it had cracked against the side of the stairs. She gasped for breath, her tears drying on her face as the effects of the shock pounded through her.

'Poppy!' Bethany shouted from further up the tower, and she continued to gasp for breath to answer her. 'Poppy! Are you OK?' Bethany yelled again and Poppy heard footsteps descending rapidly. 'Where are you?'

'I'm OK!' she said quickly. 'Don't run! I just slipped, that's all.'

The footsteps stopped and Bethany asked hurriedly, 'Are you hurt?'

'I don't think so,' Poppy said shakily.

There was a long silence from the other side of the wall; Poppy used the pause to calm her breathing. She couldn't bring up the energy to particularly care what Bethany said next. She was still too wrapped up in her own near brush with falling into the black pit below. I bet she's thinking I faked it, she thought to herself bitterly.

'Are you *sure* you're OK?' Bethany asked.

Poppy thought of the steep stairs stretching downwards and shuddered, wondering how far she had climbed and how far she might have fallen. Wrenching her mind away from the thought, she wondered for the first time how she could hear Bethany. It was as if there were two spiral staircases, not one, coiled around each other in a double helix sending them endlessly circling upwards. Taking a deep breath Poppy said, 'I'm not your enemy, Beth. I'm tired of the way things are between us. Can't we call a truce?'

There was a long silence and Poppy again had the sense that she was just talking to herself. When Bethany spoke again her answer was unexpected.

'I'm sorry I didn't believe you about being a witch,' Bethany said. 'I was wrong.'

'No, I was wrong,' Poppy said quietly, staring into the darkness and hugging her arms around her chest. 'I thought I knew what I was but I didn't know anything. Everything I thought I wanted is . . .' she took a deep breath, 'it's fading away. All I wanted was to know the truth, and after everything I'm still in the dark.'

'The Sea of Nightmares,' Bethany said softly. 'That's what you said, wasn't it?'

'Morpheus told me,' Poppy said in a colourless voice. 'I meant to stand up to him. I thought that I could choose what happened . . . that I could change things. But Morpheus said that no one controls dream. And now I'm trapped here.'

This time the silence stretched out for an eternity. Poppy listened to Bethany's breathing on the other side of the wall, pacing her own shaky breaths, until they were breathing slowly in unison in an inaudible sigh of air. It was then that Bethany spoke and her voice was changed, alive with an abrupt thought.

'He said what?' she asked suddenly.

Poppy closed her eyes, seeing the same impenetrable blackness, and tried to clear her mind, wondering what Bethany was asking for.

'He said that he didn't make the laws, he administered them, and that he . . . that no one commands dream.'

'No one commands Dream,' Bethany repeated carefully. 'But I've met Dream. In the castle and in the graveyard. I don't know what he is but he's as real as anyone else here.'

'Then you think that was what Morpheus meant? That if he doesn't command Dream . . . maybe it's the other way around?' Poppy asked, her voice alive with wonder as she moved closer to the wall. Then it fell flat again. 'But I don't see how that helps us, here.'

'Merlin told me to forget the landscape,' Bethany told her. 'He said that it didn't obey expected rules. He also said that I shouldn't be afraid when seeking my fortune.'

'I'm afraid,' Poppy admitted. 'Things have just been getting worse and worse.' She stood, trying to conjure a picture of Bethany into the blackness. 'I feel as if I'm failing this test. How can I seek my fortune when I don't know what I want any more?'

'What about going home?' Bethany asked softly and, thinking of her parents, Poppy bit her lip.

'Is that what you want?' she asked. 'To go home like Dorothy in Oz?'

Bethany started to laugh and Poppy, who hadn't been making a joke, suddenly started to laugh too.

'It's not very adventurous, is it?' Bethany admitted. Then she said in a strange voice, 'You were right before about me trying too hard to be normal.' She paused. 'Is there any way your magic can get us out of this?'

'I don't know,' Poppy admitted, before adding softly,

'In our world I can affect the way things are, but here the landscape works with what's inside our heads. How can I change that?'

'You tell me,' Bethany said. 'Try to see things from a different perspective.'

Poppy started, hearing her own words flung back at her, and was on the brink of a sharp retort when she realized what Bethany was trying to do: startling her enough to snap her out of her black mood. And with that thought she realized what her mind had been hiding from her.

'We have to go on,' she said. 'Up the stairs, however long it takes, because somewhere there has to be an ending.' In the encompassing blackness she got to her feet, feeling for the next step, trying to force herself to believe it.

There was another scuffling noise as Bethany got to her feet and as both girls made their way up the curves of the two spirals they heard each other's footsteps keeping them company during their ascent.

With Bethany listening, Poppy forced herself to keep moving, relieved that her cousin couldn't see her shaking with every step she took up into the blackness above. 'It has to end sometime,' she told herself over and over again but she didn't allow herself to hope when the darkness began to lighten. Instead, she kept on putting one foot in front of the other until she stumbled over a space where there should have been a step. Looking up, they saw a pearly grey light streaming down from the sky.

The spiral steps had finished on the slopes of the purple mountains. Turning, Poppy saw Bethany stepping past the last steps of the staircase's duplicate beside her. The cousins stared at each other and, later, Poppy could never be sure which of them reached for the other first. But when they released each other from a tight hug and turned to look across the mountainside, to see Rivalaun walking along the green bank of the river, they were both smiling.

CHAPTER FIFTY-THREE

Then felt I like some watcher of the skies
When a new planet swims into his ken;
Or like stout Cortez when with eagle eyes
He stared at the Pacific — and all his men
Looked at each other with a wild surmise —
Silent, upon a peak in Darien.

—John Keats

The Book of Secrets
Rivalaun's Book

Rivalaun had been walking alone for some time. Leaving the burial mounds and the sword lying, still untouched, beside them, he had come across the snake of the river again. For want of any other purpose he had followed it, walking slowly along one bank, only occasionally looking up at the mountains slowly getting closer ahead of him.

To his right he had seen the edges of the wasteland, the molten sea of darkness. But grass still grew on the bank of the river, and he'd been reluctant to leave it to explore so unprepossessing a vista, especially when it increasingly seemed to draw him out of the way. He hadn't seen the shape of the black tower. The constant vision on his horizon was still the shape of the purple mountains. The river flowed deep here and he paced beside it as it began the first stage of the journey that would take it through the blacklands, the hills and dales and the forest and finally back to the castle where he had begun his journey. Ahead of them the thin thread of the river stretched right up to the mountains. He caught flashes of light from where it fell from that height.

He wasn't sure when the blacklands seemed to retreat but, after a while, he was conscious of a lightening of his spirit. The grass on the riverbank grew thick and lush and the river itself was opening out ahead of him into a wide, flat lake. The path he followed grew steeper but the air from the mountains was fresh and the sky above a grey so light it was almost white.

Coming around a final bend in the river path he came suddenly upon the lake, lying like a bowl in a curve of the rocky mountain foothills, filled to the brim with water the colour of the sky. Something made him look up and, with a sudden relieved pleasure, he saw his two cousins standing a little above him on the mountainside. They waved, seeing him at the same time, and he waited while they scrambled down the scree of rocks to join him on the path beneath.

They were both smiling, at him and at each other, and he caught them both as they jumped down on to the path and gave them each a quick hug. All three of them looked at each other and then suddenly began to talk at once and, amid a flurry of explanations and descriptions, they walked slowly up to the lakeside and sat down.

'I can't believe we've finally reached the mountains!' Bethany exclaimed.

'Look,' Poppy said, still standing and shading her eyes as she looked back down the river gorge. 'It's like your father's painting in reverse, Bethany.'

All three of them looked back down across the dream landscape and then, in unspoken common consent, turned to face the mountains again. A waterfall spilled exuberantly into the bowl of the lake and purple heather covered the lakeside with soft, springy turf.

'I think we're coming to the end now,' Rivalaun said.

'The end of the quest?' Bethany asked.

'Or the end of the story?' Poppy continued, picking up the thought easily.

'The end of the world,' Rivalaun added and they stared at the bulk of the mountains.

'They don't look very climbable,' Bethany said dubiously.

'But I suspect that if we're supposed to climb we'll manage somehow,' Rivalaun replied.

'Or find some other way up,' Poppy agreed and began to look around.

'Wait!' Bethany said and, to Rivalaun's surprise, Poppy paused and sat down again.

'What?' she asked.

'I want to talk first,' Bethany said, frowning. 'About what might come next and what we're going to do about it.' She looked at Rivalaun and said directly, not hiding behind her curtain of hair, 'I'm sorry about what happened after the forest.'

'So am I,' he said quickly, before she could continue. 'To both of you,' he added, glancing at Poppy and then back to Bethany. 'I don't have any right to judge either of you.'

'You don't,' Poppy agreed at the same time as Bethany said:

'You do.'

Then they looked at each other and laughed and Rivalaun realized that, although they disagreed, somewhere along the line they had stopped arguing.

'I'm sorry as well,' Poppy said. 'For getting so carried away by the Hunt. I should have known what was happening sooner. I let them use me,' she added and her expression was blank with anger.

'We were talking,' Bethany said, gesturing at Poppy and then looking at Rivalaun. 'About what the landscape might want from us and what was supposed to happen at the end of this quest.'

Rivalaun nodded and looked down to see Poppy mirroring his gesture, reflected in the grey still water of the lake. He continued to watch the water as Bethany addressed them both.

'Well, I think we should decide now,' she said. 'What we want and what we're prepared to do to get it. I don't really want to go on before I know what you two are thinking.' She looked across at Poppy and Rivalaun raised his gaze from the lake to study his red-headed cousin as well. 'That was where we stopped talking,' she said.

'I asked first,' Poppy said and Rivalaun found her expression unreadable. 'What do you want, Bethany? What's your heart's desire?'

Bethany glanced quickly at Rivalaun and then said: 'To be special.'

She paused for a while and neither Rivalaun or Poppy spoke. Then Bethany said slowly: 'Being here has taught me a lot. But I think Rivalaun's right when he says we've reached the end and I feel as if I've hardly begun.' She hesitated before finishing. 'Poppy was right when she said I tried too hard to be normal. I haven't given this, any of this, a real chance.'

'I am ready for an end,' Rivalaun told them. 'I'm just not sure what kind of ending I want. I'd just like to reach some kind of conclusion. Just for once I'd like to have a story of my own: one I was part of from start to finish.'

'I do want to go on,' Poppy said, her voice calm with certainty. 'I'm not going to drift about here in a made-up place just letting things happen to me. I want to understand what's been happening to us and that means going forward because, really, it's the only possible choice. Going back would be admitting we're not up to the challenge. And we've come so far already.' She looked up at the peaks of the mountains and then down at her own reflection in the lake. 'I want to get to the truth of things,' Poppy concluded. 'And I don't care if that means the end.'

CHAPTER FIFTY-FOUR

~c~

Like to the falling of a star,
Or as the flights of eagles are . . .
Or like a wind that chafes the flood,
Or bubbles which on water stood:
Even such is man, whose borrowed light
Is straight called in, and paid to night.
                                        —Henry King

~ In Camomile House ~

'Wait!' said Emily and Danaan stopped, arrested in his smooth transition from Rivalaun's brown book to where the story continued in Bethany's blue one.

'Is this it?' Cecily asked, and the other adults were reminded of how Poppy had described their double act, now being replayed once more for the benefit of their two daughters who had recently assumed their own alliance. 'Is this the end?' Cecily continued.

'There's not much space left in the journals,' Sylvester pointed out. At this everyone else looked at them to see for the first time what Sylvester and Danaan had noticed some time ago: there were only a few pages left in each book.

'And when the books finish?' David asked, trying to think it through.

'What happens to the characters when the story ends?' Danaan asked and the others looked at him with trepidation.

'Or the dream when the dreamer wakes up?' Cecily

quoted softly. 'If they finish this quest or pass this test Morpheus has set for them . . . will they come home? Will they come back from the dreamland?'

'You did, after all,' Emily said urgently, looking at her husband for agreement. 'You escaped.'

'Perhaps,' Sylvester said, taking Emily's hand. 'But although it was Morpheus we bargained with, he's not a god. It's not his power that enabled us to break through the boundary between worlds.'

'What is he then?' David asked and Danaan met his eyes.

'The play's director,' he said. 'The landscape is the stage on which dreams are set and Morpheus is the architect of the plot. But his powers, considerable as they are, are limited. It is Somnus who rules the dream landscape.'

'I don't understand,' Cecily said fretfully and David tried to reassure her.

'We can't,' he said. 'But Bethany can and she will. She'll find a way of understanding it on her terms, and then perhaps she can teach us to understand as well.'

'If she comes back,' Cecily pointed out and Danaan added: 'If any of them comes back.'

His hands were not entirely steady as he lifted the next volume and no one called him to task for the comment, although they all turned to look at him in the suddenly portentous silence.

CHAPTER FIFTY-FIVE

For winter's rains and ruins are over,
And all the season of snows and sins;
The days dividing lover and lover,
The light that loses, the night that wins;
And time remembered is grief forgotten,
And frosts are slain and flowers begotten,
And in green underwood and cover
Blossom by blossom the spring begins.
—A. C. Swinburne

The Book of Dreams
Bethany's Book

When Poppy had said going forward was the only possible choice Bethany felt something inside her resonate with the thought. Rivalaun still looked uncertain but, when Poppy stood up and began to explore the side of the lake, neither he nor Bethany objected. Instead, they sat side by side on the lake's edge, looking down at their reflections in the still water.

'If I stay here,' Bethany said, 'it has to be because I want to.'

'We may not have a choice,' Poppy pointed out, wandering back in their direction. 'Our parents came from here, part of us belongs here, whatever we think about it. Morpheus set us to seek our fortune. What if finding it means that we have to stay here?'

'Perhaps it wouldn't be so bad,' Bethany thought out loud. 'After the Sea of Nightmares even Morpheus doesn't frighten me any more. But, now that I know the things I've discovered here . . . I want to go back. It's back home where I want to be different. Not here.'

Poppy shrugged.

'Too deep for me,' she said. The thought made her look down at the lake. 'I wonder what would happen if we jumped in . . .' she said thoughtfully.

'I wouldn't recommend it,' Rivalaun said. 'Remember what happened when it was just a river.'

Bethany glanced between them both and caught a slight blush on Poppy's face. Her cousin saw her looking and smiled.

'Go not to Lethe,' she said pensively. 'When I first came here I was well on the way to forgetting everything but Rivalaun found me at the brink of the river and persuaded me to go on.'

'I don't get any feeling of that here, though,' Bethany said. 'I don't feel forgetful.' She looked down at the water. 'Reflective maybe, but not forgetful.'

Her cousins both nodded and Rivalaun lay back on the springy turf. Poppy and Bethany exchanged glances across him. It seemed to them that Rivalaun had abjured responsibility for continuing their journey. They both wondered whether he would go on if they did find a way of doing so. Poppy wandered off again and Bethany watched her as the red-headed girl continued her search.

Poppy walked around the side of the lake to where it met the mountains and then circled back to the river.

Bethany watched her considering the narrow passage over the deep gorge and then caught her breath as Poppy jumped. The other girl landed safely and came wandering back along the opposite side of the bowl–shaped crater of the lake. She knelt to prod at the springy turf and walked right up to the mountain edge, where she ran her fingers over the cragged rocks and assessed it for climbability. Bethany watched her in silence and after a while Rivalaun sat up and watched too.

Neither of them spoke. Bethany had to stop herself jumping in surprise when Rivalaun reached out and took her hand. Protectively, she swung her long hair forward but, looking down at the lake, she could see Rivalaun's reflection watching hers and she smiled with him. They continued to hold hands in silence as they watched Poppy circle back and brave the dizzying jump across the river before coming back to sit next to them. Only then did Bethany drop Rivalaun's hand as she looked up and asked:

'Well?'

'All looks normal . . . well, normalish anyway,' Poppy said. 'But I've been thinking about the river.'

'Hmm?' Bethany said and Poppy nodded, her face thoughtful.

'It's strange,' she said. 'But it's been the only consis-tent thing in this landscape. We keep crossing and recrossing it and, like us, it leads up to the mountains.'

'It flows in the other direction,' Rivalaun pointed out and Poppy waved away the objection.

'Whatever,' she said dismissively. 'But look there . . .' She pointed at the waterfall that cascaded over the rocks, down from the height of the mountains, into the serenely still lake. 'I'll go out on a limb here,' Poppy said. 'And say I'm inclined to think there's something behind that waterfall.'

'Really?' Bethany stood up and looked across at the falling water. 'How much could you see?' she asked, beginning to walk over to it.

'Not much,' Poppy admitted, falling into step with her. 'We'd have to climb for a while and the rocks look slippery there, but I think it can be done.'

Rivalaun came up behind them. The two girls turned to look at him.

'What do you say?' Poppy asked him. 'Prepared to give it a go?'

'Are you going to?' he asked, looking at them both. First Poppy and then Bethany nodded in reply.

'I want to,' Bethany added. 'Poppy's right. It seems the right thing to do.'

She looked hopefully at Rivalaun, wondering if he really would leave them to go on alone. After a moment the boy sighed and then said:

'All right then, let's try it.'

All three cousins walked up the mountainside, considering the path Poppy had suggested. The rock seemed alarmingly short of handholds but Bethany thought she might be able to see a way to climb up to the edge of the waterfall. Spray from the water misted the view and they were all beginning to get dampened as they stood and watched.

'I'll go first,' Rivalaun said unexpectedly. 'I'm taller and stronger than either of you.'

'Go on, then,' Poppy said with a laugh, unafraid, and

Bethany stepped back so that Rivalaun could have a clear access to the rock face.

He ran his fingers over it, as Poppy had earlier, and then began to climb up a little way until he was about three or four feet above them.

'Hey, Rivalaun, the waterfall's *that* way,' Poppy said, pointing.

He didn't deign to respond to the taunt but did begin to edge himself sideways across to the falling spray of water.

'Can you see anything?' Bethany called out nervously, but Rivalaun's shouted reply was inaudible.

'What was that?' Poppy yelled and Rivalaun turned his head awkwardly against the rock face and looked down at them. His face was drawn and frightened and Bethany felt guilty that they had pushed him into this.

'I *said*,' he said, repeating himself in carefully enunciated syllables. 'It looks as if there *is* something. It looks like a cave.'

He climbed further into the falling spray and then shouted something else, again inaudible. Bethany held her breath. She squeaked in fright when Rivalaun's hands began to give way. He leaped awkwardly into the waterfall and disappeared from sight. Bethany quickly crossed her fingers and Poppy cuffed her arm.

'Quit it,' she said. 'He's OK. Now do you want to go next or shall I?'

'You can,' Bethany said, still not ready to brave the ascent and, for once, not minding that Poppy should be before her.

'OK, here goes everything,' Poppy said.

Unlike Rivalaun, Poppy did not climb up the rock

face first. Instead, she stepped out on to the side of the mountain directly next to them and skirted the exact rim of the lake as she climbed sideways, like a spider, towards the waterfall. Bethany, despite herself, was impressed at her daring. Halfway along Poppy turned and looked back. Her wet red hair was plastered to her face but she was grinning.

'It's awfully slippery,' she shouted. 'But there's plenty of handholds. See you in a minute.' Then she climbed doggedly into the falling water and disappeared behind it.

Bethany looked after them both. The lakeside was suddenly silent and strangely grim on her own.

'At least there's no one watching,' she said comfortingly to herself and stepped up to the rock face. She opted for Rivalaun's more cautious method, climbing up a bit first to familiarize herself with the rocks. It was easier than she had imagined, her weight hardly mattering, as she inched her way across the side of the mountain overhanging the lake. The waterfall had dampened all of the useful handholds and she moved slowly across the rock face, trying to feel her way blindly in the falling spray.

When she reached the waterfall weight suddenly became a factor again. She pressed herself hard up against the rocks so as not to be dragged back by the pressure of the veil of water. It felt strange as the water slipped past her, like silky tresses instead of the churning froth she had expected. Clinging to the side of the mountain, Bethany navigated her way by touch, blinded and deafened by the sight and sound of the falling water. It wasn't until the noise lessened a little and hands reached up to help her that she realized she had climbed around the edge of the mountain and was now through the waterfall.

CHAPTER FIFTY-SIX

~∙(∙~

Can I my reason to my faith compel,
And shall my sight, and touch, and taste rebel?
Superior faculties are set aside;
Shall their subservient organs be my guide?
Then let the moon usurp the rule of day,
And winking tapers show the sun his way;
For what my senses can themselves perceive,
I need no revelation to believe.

—John Dryden

The Book of Lies
Poppy's Book

Poppy reached out with Rivalaun to pull Bethany into the cave. She gently turned her cousin so that Bethany was facing in the right direction to see what she and Rivalaun had found. Bethany's gasp of astonishment was the same as theirs had been.

The cavern was huge, stretching out onwards and upwards into impenetrable black distances. On the far side of the cavern two huge silver doors towered above them. The path leading to the doors was through an ankle-deep ocean of flowers.

'Poppies,' Bethany said, seeing them, with a strange tone in her voice.

'I can't take credit,' Poppy assured her.

'I thought poppies were red,' Rivalaun said thoughtfully, bending to touch the white blanket that lay like snowfall over the ground.

'This is *Papaver somniferum*,' Poppy told him. 'The white opium poppy.' She looked down at the flowers appreciatively. 'I was named for this flower,' she told them. 'The ones which made Coleridge write "Kubla Khan".'

'I'd reconsider that, if I were you,' Rivalaun said. 'At least, I don't know who Coleridge or "Kubla Khan" are, but your father must have known this was here.'

Poppy frowned at the thought and Bethany shrugged, finishing wiping the last of the water from her face with her sleeve.

'I think that exhausts the significance of Poppy's name for the time being,' she said, with only a hint of sharpness in her voice. 'Shall we go on?'

The threesome walked slowly across the cavern towards the silver doors. The air was heavy with the musty scent of the poppies and they felt dizzy by the time they reached the doorway. The doors themselves glowed with a pale light, which made it difficult to make out the shapes inlaid on the silver. Poppy could see a leaf motif winding around the edges and other symbols that she almost recognized inlaid into the eldritch metal.

'Shall we?' Rivalaun asked, laying a hand on one door and all three reached forward to push it open.

Inside, they paused on the threshold and breathed in deeply. The stone castle they had seen had been magnificent in its own way, but this silver palace was something else again. For the first time in the dream landscape Poppy had a sense of completeness about a place. Every detail about it was perfect: the beaten silver of the floors, the long glowing hallways, the silver light sifting downwards from some great height to pick out details of intricacy on the walls and doors.

By common consent they kept silent, clasping hands with each other, as they walked down the long corridor before them. On every side there was something to look at. Poppy could easily imagine being held spellbound with wonder here as her eyes tried to take in everything there was to see. Other passageways led off on either side, but at the end of the long corridor two great doors stood open into a massive room. The three cousins walked softly to the entrance and looked inside with wide eyes.

It was a throne room. The silver chair that dominated the dais ahead of them was empty. But even on its own it was a commanding presence. Great silver wings lifted from the arms of the chairs, each feather perfectly detailed, and swept back to finally meet the high walls and blend with them so that it seemed the chair encircled the room rather than the other way around. At the foot of the dais was a plain black stool, placed deliberately on the right hand side of the massive silver chair.

'Morpheus's seat,' Poppy whispered, raising an arm to point at it.

'Then where is he?' Rivalaun asked, also softly.

'Not here,' Bethany replied quietly, stating the obvious. 'Let's keep looking.'

They turned and left the throne room, all feeling numbed by the sight. The silver palace was like nothing else in the dream world. It looked completely fantastical and yet impressed them with a sense of its reality as nothing else had before.

Back in the passageway they turned to the left and walked along a long gallery for some minutes. There were no paintings, but Bethany was the first to notice that the tracery of black veins inlaid on the silver showed the contours of a map. They walked on past stylized representations of the city and the castle, the formal gardens and the maze, the graveyard, the forest, the hills and dales, the wasteland beyond, the black tower and the lake in the mountains. Poppy ran her fingers over the walls, feeling the journey beneath them as a blind man reads Braille.

At the end of the passageway there was a staircase: a twisting spiral fretwork with statues instead of banisters. Rivalaun touched it cautiously, as if he expected it to melt away, and turned to show them a finger heavy with dust. As they began to climb the staircase the dust muted their footsteps and Poppy, looking speculatively at the statues, saw that their empty eyes were filled with complicated spiderwebs and that the spiders themselves were curled in the centre of the statues' eye sockets like pupils in irises.

The staircase curved up and up into darkness. Poppy looked down over the edge and couldn't even see the silver hallway beneath them. She could hear muffled noises: a soft flapping that could have come from bats or owls somewhere up in the heights of the cave. She didn't mention to the others that the occasional sighing breeze that wafted them was caused by the wings of massive moths brushing blindly past the stairway.

When the stairway came to an end Poppy was the

first to step off on to the floor. She felt suddenly dizzy. They had climbed in silence for ages, and must surely now be nearing the peak of the mountains. She reached again for both her cousin Bethany's hands and then stopped herself, taking Bethany's left hand instead, allowing her right one free for Rivalaun. Meeting Rivalaun's surprised eyes over Bethany's head she smiled but didn't say anything.

The glowing silver light was bright here and it was hard to make out anything save the existence of walls on either side and the floor beneath their feet. Poppy thought privately that she wasn't even very sure of those but she walked on, reluctant to break the spell, until they came to another door.

Unlike those they had come to before, this was a single door and not inlaid or decorated in any way. It stood at the end of the silver corridor, a plain black door made of a dark glossy substance that could have been wood or glass, with a silver handle. Poppy reached out her free hand, turned one last time to glance at her cousins, and then opened it.

~⊱⊰~

Wilt Thou not yet to me reveal
Thy new, unutterable name?
Tell me, I still beseech Thee, tell;
To know it now resolved I am;
Wrestling I will not let Thee go
Till I Thy name, Thy nature know.
—Charles Wesley

The Book of Secrets
Rivalaun's Book

Bethany clung tightly to Rivalaun's hand as Poppy opened the black door. He squeezed hers back reassuringly. Poppy's hand, on her other side, was cool and remote as she drew them both in through the door.

The room inside was full of light and Morpheus, turning to look at them as they entered, was almost washed out by it, his form barely distinguishable. He stood by the side of what Rivalaun tentatively classified as an altar. It was a black slab of stone, its stark geometry relieved by a drift of black feathers that covered the slab and scattered across the silver floor.

Lying on the slab was a sleeping figure and, even asleep, his presence seemed to fill the room. The figure's face seemed ageless, timeless even, in its steady slumber, but Rivalaun recognized it nonetheless. The black strands of hair which pooled into the mass of feathers, the translucently pale skin through which he imagined he could see to crystal bones beneath and the fathomless eyes, mercifully shut and concealed with a veil of black-bladed lashes. The figure was both strange and familiar and he cautiously identified it.

'Dream,' he said.

'Somnus,' Morpheus corrected him. 'The Night God. Death's younger brother. As Somnus he rules the night and, as Dream, he wanders the landscape of your minds. It is ever his will I have served.'

'Then he was controlling us all along?' Rivalaun asked in a fierce whisper. '*He* brought us here?'

'You brought yourselves here,' Morpheus said, his lambent purple eyes distant as he looked down at the sleeping figure. 'The landscape called to you and I set you on your path but it was you who found your way to this place.'

The Councillor of Dreams looked from Rivalaun's face to Bethany's and then Poppy's.

'Your heritage is powerful,' he said, his pale smoky face appearing more clearly than ever before from the hood of his robe. 'This is why the land summoned you. The castle has stood empty for too long. The landscape does Somnus's will, as do I, and so I returned you to your rightful place as symbols in this world: three princely children on a quest for their fortune.'

He paused.

'But you have come further than I thought possible. This is the Silent Citadel, The resting place of the Sleeping God. The heart of Dream. Since dreams first began only I have ever seen this place: watching over the Sleeping God and, like the landscape, endeavouring to interpret his wishes.'

'And what does he wish for?' Bethany whispered, staring down at the Sleeping God. 'Was it Dream who called us here?'

'I cannot tell,' Morpheus admitted. 'Since the beginning of time he has slept here. I am his Councillor, but even I can only guess at his desires. Who would dare to wake Dream?'

'We might,' Rivalaun spoke and Morpheus trembled like a guttering candle.

'Do we have the power to?' Poppy queried.

The phantom spread his arms in token of his lack of knowledge.

'You are here,' he said. 'But as to how it might be accomplished . . . who knows or dares to dream?'

The three cousins looked at each other. Then they turned to regard Somnus, enfolded in the black feathers of his wings, an almost imperceptible rise and fall of breath all that separated him from the angel of death.

'Do we have the right?' Bethany said softly. 'If we wake him, won't that change everything here? If Somnus doesn't sleep . . . if Dream wakes . . .' She raised her eyes to Morpheus helplessly. 'What will happen?' she pleaded, knowing that there would be no answer to her questions. Stepping back from the dais she shook her head. 'I don't know enough,' she said, finally certain. Speaking to Morpheus she concluded: 'You told us to seek our fortune. I haven't even begun yet. I've only just begun to find out who I am. I'm not ready to change the world.'

Rivalaun and Poppy looked at each other and then Rivalaun shook his head.

'No,' he said. 'Not me.'

'You wanted to find the end of a story,' Poppy reminded him quietly. 'This could be it.'

'No,' Rivalaun shook his head. 'I want to choose my own story. I want to make a commitment to a place and a time. I want to stay somewhere but . . . not here.' He turned to Morpheus, willing him to understand, sensing that the conclusion they reached mattered to the Dream Councillor most of all. 'I don't belong here,' he said. 'I've had too much of unreality. I don't want to live in a dream. I want to wake up.' Unable to stop himself he looked at Bethany. 'I want to go with you back to your world,' he confessed. 'And I agree with you. We don't have the right to change things here.'

Poppy looked sideways at them, a smile curving her lips, and then turned to look at Morpheus consideringly before looking back down at the dais and at Somnus.

'For the record,' she said, still looking at the sleeping figure, 'I do have some reservations about this and I'm not going to be thrilled if I find myself committed to this place without having a real opportunity to see what I'm choosing. But . . .' she sighed briefly. 'I do want to change things and . . . being here has felt more real to me than anything else in my life. So with that in mind . . .'

She darted a look at her cousins and then bent quickly and brushed her mouth against Dream's and stood back. The kiss lasted half a second and was screened by Poppy's tumbling red hair, but none of them had any doubt that it had worked. As the light in the room grew steadily brighter, they saw the god's eyes slowly open to form lakes of darkness that gathered in all the light in the room, until they couldn't be certain if they closed their own eyes because it was too dark or too bright to see.

CHAPTER FIFTY-EIGHT

~◦(◦~

Then dawns the Invisible; the Unseen its truth reveals;
My outward sense is gone, my inward essence feels:
Its wings are almost free — its home, its harbour found,
Measuring the gulf, it stoops, and dares the final bound.
> —Emily Brontë

The Book of Dreams
Bethany's Book

They opened their eyes to find themselves standing in the throne room. Bethany and Rivalaun moved instinctively to stand next to Poppy where she faced the silver throne, aware that she was now at risk in some way they could only just begin to contemplate.

Morpheus, in front of them, was seated on the black seat at the foot of the steps up to the dais. He looked at rest there; the tumbling mists that formed his figure finally stilled and the force of his authority was overshadowed by the presence of Somnus seated in the chair above him. The night god had no need of the silver throne to magnify him; he was already overpowering now he was awake. The eyes of Dream looked down at them and Bethany shivered.

Rivalaun looked up curiously at the god and Bethany saw that he was trying not to seem afraid.

'Will you answer our questions now?' he asked. 'Who and what are you really?'

'I am Somnus,' he said quietly but they all fell silent at his words. 'And I dwell on the borders of the waking world. But you who have passed into my lands and lived here as my guests may call me Dream.'

He stepped down from the dais and as he did so lost something of his presence, so that it was a boy of about the same age as themselves who faced the cousins on the silver floor of the throne room. Morpheus stood and stepped into place behind his shoulder, an expectant spectre waiting calmly for what his master would decide. Dream turned and looked back at him and shared a steady glance of complicity for one long moment.

'You have been my true councillor,' he said. 'Like this land, even if you are not entirely to be trusted you have always been true.' He looked at each of the cousins in turn and finally his gaze came to rest on Poppy. 'But you woke me,' he said softly.

Bethany watched her cousin, standing very still before Dream, and stepped forward.

'Excuse me,' she said politely. 'But what happens now?' She looked across at her cousin. 'Can we leave if we want to? Because Rivalaun and I want to go home and it's not fair to make Poppy stay if she doesn't want to, because her parents will really miss her.'

'I chose this, Bethany,' Poppy said in a small tight voice. 'I don't need rescuing.'

Then Dream smiled and they were no longer afraid of anything.

'This is my world,' he said. 'And it has languished too long without me. But there is something else the landscape lacks. Someone who stands on the border

303

between waking and dream: a ruler for the castle and a companion for its god.' Meeting Poppy's eyes he reached to take her hands in his. The circle of figures stood still as he spoke seriously.

'I would not compel you to remain here,' he said. 'But you chose to wake me and this world is yours if you wish it. As am I.'

Poppy clasped his hands in hers and then released one of them, turning so that she stood on Dream's left side as Morpheus now stood on his right. It was her cousins she looked at, but she was speaking to Dream as well as she said:

'I'll stay,' she said. 'Because I want to. But I think you should go home. I've found what I was looking for here. You've only just begun seeking your fortune.'

'I think we'll find it,' Rivalaun said quietly, taking Bethany's hand without embarrassment.

'But will we ever see you again?' Bethany asked.

'Of course,' Poppy said and she and Dream were both smiling. 'There's not that much of a barrier between dream and reality. Enough for a visit if not to stay.'

CHAPTER FIFTY-NINE

And what if all of animated nature
Be but organic harps diversely framed,
That tremble into thought as o'er them sweeps
Plastic and vast, one intellectual breeze,
At once the Soul of each, and God of All?
—Samuel Taylor Coleridge

The Book of Secrets
Rivalaun's Book

During the shift between worlds part of Rivalaun's mind was thinking and planning. With Bethany's hand still clasped in his, he knew what he had decided. Poppy might have found a truth amidst all the unreality of the dreamland but he had found his much earlier. Back in Camomile House, in a world which knew very little of the possibilities surrounding it, was not an ending but a place to begin. Without Poppy there would be a gap there that needed to be filled, a gap in a family still aching with the loss of Felix. It might not be his right to attempt to fill it but he had chosen it as his responsibility.

Bethany was beside him. She had accepted her own loss and somewhere in the dream kingdom, Poppy's kingdom now, he thought she had found something else as well. She had lost the cloud of depression that had shielded her like the curtain of her hair, and somehow she had become whole. Voices spoke out of the mist that surrounded them. He thought he heard words he recognized. He could heard Morpheus and Poppy and Dream, whose voice was also that of Somnus the Night God, and other voices too: the Elf Queen's and Quarry's and the thousand unnumbered voices of the shadowy crowds who had so often filled the blank spaces of the landscape with their own tenuous reality. Beside him he could feel Bethany also listening and wondered what she could hear in this space between worlds, where all possibilities were, for a short space of time, open to them.

Rivalaun held Bethany tightly and determined that his cousin would be the first to know of his decision to stay, because there were things he intended to ask her about and promises he hoped they could make before the spell of the dream landscape left them.

He didn't know what would happen on their return but he felt exultant at the idea that this time he would stay and find out. He had found the truth at the centre of his father's secrets somewhere in the midst of secrets and lies and dreams.

CHAPTER SIXTY

~⊰⊱~

Let us stay
Rather on earth, Belovéd — where the unfit
Contrarious moods of men recoil away
And isolate pure spirits, and permit
A place to stand and love in for a day,
With darkness and the death-hour rounding it.
—Elizabeth Barrett Browning

~ In Camomile House ~

Three books lie on the polished wooden desk. Each of them tells a story. Professor Greenwood, whose desk this is, has reason to believe it is the same story. But the titles of the books would appear to contradict him.

But those contradictions have ceased to worry the protagonists of the story, as they stand outside the front door of the solid Cornish house underneath a misty grey sky that seems both real and unreal to them.

'You don't need to explain,' Emily, her eyes wet with tears, tells Rivalaun.

'We were there with you every step of the way,' Cecily adds, hugging Bethany tightly.

'You did well,' Danaan adds, quiet approval in his gaze as he meets Rivalaun's eyes.

'Choices are never easy,' Sylver agrees, putting his arms round his wife and allowing his silver-topped cane to fall to the earth beside him. 'But through decision comes maturity. And eventually, for us . . . perhaps even acceptance.'

'But that's not all that happened,' Bethany insists, looking eagerly up at them all, her hair pushed back from her face. She has been told about the journals and is keen to explain something.

'Poppy gave us a message for you,' Rivalaun adds, looking at his uncle and aunt seriously as if he can see through their eyes like looking through windows.

'She said . . .' says Bethany, only half sure herself what the message means, holding out a thin silver chain with an enamelled white poppy strung from it. 'She said to say thank you . . . for naming her Poppy.'

Sylvester bursts out laughing. After a moment Emily joins him. The other adults smile also in relief that, for a second, Poppy's parents can share in their own happiness.

'It was always going to happen,' Sylvester says. 'There are some things that can't be kept secret for ever.'

'And who knows?' Danaan added. 'Visiting works in both directions and now that the quest is over perhaps Morpheus will release his ban.'

'We made a bargain,' Sylvester says but Rivalaun shakes his head.

'And we made another,' he says. 'Things will change in the dream landscape now that Somnus is awake. And somehow I can't see Poppy allowing Morpheus, or Dream, to make all the decisions.'

'Oh God,' Bethany says, thinking of essay-composition titles in her head; 'What I Did in the Summer Holidays' read out to a class of Ashmount students. 'That would be so typical of Poppy. Now it'll be both of them messing around in our heads.'

'Well,' says Rivalaun thoughtfully. 'It could have been any of us, really. I think she'll remember that we gave her the choice. In the end, it wasn't a competition.' He still hasn't released his grip on Bethany's hand as he adds: 'We all got what we wanted after all.'

EPILOGUE

~❨~

When I lie where shades of darkness
Shall no more assail mine eyes,
Nor the rain make lamentation
When the wind sighs;
How will fare the world whose wonder
Was the very proof of me?
Memory fails, must the remembered
Perishing be?

—Walter de la Mare

~ *In Dreamland* ~

Two figures stand on the battlements of a stone castle. The sky above is black. Colourful fireworks shoot up from the whirling shadowy crowds of the city at the bottom of the hill to scatter the curtain of night with stars.

The dream landscape is celebrating a coronation and a new awakening but, at the top of the castle, looking out across the land, two figures are celebrating the end of a dream.

'Is it all over?' Poppy asks suddenly, a silver crown twined through her brilliant red hair. 'What happens now when everything is ending?'

Dream laughs, a shout of pure delight.

'You're asking me that?' he says. 'Whatever you want, even uncertainty. What else is there to do at the end but start another story?'

310

AFTER TEXT

~⟨~

Acknowledgements

The author wishes to thank the following for permission to reproduce copyright material. All possible care has been taken to trace the ownership of all quotations included and to make full acknowledgement for their use. If any errors have accidentally occurred, they will be corrected in subsequent editions provided notification is sent to the publisher.

Extract from 'The Way through the Woods' by Rudyard Kipling, from *Rewards and Fairies*, by permission of A. P. Watt Ltd, on behalf of the National Trust for Places of Historical Interest or Natural Beauty.

Extracts from 'No Second Troy' and 'Sailing to Byzantium' by W. B. Yeats, from *Collected Poems*, by permission of A. P. Watt Ltd, on behalf of Michael B. Yeats.

Extracts from 'Snow' and 'Prognosis' by Louis MacNeice, by permission of David Higham Associates.

Extract from 'One Foot in Eden' by Edwin Muir, from *Collected Poems*, by permission of Faber & Faber Ltd.

Extracts from 'The Hollow Men', 'Four Quartets − Little Gidding' and 'The Love Song of J. Alfred Prufrock' by T. S. Eliot, from *Collected Poems*, by permission of Faber & Faber Ltd, on behalf of the Estate of T. S. Eliot.